THE NEAR MISS

FRAN CUSWORTH

Copyright © Fran Cusworth 2017

Twelftree Press, Melbourne, Australia

The right of Fran Cusworth to be identified as the author of this work has been asserted by her in accordance with the Copyright Amendment (Moral Rights) Act 2000.

This work is copyright. Apart from any use as permitted under the Copyright Act 1968, no part may be reproduced, copied, scanned, stored in a retrieval system, recorded or transmitted, in any form or by any means, without the prior written permission of the publisher.

Cover design by Michelle Payne, HarperCollins Design Studio and Bec Yule, Red Chilli Design.

Images by shutterstock.com

Formatting by Ebony McKenna using Vellum

National Library of Australia

Cataloguing-in-Publication Entry

Cusworth, Frances Ann

The Near Miss/Fran Cusworth

Printed by IngramSpark

ISBN: 978-1-64136-892-6 (paperback)

ISBN: 978-1-46070-609-1 (eBook)

Reviews for The Near Miss

Fran Cusworth's fourth novel shows an author in her prime.
—The Big Book Club

A tale of all our interconnected lives: intimate, insightful and gripping.
—Kelly Gardiner, author of *Goddess*

Fran Cusworth has captured the adolescence of mid-life so well. *The Near Miss* is funny, smart, and emotionally astute.
—Myfanwy Jones, author of *Leap*

Quality writing and a gripping storyline … contemporary fiction in the Liane Moriarty vein.
—Bookbirdy.com.

A very talented author with a strong and relevant voice.
—TahliaNewland.com

Reviews for Fran's earlier novels

Strong female friendships, the grief that comes from losing a child and parent-child relationships are tenderly observed and caringly rendered.
—The Herald Sun

Cusworth handles the provocative issues in Sisters of Spicefield with keen insight and compassion for their

complex emotional nuances. Well written, this novel is thought provoking, topical and engaging.
—Book'd Out

Friendship, grief, marriage, divorce is the stuff of life and Cusworth offers a tale brimming over with the realities of modern families, be they blended, broken or created in a test tube. Serious issues wrapped up in a well told,
feel-good story.
—The Hoopla

A rare description of life in a mining town … Hopetoun, like Cusworth's first novel *The Love Child*, is a highly enjoyable read.
—The Age

Apart from offering a wonderful insight into the lives of mining families and the ripple effects of a boom the like of which has never been seen, this page-turning novel intricately examines the importance of female friendships, flawed relationships and the need to belong and stand alone at the same time.
—The Herald Sun

In the security born of many harmless marriages, it had been forgotten that Love is no hothouse flower, but a wild plant, born of a wet night, born of an hour of sunshine, sprung from wild seed, blown along the road by a wild wind.

The Forsyte Saga, John Galsworthy

CHAPTER ONE

One hot day, a young woman rushed her child's stroller through spotlights of glaring sun, and lingered in rectangles of shade cast by the butcher, the baker, and the two-dollar shop. The woman's four-year-old daughter was too large, really, to be strapped into the flimsy stroller — if the child had thought to stand up and walk, she could have carried the contraption on her back, like Atlas bearing the world. The girl pressed the backs of her sandals onto the stroller wheels, making them shudder to a halt, and Grace stumbled.

'Lotte, *please.*'

Lotte narrowed her green eyes. 'I want to *walk.*'

Grace stopped outside the newsagent to stare at the caged news headlines: *Wildfires Rage. Ten Homes Lost. Train Rails Buckle in Heat.* Nothing yet about the dreaded mortgage rate rise. Maybe they should give up Lotte's kindy gym classes. Or eat less. Or rent out a room to a student, a nice quiet girl who liked housework. Maybe Grace should work more. Or Tom should work more. Later, going over the events of that afternoon, she would see that her hot exhaustion, and her worry about money, had distracted her from the child.

'When are we getting an ice cream?' Lotte twisted in the stroller, which creaked at the joints. Please make it through one more trip home, oh piece of junk. It was like so many things these days: cheap, and bound to break. They passed a billboard ad for the local university: *You Weren't Born To Wait*. As if some people might be born into some waiting caste, but not you — you had scored the lucky non-waiting card.

'Soon.'

'I want to get *out*.'

'Just ... wait.'

At the ice-cream shop, people with sweating faces and glazed eyes spilled out of the doorway. Grace parked the stroller and unbuckled Lotte. She lifted her daughter, and held her on her hip.

Nearby, a woman in a green tie-dye dress shared a tub of ice cream with her son. She raised a spoon to his mouth, revealing blonde armpit hair, slick with sweat. The little boy wore a shirt open over his milk-white chest, and a tattered straw hat. Check the woman's dreadlocks, almost to her waist! Such commitment to a life less ordinary, probably spent in sharehouses traced with fragrant smoke, littered with motorbike helmets and half-painted canvases, where nobody had mortgages. Grace momentarily ached for such a life.

She sighed. She should have done more in her twenties, taken a few more risks. She should have travelled to the Incas, even though there might have been bandits; she should have taken that Contiki tour of eastern Europe with her uni friends. Her back hurt; Lotte was too big to be carried. She lowered her daughter to the path. The red

Subaru, somewhere to the north, speeding towards them, could not yet be seen.

Melody watched the woman and the little girl, who was about Skipper's age. The girl's mother let one handle of her shoulder bag drop and she pawed through the bag, looking for something. She tsked, and sighed, and glanced around herself, catching Melody's eye. She hastily looked back to the bottomless bag; the answer to her problem was obviously in there. She frowned. Maybe infrastructure shares had plummeted, or the nanny had taken the day off? Maybe her Master of the Universe husband was having an affair with his life coach? Melody looked away. Oh, if she was going to survive back here in the big city she would have to learn to stop watching them all, and judging, or her head would fill up with stupid thoughts.

Melody crouched in front of Skip, and fed him the final spoon of pistachio and chocolate ice cream, bought with the very last of their money. The universe would provide. A man walked across the hem of her green dress as it pooled on the pavement.

She carried on her back a day-pack stuffed with groceries from the small supermarket next door. She had paid for the rice, but the cans of chick peas, the tofu, the olive oil and the curry paste had been slipped in when no one was looking. She didn't shoplift much anymore. It was bad karma. But they had to live.

Around them, ice cream melted over knuckles, and faces tilted this way and that, tongues protruding to catch drips. Old Italian mommas stood back-to-back with men in suits, and young women leaned on prams. City people all, their synthetic fabrics rustling, a different species from those Melody and Skipper had left behind on the commune. Here in the south, they were fatter. Whiter. Shinier, from their walnut-gloss heads to their coloured nails, their thin threads of overplucked eyebrows and their bald, shaven legs. Love yourselves, people! You are all beautiful blossoms of Nature. Even you, spotty teenage boys showing your underpant tops, and you, fat Greek men in belted pants.

She checked her drawstring purse again for cash. Nothing. Just the stubs of two Greyhound bus tickets from Byron Bay to Melbourne. She sighed. There would be no going back. The commune had been heaven, until the druggies got in, with their money-belts of plastic baggies. The woman's fatal overdose could have been predicted; but the death of the woman's six-month-old baby through neglect had defeated all imagination. Melody had not known the woman well, but everything good died with the baby. The mangoes rotted on the trees, the waterfall ran dry, the lantana seized its chance to strangle veggie patches. Melody had packed her and Skipper's backpacks, hitchhiked into Lismore and left on a bus heading south.

Now, licking the bare ice-cream spoon, she glanced over at the small supermarket. An aproned man stood in the door, and raised a hand. Melody looked around, but it was at herself he was waving. He appeared to be wielding a phone. Her backpack of stolen goods grew heavy on her shoulder. Oh, please don't let him have filmed her stealing. Anything that could land her in court, that could separate her from Skipper, could not be risked. She moved, and the cans of chick peas clunked in her pack. They had fallen to the bottom, and their metal corners stuck into her lower back. Her skin burned.

Eddy Plenty, senior corporate risk analyst, drove his new red Subaru home. He had been out to the university to give his annual talk on risk management to the summer school business students, the driven types sacrificing a fortnight of sunshine and beach to knock off a whole unit on a deserted campus. He felt the usual post-seminar relief that it was over, the usual hope that he had inspired some to see the beauty in risk analysis (shrinking each year), and the usual wistfulness for the student days now behind him (growing each year). He turned west, his turbocharged H4 firing up to pass another car; the stability control system waiting to correct any errors. He had selected this car for its safety features, which included overhead airbags and pretensioner seatbelts. He had chosen many things in life according to his professional principles of risk reduction — many things except his girlfriend, he reflected, possibly the most important life choice of all. Love had selected his girlfriend for him, and Love, judging by her choice, had only scorn for mitigating harm probability or severity of failure categories. If Love were a person, she would be a fat, shrewish woman leaning on a kitchen counter and sucking on a cigarette with garishly painted lips, letting ash fall on the floor, and cackling manically at him. 'And you, you measly, small-hearted scared-of-everything little man! For you, I pick someone who will keep you on edge, nervous, every day of your life! Ha ha ha ha!'

Eddy had for some weeks now been carrying a diamond ring in a small velvet box in his pocket. Risk: such an open declaration of his love might make the restless Romy flee from him forever. Consequence: Severe to Catastrophic. Probability of her flight: well if he were honest, over fifty per cent, or Medium to High. A Severe-to-Medium matrix was never to be advised in business, but this was a matter of the heart, and Love did not brook such interferences as rational thought. He could hear Love sucking on her fag and cackling at the very thought of his risk matrix. Anyway, it could be argued (he whispered so Love could not hear) that the possible rewards of a secure life with Romy – children, a family – changed the matrix.

He turned up the air-conditioning. He needed fresh air, the car was stuffy, but the aircon would not be optimised if he opened a window. Romy should have finished her waitressing job by now, and be heading to their modest, three-bedroom brick home in a nice street, in a desirable area. No doubt checking her phone as she did every hour, for a message from the acting agency; the message that never seemed to come. Not a failed actress, as Eddy's surly father had once called Romy behind her back, to Eddy's indignation. Just someone who dreamed of a bigger life.

Romy had complained less about her menial job in recent weeks, newly distracted as she was by an event which had shaken both their lives. She had cheated on Eddy and slept with her yoga instructor — just a one-night stand, but still; sex, true sex, with another man. It had shocked them both, after five years of monogamy. Romy had confessed to him within days of the act, and then proceeded to confide in all of their friends with an endearing and handwringing honesty, which made people murmur soothing things like 'Don't be too hard on yourself'. Advice which Eddy privately thought was well-intentioned, but not, it appeared, *desperately* called for. There appeared no danger of true, heartfelt self-flagellation on his girlfriend's part.

For himself, he reflected that, had he seriously contemplated such a possibility in risk-analysis terms, he would have dramatically underestimated the *likelihood* of its occurrence, but probably could have guessed its *consequence* — the level of his pain — at about right. He was gutted. He would rather have endured a physical beating to his body than the agony of this intimate betrayal. Almost as bad had been her need to share the titillating details with *all* of their friends, even if it was in a spirit of self-recrimination. But such soul-baring was typical of Romy. She had even *blogged* about it.

However, he had survived the infidelity, and the subsequent broadcasting of it to half of Melbourne and general cyberspace. Things were healing. They would get through. And maybe, just maybe, moving to the next level of commitment would help.

Driving now along the main street, Eddy slowed. He was drawing near the strip of shops which clustered near the train line, and traffic here was always a stop-start affair. Cars pulled out of parallel parks; pedestrians darted into the centre of the road and quivered on the white line, waiting to dash to the other side. A bus heaved itself out from a stop like some massive, weary beast and blocked his vision. Eddy politely let the bus in, and two more cars took advantage and darted in front of him into the stream of traffic.

'You're welcome,' Eddy told them. He pressed down on the accelerator and set off.

Up ahead was an ice-cream shop; the busiest outlet in the street, of course, on a day like this. The sort of crowd the TAB drew on Melbourne Cup Day. People spilled from the door; others moved towards it. They held cones and tubs with spoons. A little girl emerged at the edge of the crowd and stepped onto the road. Eddy watched her, wondering what he could make for dinner. Maybe something on the barbecue outside, not the stove, so as to keep the house cool—

The child darted onto the road, right in front of his moving car. Eddy saw the streak of her white dress like a torn page, and in one frozen moment he saw the child's laughing face, all mischief and loveliness, at the lower edge of the window. He slammed hard on the brake, the ABS fluttering beneath his feet to stop the car fishtailing. The child's dress had scalloped edges, and she held a cone topped with pink ice cream, and her face was too close.

'*Shit!*' he shouted.

But in that last second a woman in a green dress appeared; thin, with golden hair in long ropes, and long brown arms that shot out and snatched at the child. Bystanders' ice creams fell or melted unseen down their fingers, people's faces distorted in gothic, open-mouthed denial. *No!* Every face turned towards him. Movement everywhere. There was the plastic crunch of a second car accident somewhere in the traffic behind him.

Had he hit the kid?

Eddy flung open his door, and he leapt out into the heat.

CHAPTER TWO

Skipper slept in Melody's lap, his feet up on the hard plastic bench. An elderly man inched past, placing a walking frame ahead of himself and shuffling his feet to catch up to it. A woman in uniform stopped to straighten the sheets on a stretcher. She refolded a blanket, and strapped it in with a safety belt, pulling the straps tight over the cotton weave. She pushed the stretcher away, and fluorescent lights glinted along its rails. Nurses walked past wearing blue pyjama outfits and pocket belts loaded with pens and small tools.

Melody plucked a toy train out of Skipper's loose fingers and turned it over. She pushed the engine along the palm of her hand and the coupling rods rose and fell. Under the train's belly was a movable piston, and a key.

The man from the accident sat one seat away. He rested upright with his eyes closed, his cheeks hollow and slightly flushed, lips fluttering as he breathed. His coat hung open; his wallet peeked from the pocket and displayed the edges of a wad of fifty-dollar bills, close enough to smell.

He should be more careful. Someone could take advantage of that.

And where was the woman? Melody had not seen her since they had arrived at the hospital. Melody herself had been crouching down to Skip's level when the mother put the little girl down on the ground. The child had rubbed her hands with satisfaction, as if brushing off her mother's touch. She looked at the road as if it were a great opportunity, and then she ran straight onto it.

Melody was amazed, later, at how much she could fit into a fraction of a second. She had dropped Skipper's hand and turned into the wake carved through the hot air by the little girl. She took giant strides, calculating the exact point at which she would have to stop and centre her weight, to pull them both back from the path of traffic. She squatted slightly amid the blur of wheels moving and the exhaust of cars and she snatched at the white of the child's dress. She brushed it, then she got a handful of broderie and yanked it back, scrambling with her other hand to get a purchase on more than the cotton fabric; she would not stop until she felt warm flesh. The red car was upon them. She met the man's eyes, saw their whites. She seized the girl's upper arm, frail as a chicken bone, and she yanked it hard, knowing she might break it, and that it didn't matter.

There was a tap as the car hit something, the child's foot, just the tip of her sandal, and the little girl released a fire-engine scream.

Melody had the whole child now, her arms wrapped around her warm belly, tyres burning and shuddering all around them on the hot bitumen. She whisked the girl up and away. A white car swerved to miss the red car, and hit a parked car; a third car hit the white car. The child screamed, each chainsaw howl ending in a *hoo-hoo-hoo!* before winding up again.

She was writhing in Melody's arms, and Melody carried her back to the footpath and the crowd of breathless onlookers, and the ashen-faced mother. On the road, people stood beside smashed fenders and waved their arms, then tapped each other's insurance details into their mobile phones. Melody handed the child to her mother and everyone sighed. Death had blown through them like a cinder-laden wind on a bushfire day, but he had missed his chance.

'Nice train.' The man blinked in the glare of the hospital lights, cheeks pink with sleep. He was tall and lean, his head cut back to the one-degree shave favoured by balding men of her generation. She envied anyone who could fall asleep where they chose. It showed an admirable level of comfort in your own skin. His stooping posture indicated that he was one to lean towards the world, as if curious and concerned about it. Even his bent nose followed his forward lean. His suit pants were too loose, and higher than was fashionable, like those of an older man. He had been quick to run from his car, the one to comfort the mother and take them to the hospital.

She held out the train and he took it, and tried the key.

'It doesn't work,' he said.

'I know. I bought it on eBay.'

'I think I could fix it.'

She shrugged. 'We like old things.'

'Old doesn't have to mean broken.' His fingers pushed the coupling rods so the wheels turned. Melody leaned her head back and exhaled. Her father had been like this, trying to fix everything. If she opened her eyes just a narrow slit, she could see the cash peeking from the man's coat pocket.

There really were a lot of fifties there. He couldn't possibly need them all.

'You must be hot in that jacket,' she said.

He smiled and absently shrugged off the jacket. He laid it on the seat between them.

Grace stood at the door of the waiting room and watched these three strangers, man, woman and child, and breathed a fresher air than the air she had left behind in the ward, where blue face masks and plastic tubing absorbed all the oxygen. Around them here, families gathered in little clumps, some staring at her with surly envy. They wanted in. Children wailed and coughed and grizzled. Grace went over to the man and woman.

'She's going to be okay,' she told them. 'She's strained a ligament and bruised her foot. But it's relatively minor.'

'Lucky,' said the woman. She had extraordinary blue eyes.

'Lucky you were there,' said Grace steadily. 'What's your name?'

'Melody. We just moved here last week. From up north.'

'Where up north?'

'A commune. Tuntable Falls. Have you heard of Nimbin?'

'Of course,' said Grace. Drop-out 'sixties scene, up in the rainforest mountains. Explained the dreds. 'I didn't think there was anyone up there under sixty.'

'Plenty,' said Melody. 'Their kids.'

'You grew up there?'

'No, here. Donvale. Most boring suburb in the world. Probably why I fled to Nimbin as soon as I could.'

Grace nodded. 'Well, I for one am glad you came back! Hey, do you think you could both come for dinner one Saturday night? My husband Tom and I, and Lotte, we live just near the ice-cream shop. We would like to say thank you.'

The man beamed and looked absolutely delighted. 'Can I bring my girlfriend?'

'Of course.' She looked at Melody. 'Do you want to bring someone? Besides your son?'

'Uh. Maybe.'

'Is your car alright?' It was the polite thing to ask, although Grace could not have cared less about the car. *I do hope my child's body didn't dent your fender?*

Eddy blushed. 'It's fine. We drove here in it, remember? From the scene of the crime.'

'Oh, yes. Sorry.'

'So to speak. Wasn't really a crime.' The man spoke hastily, as if sensing Grace's burning guilt, and the two women turned as one to study him for a moment.

'I'm so sorry,' he said, his hand on his heart.

'It wasn't your fault,' Grace said gloomily. It would have been nice to blame something other than her daughter's lunacy, but in this case it was not possible. 'She's always been a runner. I'm just lucky you both have quick reflexes.' She tore a corner from a magazine and wrote. 'So here's my address. I'll see you.'

At her feet, the boy, who must have been Lotte's age, shrieked and pointed. A tiny tin train peeled away from his feet and skittered across the floor merrily, over the linoleum, under seats and between feet, carving a straight line through the lives it passed. The hippy looked accusingly at the man.

'You fixed it.'

He looked sheepishly proud, and crouched by the squealing, delighted child.

'Yeah.'

'So this little girl, she was nearly killed.' Eddy followed Romy into the kitchen. He kept one hand in his pocket, cupped around the small velvet ring box, blocking it as if it might leap out of his pocket and propose of its own free will. Had Romy heard the first part of the story? 'We were so lucky someone grabbed her in time. Are you listening, hon?'

'We're out of coconut milk. When did we run out of coconut milk?'

'I used the last can the other night, in the curry. Hey, did you take money from my wallet? I was sure I had about ten fifties, and now there's only one. It's okay, it's just that—'

Romy whirled and stabbed her finger at a piece of paper pinned to a wall. 'You haven't added coconut milk to the list!' she said accusingly. Triumphantly, almost, Eddy could have said. Maybe she thought enough of these minor transgressions on his part would mount up to equal her infidelity. Maybe she was scrambling for the moral high ground. Oh God, what was he thinking? Romy was always like this. She had made love with some strange man without setting a foot off the moral high ground. He rubbed the velvet nap anxiously.

'I'm trying to tell you about something that happened to me today,' he said mildly. 'I wish you'd listen. This was huge. A little girl was nearly killed.'

'And yet, she was fine, *si*?'

'She was, well her foot was bruised and she strained a ligament, but it could have been so much worse— Oh God, there it is!' He crossed the room to the remote and turned up the television. 'This is it!'

There it was, on some current affairs show! First Melody and her son, sitting eating ice cream, probably shot on someone's phone camera. Then something flashed white behind Melody and there was the little girl running into a river of moving cars, her head not much higher than a car bonnet.

'That's me!' He pointed at the red Subaru, sliding into frame, Melody already spinning and flying after the child, in a whirl of green dress and golden dreadlocks and sunbeams.

'Shit!' breathed Romy.

The brakes on his television car screeched, the camera frame wobbled, unseen people gasped and screamed. A broadcaster spoke solemnly over the top.

'This near miss today in the Melbourne suburb of Meadowview graphically illustrates the dramatic findings from the government's newly released traffic accident report. If not for a quick-thinking bystander, this child would have become a statistic, one of the twenty per cent who ...' The footage was replayed, in slow motion.

Romy shook her head. 'Where were the kid's parents?'

'The mother was there. She was so grateful.'

'That you hit her kid?'

'No, because I braked in time and it wasn't worse. And I took her to hospital. The kid is okay. It's minor. And the mother has asked us to dinner. You, too.'

'A thank-you-for-not-hitting-my-child-very-hard dinner? Kooky.'

'You said you wanted to meet new people.'

'Maybe.' She finally seemed to wake up to his presence and slid her arms around his waist. He exhaled and leaned back against her arms.

15

'You sure you didn't take four-fifty from my wallet? I don't mind, I really don't. I'm just hoping I didn't lose it.'

Romy broke away from him and returned to staring into the pantry.

'No, Eddy, I didn't.'

When Skipper said he was scared to start at the new kindy, Melody told him to bring his invisible friend, Mr Sumper. Mr Sumper varied in age. At times he was old enough to go to primary school and drive a car. He could teach Skip how to do things. But then Skipper would say that he remembered when Mr Sumper was a baby, when the only person he liked was Skipper.

'He was shy,' Skipper reminisced nostalgically. 'And I held him, like this.' By the neck, it appeared, and possibly tucked under one arm.

'And could he talk?'

'He could only say "Mo-mo" and "tooka".' Skipper generally gazed into the air at some point to his left when discussing Mr Sumper, as if channeling some being who was poised up next to Melody's right ear. Bless him, he probably was.

She grew to love Mr Sumper. He was the sibling Skipper didn't have, and didn't look like getting anytime soon. How simple, that Skipper had created his own. She pictured him as an elfin man of indeterminate age, with a green hat no higher than her knee. She could say to Skip at any moment: Is Mr Sumper here? And Skip would stare off to the place by her right ear and finally say either no, he's in Sitter-ny (Sydney) or yes, he's just sitting over there. And Melody would nod in the direction of the small green man, and give him a wave. Who knew, maybe there was something there that only a four-year-old could see?

Now, she crouched in the kindergarten home corner, hoping Mr Sumper was not too far away. A brown baby and a white baby lay in a small wooden bed and stared sightlessly at a sky fluttering with finger paintings. Melody fed the brown baby a plastic lemon, and made kissy noises to simulate eating, while Skipper supervised approvingly. From the corner of her eye, she saw the little girl enter across the room. Lotte. She limped a little, but not much. Already better, Melody thought, with a twinge of possessive pride at the sight of this little human she had snatched from the jaws of death. Lotte trailed around a group of girls for a bit, but they turned their sharp little shoulder blades towards her, as if they knew *her* only too well. The child ran her fingers over the book display, and passed the unattended play dough table, where she stuck her finger into each of the four perfect balls of dough waiting to be discovered. She reached the home corner, and stopped and stared at Skipper.

Melody picked up the brown baby and waved its hand at her. 'Hi, Lotte,' she made the doll say, in a squeaky voice.

Lotte gave Melody a baleful look and turned her attention to Skipper.

'Skipper's new here, he's starting today,' offered Melody.

Lotte regarded him. 'Would you rather be eaten by a rhinoceros or a giant turtle?'

Skip thought about it. 'Turtle.'

Lotte nodded. He seemed to have passed some test. 'Do you want to come outside?'

Melody tucked in the baby and rose to her feet, feeling self-conscious. The other mothers stood in small groups, wearing little pastel dresses and shorts, feet slapping in thongs. She twisted the silver studded band on her upper arm, until it let go of her hot skin, and she let it settle again in a cooler place.

She couldn't keep lurking here in the home corner. She had come to Melbourne to give Skip a normal life, a safe life, and that meant making friends. She spotted Grace in one of the clusters, and ventured over nervously. The little group fell silent and parted at her approach, the women smiling questioningly at her.

'Oh! Melody!' stuttered Grace. 'It's great to see you here! What a coincidence! What's your little boy's name again?'

'Skipper.'

'Of course! Well this is Nina, and Anna, and Verity. We were all in mums' group together.'

'Hi,' said Melody, in what she hoped was a pleasant manner. She felt like an elephant, three metres wide and high amongst these svelte, girl-women. One of them, who had a pointy face with a sharp nose, stared up at Melody's hair. Another, with a full mask of makeup, stared down at Melody's boots. The other, whose face was kind and smiley, met her eyes.

'You were on the telly! About the accident!'

'Oh!' Melody was startled. She had not watched a television for years, and had draped a sarong over the set in her rented flat. 'I haven't seen it. Was it okay?'

'Amazing! You looked great!'

'And I'm *sorry* if I never thanked you for saving Lotte.' Grace sounded wounded. 'I mean ... I *thought* I did.'

'You did,' said Melody.

'Well *I* thought I did. The reporter, she just made it sound a bit—'

The woman with all the makeup broke in. 'Like you hadn't thanked her.'

'But I'm having Melody for dinner. *And* her son.'

Melody wrapped the handle of her hessian bag around her fingers until they turned white. 'The reporter asked me that question, and I didn't really understand what she meant. If it sounded ... I really didn't mean ...'

'Oh, it's okay. That's television.'

'And we're looking forward to dinner ...'

'Amazing footage. Lotte was *so* lucky you were there,' said sharp-face. Grace shot her a look.

'Just a fluke,' said Melody.

'Lotte's a runner,' said Grace. 'She's crazy. I don't know what to do about it.'

'She'll grow out of it,' said the kind-faced woman. 'She has a big spirit.'

There was a commotion from the home corner, where Lotte had returned to tip babies out of their cradles and hurl plastic food, piece by piece, from the fridge. Two little girls shrieked at her to stop. Skipper turned away to press his palms against some play dough. Lotte finally gave up the house-trashing and went to sit beside him, punching her little fist on a ball of red dough.

'She's lively,' murmured the kind-faced woman, while sharp-face and makeup exchanged glances.

Later, Melody picked Skipper up on her bike, and on the way home they stopped at the big bin behind the shopping centre. Melody checked no one was watching, then stepped up on a milk crate and peered over the edge. In one corner was a box of eggs, cartons slipping and sliding all over each other, yolks dried shiny and awful. She climbed up on the edge and reached down for the cleanest carton she could see. Picking through the landslide, she found six unbroken eggs.

There were more but she did not want to linger; women were walking in the distance with prams and strollers. They might be kindergarten mothers. She climbed out and showed Skipper her find.

'We'll check them later, to see if they're fresh.' She still had the nine fifty-dollar notes back in the flat, but she wouldn't spend them until she had to.

'How?'

'We put them in a bowl of water. If they float that means air has got in and they're bad. If they sink, that's good.'

'Sinking is good.'

'Funny, isn't it?'

They walked through the pet shop and stroked the kittens in there, and ate some samples of cream donuts out the front of the bakery.

'Can we go to Lotte's house for a play?'

'We're going there for dinner. On Saturday night.' God, she had forgotten to mention that they were vegetarian. It wasn't even necessary up north. Maybe she could tuck a note in Lotte's kindy bag.

'Can we go there now?'

'No. But that's nice, that you knew someone at your kindy. Did you play with her some more?'

'Yes. Always I played with her. She finded me all the time.'

He climbed onto a low wall and into his bike seat. She put the eggs in her bike basket, and they set off. If they were quick, they could get home before those rain clouds burst.

That night, Skipper said, 'Lotte says Mr Sumper's not real.'

'So? You know he's real.'

'She says you can't see him, so he's not real.'

'Tell me, Skip — do I love you?'

'Yes.'

'Can you see my love?'

'In my heart.' He patted his little chest. She had told him this.

'But you can't see it, can you?'

'No.'

'But it's real, isn't it? Just like Mr Sumper is.'

He gave her a look.

'That wasn't very nice of Lotte to say that.' Melody pursed her lips and he saw.

'I like Lotte. She never be's mean to me.'

'She'd better bloody not,' muttered Melody, momentarily reflecting that she had saved the life of the little girl who may end up killing Mr Sumper, Melody's low-maintenance second child.

Skip frog-hopped through the kitchen.

'I *love* Lotte.'

Somewhere in the universe, Mr Sumper thinned into vapour and vanished.

CHAPTER THREE

A computer engineer, Tom had always tinkered around with inventions in his spare time. He had invented a robot to do basic tasks for elderly people living alone, only someone else had got their version to market first. Then he briefly tried to create an electromagnetic motor which could produce its own free energy, and the spare room was strewn with the spare parts of that doomed venture. His latest brainwave was solar-powered roof tiles, cheaply produced from recycled water bottles.

Grace had once been affectionately amused by Tom's spare-time creative efforts, and even believed in them, but now she wanted to have a second baby and take time off. She wanted their mortgage to grow lower, instead of higher. She wanted Tom to stop spending so much money on spare parts and materials, and so much time on making stuff. And she wanted her guest room emptied of all the invention junk which had crept inwards from Tom's back shed. This was why she resentfully kicked yet another garbage bag of empty plastic drink bottles aside as she stalked out of the house on her way to work.

She caught the train, holding onto a strap and the luxury of twenty-eight minutes of unscheduled time. Time to think and stare out the window. Lotte would be fine, the bruising on her foot was healing already, but the accident had frightened them all. Grace needed a second baby. She needed a spare.

Grace mentally roamed through her smorgasbord of worries. Would the foundation at work fold if she wasn't successful in winning a new grant? Was Lotte always going to be so temperamental and strange? How could she persuade Tom to apply for a better, higher-paying job, and how soon could they start trying to get pregnant?

She had once believed that Tom's inventions might pay off, that he could win the lottery of creativity and make a big sale to a multinational. But they had been disappointed so many times that she had lost the faith. Yes, she had once dreamed of a world where they could have all the things, and all the time, they wanted. A get-rich-quick scheme, for God's sake, like any stupid, greedy hick. What a fool. She wouldn't risk her fertility on that again. The silver lining of Lotte's accident was this clear-eyed sighting of the way things were.

Grace's job for the past ten years had been writing grant applications and scrounging up occasional media at an organization called the Mental Wellness Foundation, where her manager Barbara Boiler was in constant hungry pursuit of more grant money, and more media coverage. This morning she stuck her head around the door and barked. 'Page six of the *Morning Star*? Read it yet?'

Grace sighed. 'I'm well thanks, how are you?' she muttered to herself. She opened the paper on her desk to the page already marked accusingly by a coloured Post-it note. Ah. *TV Soap Sparks Suicide Risk, Black Dog Trust CEO Helen Strutter was yesterday outraged at suicide storyline in* Home and Away.

'It's hard, Barbara," she said. 'It's a bit of a one-day story, but I'll get onto the *Star* and see whether they're planning a follow-up for tomorrow, and whether we can get you a comment.' Grace's boss's goal in life was getting more publicity than her rival Helen Strutter from the Black Dog Trust, and she believed Grace was incompetent for failing to achieve this. Grace watched her go and let herself momentarily unravel.

Oh, that woman. She ran her nails over her scalp, just to reassure herself she was still alive, and picked up a picture of her daughter from her desk. Lotte, captured one frosty Melbourne morning in her Incredibles nightie. Lotte with her legs bare, standing just outside the back door, breathing with purpose into the icy air, and raising her hands to touch the steam of her own breath. The visible breath had become invisible in the picture, and Lotte's hands and eyes seemed to reach up to something godly in the silvers and greys of the winter garden. Grace stared at the picture, searching for anything new in it, and felt the tiny crack in her soul widen a little further. She had had insomnia every night since Lotte's accident, the vast dark universe of the bedroom ceiling above falling into her open eyes. Loss of appetite, dislike for food. A toxic, unending anxiety that was a constant taste in her mouth, and a craving to have another child.

That day, she was meant to work on the association's application for a state government Good Works grant. This grant had taken on a new urgency since the association, incredibly, had missed out on the large, triannual Healthy

Australia grant from the federal government that had been the cornerstone of its funding for the past decade, a snub that had favoured the newly enriched Black Dog Trust. Now, it appeared, Grace was expected to put all that aside and write a press release starring Barbara Boiler, which would go out by lunchtime to hook into a story which was already dead.

She drank her tea, and for the thousandth time calculated how much twelve weeks' maternity leave on her wage would be. How many work-free, Barbara-free days it would represent.

Grace would wake at night and feel for Tom beside her, and find only flat sheets and blankets. She would then pad through the house and look out the back window towards the garden, where light would shine from along the joins of the tin shed, outlining it like a child's line-drawing hovering in the dark. Night after night, Tom crept out there to work on his inventions. When she confronted him about it, he shrugged. 'I went out for a piss, and I just thought I'd check on the shed.' Or 'I only popped out for twenty minutes', when she knew he'd been out there for hours.

She rang him at work one afternoon, and got his colleague, an engineer called Deepak. 'He's asleep,' Deepak whispered. 'In the store room.'

'He's what!'

'He does it every day now. What do you *do* to him at night?'

'Nothing!'

'He's always exhausted.'

No wonder. How long had he been sneaking out to the

shed to give the best of himself to his tiles, leaving the sleepy dregs for his day job, the one they relied on. Being a programmer for a global IT company earned good money, nearly twice as much as a media manager at a charity.

'He's taking nanna naps?' said Grace.

'Exactly.'

'Bet his boss loves that.'

'He doesn't know,' whispered Deepak. 'We're all doing our best to cover for him. But it's getting too— Yes, thanks,' he suddenly boomed. 'Just send that order as requested thankyouverymuch haveaniceday. Excellent. Goodbyesir.' The line went dead.

'We could always sell the house,' Tom said that night.

'Oh, ha ha.'

'I'm serious.' He stood in the bedroom and stripped off his business suit as if it were alive and crafted from reptiles. He dropped the jacket on the floor and wiped his hands of it. Kicked the pants into a corner. The cat kneaded the fabric with her claws. Lucky they were millionaires, with money to treat suits like they were disposable raincoats.

'Hey, hang up your suit. The cat will wreck it.'

'Good.' He pulled a dirty T-shirt on above his jocks and stepped into his favourite khaki overalls. 'I hate it.'

He had taken an entire year off work recently. He had pleaded with her for it: support us for one year and I will get the robot over the line. During this year, he had spent almost every minute in overalls. It was his uniform when he was working on the Oldbot, and he did everything in them — invent, drop Lotte to kindy, cook dinner. Finally, when that year had finished, there was the bitter disappointment of the

Oldbot's failure to sell, and once again Tom emerged in a dark suit, his hair newly cut, his grim jaw clean-shaven. He looked so handsome, despite that sullen work face.

Now, his whole body sighed in relief. He sat on the chair with his legs spread and his arms dangling.

'Sell the house?' She recoiled.

'I'm serious.'

'You *love* this house.' Every time he came home, he slammed the door behind him and shouted it to the peeling, leaky ceiling: *God, I'm sooo glad to be home.* He was a practical man who would pounce on small tasks; he would replace a washer before dinner, or oil a squeaky door.

'I want to quit my job.'

Grace followed him out to the back shed where his workshop was, and perched on a dusty chair in the pool of light that spilled from the doorway. Cicadas creaked gently around them; the squeaky doors of warm nights. She kept an ear out for Lotte, who was in bed. This was her first night since the accident to sleep without painkillers. The medicine and measuring cup sat at the ready.

Trains hooted lonely warnings as they rattled empty along the tracks, back to suburban railyards to await the morning's office workers. Across the neighbourhood, doors and windows swung open to catch sea-scented southerlies after a hot day; the low rattle of television news voices told of bushfires and of children starting school; preps on their first day. That would be Lotte in a year's time. Too fast, she was growing up too fast. Dishes clanked in sinks, children called from bed for glasses of water, a mother's voice sailed over the fence: *Don't touch the fan.*

'Well, I hate my job, too, you know, Tom. I've hated it for fifteen years.'

'I know, baby. You don't seem to mind hating it, but I

hate that you do. That's my dream: to make the solar ceilings and we will never have to work again. Unless we want to.' He knelt before her, his arms along her legs, dusty overalls brushing against her black suit. 'You used to believe in me. In the Oldbot. In my inventions.'

'Yeah, I know.'

Various incarnations of his last invention, the Oldbot, sat around the shed. The dream of the robot had been a solid part of their marriage; it had entwined itself around them like cement around bricks. They had sat up nights, talking and dreaming, and during the year Tom had taken off work it lay behind everything they did. Tom refined the design and Grace planned the marketing. They collected news articles about similar inventions, they anxiously followed the progress of other inventors travelling down the same path of creation, who might cross the finish line first, they imagined a world where small robots with emotional intelligence could watch over lonely old people, and, worst of all, they imagined the money they might earn from such a creation. And even as they went backwards on the mortgage, they dreamed of a life of no debt. Oh God, the freedom. Annual overseas travel and nice cars and expensive hobbies. A proper workshop for Tom, instead of a little tin shed. Grace would quit her job and start some private marketing consultancy with a fancy website and prices so high she would only accept one job a year, and they would have to fly her to Paris for it, and then maybe Stockholm and Geneva. Oh, their dreams had once united them.

But then Tom got a couple of knockbacks from companies that had once been keen, and those companies bought instead from other inventors. Grace saw the time flying by, and the mortgage getting larger, and the robot not selling, and her chances of a second baby slipping away. She had never known how much she had wanted children until she had one, and then she never knew how much she wanted a second until everything seemed stacked against her.

She went to her doctor who said, are you trying? And Grace said, well no, my husband is not working, we can barely afford the house, we thought we would wait. And the doctor shook her head and said thirty-eight is too old to be waiting, there is a window. And it closes. And Grace felt cold all over, and she said but Cherie Blair? Carla Bruni? And the doctor said oh God, don't think about them. Rich people. Lucky people. Get on with it, Grace.

So Tom had reluctantly returned to his day job, three months ago. But then, after trying the electromagnetic motor and discarding that, he had come up with the solar tiles idea, and her home had filled with old plastic bottles, and his passion for them grew every day, and she really didn't like the direction in which this was heading.

She sighed now, and felt another day of her life passing by, tick-tock. The near-loss of Lotte had made everything sharper, keener, more exquisitely fragile. Even sitting here. It was one of her favourite places in the world, this chrome-legged kitchen chair with the torn vinyl seat that sighed when she sat on its cushion, puffing resignedly out of the foam-filled gash. Weeds clung to its legs, a pile of twisted metal sat off to the side. Leaf litter flapped against Tom's workbench. Tom got up and closed his laptop, slapping it with loose fingers as if it had let him down. He turned and faced her.

'So, we both hate our jobs.'

'Well, big deal! It's not the whole of our lives. And we like our house, and our jobs pay for our house. And for another *baby*, Tom. We can't have another baby if you chuck in your job.'

Tom sank in a little on himself, like a deflating balloon, and studied her for a long minute. He looked at Grace in the way he might look at someone he didn't much like. He started to speak but the words puttered out, and he shook his head.

He tried again. 'If we both hate our jobs, then let's just quit. Sell the house.' He shrugged. 'There's more to life than this. And I want to give myself a year, just one more year, to work on this and get it over the line. I know I can. *This* is a good one.'

'Tom, I couldn't bear to sell the house. A house is everything. Security. And I want to have a baby. That was the deal: you'd have your year, you'd go back to work and save enough to have a baby for *my* year. And you've been back at work three months. Three months!'

'Yeah, three months. And I hardly ever see Lotte now. I'm lucky to get to say goodnight to her when I come home. If I was home she could do less time in childcare, and I could pick her up from kindy. Why would I have a baby when I hardly see the one we've got?'

'You had lots of time with her last year.' A little too much, thought Grace jealously. All the little rituals father and daughter had developed; milkshakes at the café with the bear sign, and chats to the old lady with the cat on the walk home from childcare, and Lego out in the workshop while Tom worked on the robot.

'What about those people down the road? The Trappers? They have five little kids, they rent, they live on one income and they're always happy. That guy's always sitting on the front porch playing guitar, the kids are always running around, laughing.'

'They've got a house that's too cold in winter and too hot in summer, a car that breaks down every second day. I talk to

Anna. Those kids couldn't even afford to go on the three-year-olds' kindy excursion last year.' She stared at him.

'No?' he said mildly.

'No. They had to take the day off and stay home with their dad.'

'Oh. My. God. You mean they missed the Munich Children's Opera, on its eighth Australian tour? Should we call Human Services?'

'Fuck *off.*'

'Mummy?' The word trailed from a nearby window.

Lotte. They went inside and to her door. She sat up, a shadow in the darkness.

'It hurts.'

'I'll get your medicine.' Grace brought the little cup and sat on the side of the bed and stroked back her precious girl's hair. The mattress sank as Tom sat behind her and patted Lotte's leg. Lotte drank her medicine and her parents sat together and breathed in her smell. Around them swirled the horror of the accident, the near miss, the knowledge of how close they had come to losing her. Nothing else mattered.

Finally, Grace spoke in the darkness. 'Two years, Tom. If you could just work for two years while I take time off for a baby, then you can have your year off. How does that sound?'

He sighed deeply, lying down to snuggle beside Lotte. 'It sounds like hell,' he murmured.

'Oh.'

'Would it include the three months I've already worked?'

'Yes.' She had to hide the sympathy she felt. Her clever man, full of passion for his clever dream. She did not want to be his jailer.

'I guess I could keep working on the solar roof at weekends.'

'And nights,' suggested Grace. It was a peace offering; she was sick to death of him working out in the shed every spare minute of his life, but if that was what it took.

'It would be nice to have another baby,' said Tom. He stroked Lotte's shoulder. 'She's so beautiful.'

'If anything happened to her …'

'We're so lucky.' That horrible luck that they had genuflected before since the accident. 'When is the woman coming over, the one who saved Lotte?'

'Saturday.'

'I really want to meet her. And say thank you.'

'I wonder if she's vegetarian.'

'Of course she's vego. She has dreadlocks.'

'It's not the law.'

'It is. Dreadlocks, vego.'

'Maybe.'

'Mm. Goodnight.'

'Should I make the pilaf?'

'Lovely.'

'The banana curry?'

'Hmm.'

'I know, no protein. Vegos hate that.'

Lotte gave a little sigh, a puff, as if she had sunk deep through leagues of ocean and landed on the sandy floor of sleep, towing her father behind her on the seaweed strings of dreams.

'What about the lima bean dish, but without the bacon?'

Tom snored and Grace smiled. She was pretty sure a deal had just been struck.

That night, Eddy breathed in a steam of peas and gravy, and

watched his mother stab another slice of overcooked roast lamb and shake it off onto his plate. He nodded to his father's offer of wine, a startlingly bohemian turn on the part of his parents in recent times, who had drunk beer or Coke with their meals forever, and then he picked up his knife and fork and assembled his most incredulous face.

'This looks *fantastic*, Mum!'

Merle beamed. 'Oh, phooey. It's nothing.' She flicked him one last potato quarter.

Romy raised her knife and fork cautiously. She had two microwaved Sanitarium tofu burgers on her plate; the same as every time they went to Merle and Ray's place for dinner. Merle must have a sack of them stashed in the deep freeze. To the side of that, Romy had four dry roast potato pieces, with no trace of the Gravox and chicken-fat gravy, and a tablespoonful of rehydrated peas. In addition, as if to acknowledge and apologise for her paltry understanding of what on earth a coeliac vegetarian did eat, Merle had added something new; a little flourish. It appeared to be pineapple which had been sliced and then fried, in a mix of breadcrumbs. Or something. Eddy followed Romy's stricken gaze and saw where it rested. Surely that could not be …

Merle leaned between them, her kind eyes turning back and forth reassuringly. 'Do you like pineapple, Romy? I just wanted to make you a little something …'

'Is that bacon?' Romy poked at it with her knife. Ray rose across the table to join the examination, his face full of a sullen threat that was not directed at the plate.

Merle nodded encouragingly. 'It's a Pacific dish. I got it from the *Women's Weekly* cookbook, because you were talking about Pacific foods last time you came over, remember?' Her tone turned instructional. 'You just mix a bit of all-spice and a handful of bacon chips …'

'I don't eat *meat*.' Romy made the statement, its contents only too well known in this household, with apparent satisfaction. Gotcha. Nowhere did she cling to her vegetarian principles quite as firmly as in the home of her boyfriend's parents. She had been known to scoff the odd sausage roll in the wee hours after a night of drinking; she would sometimes absently take a marinated drumstick from Eddy's hands and gnaw off the crispy exterior as if she were in a trance-like state, as if eating your boyfriend's meat would not count before a jury of the great meatless. But at the Plentys, her state of ecological, gastronomic purity was complete. Here in this suburban home of plastic plants and macramé owls, here she was as meat-free as the Dalai Lama.

Merle's horror was tidal, physical. She seized handfuls of her own face, she shrieked into her hands. The origins of bacon chips had obviously somewhere slipped off her radar, and she had recategorised them as a spice, or a flavouring, or something.

'Oh, darling! Oh, I'm so sorry! God, what was I thinking! Bacon chips! Bacon! Of course! Ray, I'm going crazy! Ray you sat and *watched me* cook this for Rommers, and it didn't click with you either, did it?'

'Nope. No, it did not.' Ray pointed the remote control at the television. His mouth twitched, and he appeared to be chuckling at a quite serious news item on the collapse of the Greek economy. 'Didn't notice a thing, darl.'

Now that guilt had been established, Romy was all forgiveness. 'Oh, Merle, please, don't *you* be sorry. I should be sorry, inflicting my dietary needs onto you. And it looks like a ... such an interesting ...' Here she poked at the yellow mush with her fork. '... concept. I'm sure *Eddy* would love to try some.'

Eddy leaned over the dish again, his hands pressed

between his knees under the table. 'Oooh, I'd love to. I reckon vegetarians get all the little treats we carnivores miss out on.'

'Except it's not vegetarian,' Romy corrected him sweetly.

Ray stood and whisked the dish away. Their faces turned to him in a silent chorus of astonishment as he marched it over to the bin and scraped half the contents of the plate into the bin. He then crashed the plate back down on the table, tofu burgers skittering, before Romy. She put her hand to her throat and winced away from him, turning one shoulder slightly as if fearful of a blow.

'Hey, Dad. I would have eaten that,' Eddy protested.

'Ray!' Merle's mouth sagged with distress. Ray clattered his chair around like he would break it against the floor before he reseated himself. He took his cutlery in his big, farming fists, and started eating, glaring at the telly.

'I'm sure we don't want to *force* anyone to eat anything.'

Romy lowered her head like a nun in prayer, and nibbled at her tofu.

Eddy sighed, and ate. So often it ended up like this, Romy and his father growling like two dogs on a leash while his mother and he smiled their faces off and tried to keep the peace. Your father and I are so different, Romy always said in the car on the way home, shaking her head. A red-necked, bullying old man and a new-age, feminist young woman, she would marvel. So different! The classic confrontation of generational power! Eddy often reflected privately that Romy and his father were actually scarily similar. It was just that stubbornness, like second-hand clothes, looked stylish on the young, and plain dowdy on the old.

Eddy and Romy had met at Romy's parents' wake. His parents knew her parents through the church, and when Carlos and Francesca Fernandez were killed in a car crash towing their caravan up the Hume Highway, his parents went to the funeral. Their own car was in for servicing that week, and Eddy was driving them everywhere; to golf, to the doctor, to the supermarket. When he heard about the funeral, he offered to drop them off and pick them up. His mother saw it as a good chance to show him off to her acquaintances. Eddy was the sort of son you showed off. He had a good job and nice skin and he had no tattoos or earrings. On the downside, he could come across as a little embarrassed in his demeanour and not very confident, although he had an endearing gentleness and excellent manners.

But when he laid eyes on Romilda Fernandez, he forgot his manners immediately.

'So, got yourself a girlfriend?' Roger Davis from the golf club had enquired, winking at Eddy's dad. But Eddy pushed past him without responding and crossed the room.

'I'm Eddy,' he told the pretty, dark-haired woman with the swollen red eyes. 'You must be Carlos and Francesca's daughter.' He had heard she was living and working in London, had been called by the Australian police in the middle of the night to hear the news that her parents were dead. Had flown back from an English winter into a blistering Melbourne summer.

'My name's Romy.' She pressed her hands to her eyes and walked out the back door to where the sun was setting and fruit bats wheeled through the branches of a giant fig tree. He followed, and offered her a clean hanky. She took it.

'I just ... wish I'd been able to say goodbye.'

'You're living in London?'

'Streatham,' she said. He nodded, having never heard of it. Should he run and get her a seat? But then he would have to leave her.

'Are you going back?' He couldn't believe the greed of his own question; too desperate to hear the answer to mess around with niceties like *what a loss, so sorry to hear, pillars of the community.*

'Yes. I was an actress there. I'm part of a show, so I have to go back.'

A double knife to the heart. First she was going back, and second she was an actress, something so incredibly glamorous and interesting that her geographical placement on the other side of the planet was a mere pebble of an obstacle when compared to this. He had held up a drink with a straw for her to sip from, through her tears, and wondered how illegal it would be to kidnap her and physically stop her from leaving the country.

But in the end, it wasn't necessary. Heartbroken by her parents' death, Romy was easily convinced she was in love with Eddy. A wise elder in her life might have advised her to return to London and her show; suggested that this was not a time to make big decisions, or to abandon a hard-won career break. But there was no such person left in Romy's life, and, although Eddy felt a vague sense of guilt about pressing Romy to stay in Melbourne, it was outweighed by his greedy love, and his overwhelming desire to care for her.

Romy moved in with him in Melbourne and found waitressing work. For a few years, the two of them were happy. Her grief about losing her parents was so solid at first, that it was almost a third member of the household, but he grew used to it. In his heart, he knew this grief was his ally. She was a creature he had captured while broken; an exotic bird with a damaged wing, who he had tenderly nursed back to health. Romy's sexual infidelity with the yoga instructor had shaken him, but he thought of it now as a momentary glitch. A fluttering of those once-damaged wings, a stretching of them. It didn't occur to him that those wings might have healed, that that bird might be beating her chest against the bars of her cage.

No, no. Romy had always needed him, all their relationship, and he had always looked after her. That would never change.

CHAPTER FOUR

The doorbell rang, and Melody ran down the stairs. 'Van.'

She held her friend for a moment, inhaling his scent of smoke and sweat and metal. He followed her back up and through her doorway, and let a small backpack slide to the ground. He wore a short-sleeved Hawaiian shirt under a sleeveless leather vest, and black fisherman pants, his thin ankles bare. In Birkenstocks, small silver rings gleamed on his toes, and a tattoo marked the top of his right foot.

'Some supplies.' He dropped a shopping bag on the table. She rifled through tofu, bok choy, a packet of the chocolate teddy biscuits that Skipper loved.

'Thanks so much for finding the flat.'

'It's cool.'

'Thought you had a job this week?' she said.

He shrugged. 'Put it off.'

'Uh-huh.'

Melody had once had a twin, Esme, and Van had been Esme's boyfriend during high school, until her death from a heart infection contracted after getting a tattoo. Melody had known Van as a skinny weird kid, then as an art school student, briefly as a fashion designer, then as a photographer, then he had seemed to create a niche as a stylist, then there was that bit where he imported things from overseas, things that were never really explained. She suspected drugs, but made a point of never asking. Nowadays he seemed to own real estate around the country, and to make unexplained business trips.

'You cut your hair,' she said.

'Too hot for dreads.'

'No. Dreads are cooling. Like insulation.'

'Does everyone stare at you here?'

'I don't know. A bit. Hey, are you doing anything Saturday night?'

He shrugged. There were things he didn't tell her. But she knew he would drop everything to help her.

'It's just this woman, the mum of the kid that I —' she raised her eyebrows and mimed dramatically '— *saved*, she's asked me for dinner. And said I could bring a friend.'

'Oooh.' He fluttered his eyelashes and squeezed up his shoulders in a camp way. She laughed.

'*Melbourne* people.'

He agreed. 'They *love* to do dinner parties.'

'And they plan things *so* far ahead. Skipper's new kinder have arranged a playdate for all the children in *three weeks*' time.'

'I hope you've logged it into his iPhone.'

'Of course.' She laughed, but felt uncomfortable. She was desperate for Skipper to make friends. Bad karma to be badmouthing the mothers.

'So you got him into a kindy. Montessori?'

'State government. Just around the corner. It's sweet. So, anyway, will you come?'

'To the free dinner?'

'Yes.'

'Sure. Why not?'

She smiled and stirred her tea. What was the rhyme the children had chanted each morning back in Tuntable, under the painted sun and stars of their ceiling, cross-legged on mats woven with wool from the kindy's own goats?

Here is the earth,
Here is the sky,
Here are my friends,
And here am I.

Grace toasted the almond flakes, banging the pan on the stove as the nuts browned. The strangers were due in fifteen minutes and she wished she'd never asked them. The last thing she felt like now was facing people she barely knew, and making conversation for a whole night. What had she been thinking? What was wrong with her? Couldn't she have just sent a thank-you card? This was beyond gratitude; she must have been punishing herself for the accident, and her own negligence. Maybe she could ring and cancel. That was it, she would say that Lotte was sick, a very contagious child thing, chicken pox maybe. No doubt the hippy didn't vaccinate. She froze, immobilised with hope and fear. Was there time? She stared into the almond flakes, now turning from brown to black. Should she invest the remaining fifteen minutes in finishing the stir fry, putting on the rice, checking that the broken toilet seat was at least clean, or should she throw her bets on finding the kindy contact list in the hope that Melody had been included, despite Skipper's late enrolment. Although there was a look about

Melody as if she might not even have a phone. She might live in a cave. Grace stepped towards her little desk, overloaded with a laptop and electrical cords and unpaid bills and lists, and then she stepped back and looked at her black almonds and her stir fry. But the guy, Eddie, she certainly didn't have *his* number.

A knock rapped through the house, signaling an end to the decision. Was it them? Were they early? Curse them to Hell and back. Not even ready. Grace cast one despairing look around her and strode up the hall, with what she hoped sounded welcoming, Gosh-I-can't-wait-to-get-to- that-door-and-see-you footsteps. Grace had already decoded the initially faltering knock, now being repeated too aggressively, as that of a child. She swung back the door and crouched to be on the same eye-level as Skipper, who wore a little checked shirt and some cargo pants. He carried flowers, which looked as though they might have been picked from nearby front yards; Grace thought she recognised the wattle from the Trappers' rental.

'Did you bring them for us?' Grace took them. 'How beautiful! Come in, come in!' Then she stood and saw Melody had brought someone; a man with a shaven head and a leather bikie jacket that gave him the look, in the shadows, of a cartoon super hero; as if he should have a logo emblazoned across his broad chest. He stretched out an arm to shake her hand, and the leather sleeve shifted to reveal tattoo ink on a muscled forearm. The silver rings on his fingers were an oddly feminine touch. His warm and rough hand enclosed her small one, and she felt the physical jolt of contact travel straight from her palm to her thighs. He stepped close to her and smiled. She blushed and glanced around; where was Tom?

'This is Van.' Melody dropped a bike helmet onto the step with a clunk. The long beige knots fell down her shoulders and her blue eyes were serious. She wore no makeup and her features were little-girlish: a pert nose, soft-looking cheeks with faint freckles, and a mouthful of what looked like a pre-schooler's milk-teeth — small and shell-white, slivers of space between each.

'Fan, was it?'

'*Van.*'

'As in Morrison.' God, the voice on him, the sort of spine-tingling vocal damage that took a lot of drinking and smoking and probably shouting to achieve. A faint American accent. Grace stood back to let him move further into her home, against her better judgment. She leaned to see where he was going and bumped her head on the coat hooks. Where was her daughter?

'We didn't get chocolates because they make you fat,' Skipper told her.

'Oh, of course.' Grace blushed and twinkled at Melody over the little boy's head, and hoped he wasn't about to tell her his mother had said she was fat, as only a four-year-old could do. She hastily headed them all off on a tour of the house. 'Here's the lounge room. We still have to fix that crack and we're choosing a colour for the feature wall, but it should be finished by the time we're ready to move into the old folk's home.' She laughed shrilly. 'Over the hall is our bedroom ...' Grace always did this on her house tours: launched into them and then faced the dilemma of whether to include the master bedroom. It always felt a little intimate to show people one's married bedroom — 'this is centre stage,' one bawdy friend had introduced her own boudoir as

— but then it was also a little reserved to hold a part of yourself back. And she owed such a debt of thanks to this woman, she would hide nothing, absolutely nothing, even the pile of clothes on the bed, obviously revealing she had tried on at least a dozen outfits. 'Excuse the mess, I'm just sorting through things to throw out.' She marched around the bed, determinedly waving at the wall of blankets down the middle of the unmade bed, the cluttered, dusty side tables, and the towels on the bathroom floor. She could see herself through Melody's eyes; oh-so-boring and middle-class suburbia.

'Nice curtains.' Melody stood in the bedroom doorway and fiddled with the zipper of her jacket. She cast a look down the hall. 'Where's ...?'

'Oh, they've found ...'

Skipper and Lotte had indeed discovered each other. Their reunion was reminiscent of an old movie; they saw each other down the length of the hall and they ran. Once face-to-face, they stopped and regarded each other from a hand's width apart, and then Lotte put her hands around Skipper and hugged him. Skipper looked thoughtfully over Lotte's shoulder while this occurred; he didn't respond until she went to pull back, at which he raised his fists and squeezed her until she gasped.

'Oh, sweet.'

'Don't hurt her.' Melody smiled. The children moved apart.

'Doesn't hurt!' Lotte shrieked. 'Come and see my room!'

Tom emerged, in King Gee shorts and dusty boots and hair thick with grease. 'This is Tom!' Grace smiled at him threateningly.

He offered the newcomers his hand, and then looked at its oily state apologetically and withdrew it.

'So you saved our little girl's life.' Tom said. 'How do we thank you?'

Maybe by having a shower, thought Grace. Melody winced modestly and raised a hand as if to bat away gratitude. Grace could see they would have to stop thanking her; she didn't like it. Which would make it even harder to find things to talk about. The man she had brought smelled so strongly of cigarettes and alcohol that her eyes watered. She had a sudden and passionate need to steer them out of this passageway and into the lounge room.

'Come, sit down. Tom, go and have a shower and hurry up!' A mock scolding tone for the benefit of the visitor, who should have smiled in appropriate amusement at the foibles of men. That was what women did. Melody, however, just watched Tom leave with grave eyes.

Eddy held the ring box in his pocket and jiggled it between his fingers. He had spent the week in an unhealthy, sleep-deprived anxiety, and he knew he was now obsessed with finding the right place to propose marriage. It was Romy's own fault, with her superstitious belief that the way things began determined their outcome. He knew she would put unnecessary emphasis on how the proposal was made, and, if she said yes, she would for the rest of their married lives link events back to the circumstances surrounding this momentous question. For her sake, he wanted it to be perfect. But was it for his own sake, too? Did he want to give himself the best chance? Was he in fact not sure she would say yes? But who could ever be sure of anything, he wondered, as he sat on the bed and folded a cotton handkerchief into the pocket of his pants. Romy had been in the bathroom for half an hour now, and Eddy really needed to urinate. He went to the back garden and peed on the lemon tree, zipped himself and put his hand back in his pocket, stroking the velvet of the ring box as if it was his future. Their unborn children would one day ask him *Dad, how did you propose to Mum?* and he wanted to have something passable to tell them. Should he book a flash restaurant? Such a cliché, though. No, tonight was full moon, a fortuitous coincidence he had seized upon when Romy had mentioned it this morning, and the forecast was fine. They would go to this dinner at the family of the rescued child, and spend an evening basking in the gratitude of these thankful people — Grace seemed very nice, and her husband, Tom, was an inventor, Romy would like that. Then, on the way home (moon rise was 11.07pm, he had checked in the paper), he would take a detour to the Royal Botanic Gardens in South Yarra, park under the elm trees on the east side, and take Romy to the low part of the fence where they had entered in the first week of their relationship, five years before. On that night, another full moon, they had frolicked through the dark park like Puck and Titania, finally stopping in a copse of endangered cycads to fuck awkwardly under some palm fronds, the far-off torch of the wandering park guard forcing them to choke back their giggles. Eddy had never before done such a thing, and he knew he had scored full points for it, and it had taken years to occur to Romy that he probably would never risk it again. Anyway, he would take them back to this holy site and hope to absorb some of that Puckish spirit, and make a proposal that would be remembered for a lifetime. Hopefully she wouldn't want to actually shag there again; Eddy's heart raced with anxiety at the very thought. The frightening possibility of getting caught, the discomfort of sex under trees, the added logistical difficulty of ensuring Romy reached orgasm in such an environment, while he would, conversely, ejaculate prematurely from sheer stress. No, his bedroom at home was by far his preferred venue. Although hopefully a marriage proposal *would* spark a shag. It had been a while now.

Romy came out of the bathroom and went to rummage for an earring. Her buxom figure was clad in a black dress which showed off her olive skin; the tops of her breasts.

'God, you're gorgeous.'

'Don't mess up my hair.'

'I love these underpants!'

'Eddy!' She wriggled her dress back down and kissed him maternally on the forehead. He fell back on the bed and smiled at the ceiling; velvet between his fingers. His future was in that body; that courageous spirit, the already-existing organism that was Eddy-and-Romy. His heart was so full he had to bite his tongue, hold back his ring-loaded hand. Just four hours and he would feel the bliss of depositing this impatient load.

'So how long have you and Van been together?' Romy used her knife to nudge the last grains of rice onto her upturned fork, as she murmured the question to Melody. Van had sauntered outside to smoke. Melody hoped he was not rolling himself a joint. She really needed to make some friends for Skip, to start building a normal life.

'We're not together.' Melody paired her knife and fork and laid them across the plate. She had answered this question before, in other situations, and was unsure why it made her internally wince. It felt even more uncomfortable when asked in Van's presence, although he only smiled at it.

Was it simply the resistance to being put in an Married/Unmarried box, or the weird thought of being in a relationship with Van, or was it, worse, a flicker of guilt about this friendship, a sense that she should have cooled it a while back? 'We're just friends.'

'Really?' Romy looked towards the door where Van had exited, through which he could be expected to return. She was an attractive woman who had played to the table throughout this dinner; charming Tom with flattering questions about his invention, beseeching Melody for every detail of Lotte's rescue, crouching on the floor to talk to the children about their toys, although she quickly lost interest in that when the adults stopped watching. A woman who enjoyed attention, who had the enviable knack of being able to duck out of boring turns in conversations, who could steer the subject quickly back to herself. A lovely rich aura; maybe a deep, dark rose.

'He was my sister's boyfriend.' Melody shrugged. She thought of the cat with the forked tail that used to hang around their family home, that Van and her sister had adored. Eddy gazed at his girlfriend; he was a planet to her sun. He was in love with her, and the woman was in love with being loved. Melody had seen it before.

Grace and Tom's house had a comfortably messy look about it, as though one day, long ago, there had been a theme, an effort made at Understated Style, but in the manner of many with a young child this had been superseded by the theme of Just Surviving. The glass of shells in the window sill was coated in dust, and a fly had died amongst the sand dollars and baby's ears. Picture books were piled on a chair, in an attempt to clean up, she deduced, and in fact it was clear that someone with a propensity for grouping like objects rather than actually putting them away had been placed in charge of cleaning duties. Phone chargers were tangled in a bowl; one full washing basket was placed on another and tucked under a table; hair pins and spare change and miscellaneous small objects sat in their respective piles on the mantelpiece.

Melody surreptitiously checked her watch, and wondered whether she should suggest sitting outside, under the rays of the full moon. They were nice enough people, but the night had somehow, so far, not quite gelled, and she had given up hope that it would ever leave this realm of getting-to-know-you questions, punctuated with Romy's flirtation and Grace's teary gratitude for Melody's lifesaving act. Grace's husband, Tom, seemed heavy and quiet, as if he would really have preferred a night in bed with a takeaway and the cricket on telly over this high-pitched dinner party. He had used his wife's outbursts of thankfulness to nod mutely and slip off to the kitchen, from which the day's cricket highlights could be heard murmuring on the radio.

Grace herself had felt the urge to show Melody Lotte's birth and newborn baby pictures, as if in stopping the child from being killed, she was somehow in the same category as a mother who gave her life. Melody had quite enjoyed the pictures, she was always interested in births, but was privately dismayed by the arsenal of medical equipment Lotte had been plugged into upon entry to the world. Skip had been homebirthed on the commune, on a warm moonlit night like this, and it was one of Melody's sweetest memories.

'I'll go check on Skip,' she said hopefully, rising from the table. 'And Lotte.'

'They're fine,' said Tom gloomily, having already unsuccessfully tried this excuse to gain respite. 'You'll have trouble tearing them apart.'

'Oh.' She sank reluctantly back into her chair.

Tom sighed, and attempted a smile. 'What do you do?'

'Now? Look after Skip.'

'Ah ...'

Money. She could see his brain ticking over, with city thoughts and calculations. 'We get by,' she said calmly. 'I never worry about money.'

'Really?' His mouth hung open. She had his full attention. He leaned towards her as if she had signaled she was about to make some great announcement. She felt compelled to make one.

'The universe will provide. It always does.'

He fell back in his chair, his cheeks drained of colour, his eyes wide with shock.

It was all too weird. Melody excused herself and went to look for Skip.

'Home time, Skip.'

'Noooo!' Skip skittered under Lotte's bed like a crab. 'I want to stay here.'

'Aren't you getting tired?' She crouched and raised the blanket. The two children pressed themselves into the dark cavity, their heads together. She gave up, and straightened herself. 'Well, *soon*, Skip. Five more minutes.'

She dragged her feet back to the dining table. There they all were, in varying stages of social torture. It was like an Oscar Wilde play gone wrong; it was the most boring dinner she had attended in her life. On weary examination, she found that her seat had been taken, with Romy leaning on one arm to chat to Van, who sat in a cloud of marijuana smoke. Romy tilted her head, and played with her hair. Melody stood behind her chair and crouched for her bag, pretending to look for something inside it.

'Oh, I've taken your chair!!' Romy giggled mischievously,

and wrinkled her nose at Van, as though they had done it together. Across the table, Eddy was distractedly involved in a conversation with Grace about teaching standards. He was pale and thin-lipped, and answering Grace's earnest queries with sing-song generalities. 'I guess there never would be enough money in the system to make people happy, would there?' His eyes drifted back to Romy. He laughed loudly at a comment Van had made, seeking to thrust himself into their conversation, but Grace, by his side, was insistent.

'This government needs to really examine its policies, and it needs to get the people on board. For example, they need to transfer control of kindergartens to the Department of Education. What's it doing in the Department of Human Services, alongside aged care and immunisations? Everyone these days knows — everyone — that the first few years are when you lay down the foundations for a human being's life ...'

'Oh, precisely.' Eddy sounded faint. 'Let me educate the boy and I will give you back the man ... Romy, who is it we know who always says that?'

Melody couldn't get out of this place quickly enough. She cleared her throat. 'We should probably think about ...'

'Would you like your chair back?' Romy broke off her whispering with Van and smiled up at Melody, at the same time lowering her chest to the table as though to suction-cup herself to it.

'No, no, I'll sit here.' Melody crossly took the chair beside Eddy.

'I've never done it!' Romy breathed at Van. Melody tried to catch Van's eyes, so she could roll her own heavenward at this silly woman, but he would not look at her. He was idle, and stoned, and therefore dangerous. She should not have brought him, should not have tried to mix the old world and the new. He sat back in his chair and regarded his new friend with what Melody recognised as curiosity, the same emotion with which he might have inspected an interesting beetle. He was not a man any woman should trust. He had never fully recovered from Esme's death, and had a sliver of ice in his heart. He had taken off his leather jacket, and he wore a red T-shirt with a Chinese symbol on the front, and his muscular arms rested on the table. A small silver earring twinkled in his ear and his face was unshaven. Despite everything, he appeared to be the social success story of the evening, while Grace and Tom's effusive speeches of gratitude to Melody had nervously withered away an hour ago in the face of her own lack of interest.

'We could do it right now.' Van leaned forward, his elbows on the table and his muscles twitched, smiling down at Romy. The silly woman widened her eyes, squeezed her hands together and breathed 'Yes!' Everyone listened, although other conversations limped along as people tried not to look at the only two people enjoying themselves.

'We all know how important kindergarten teachers are, and yet they get paid less than primary teachers!' Grace orated, determined. 'About twenty per cent less, according to the last Education Union surveys. I bet most people aren't even aware of that. Did *you* know kindergarten teachers get paid twenty per cent less?'

'We could!' Romy's face was alight. She pushed back her chair and stopped, as if waiting for Van to do something.

'Well.' He stood and put on his jacket, and strode to the door, stopping to cock an eyebrow at Romy as if daring her. She practically ran after him.

'What are you guys up to?' Eddy tried to make a joke of it.

'Just taking Romy here for a spin.'

'Van!' Melody said. He could not do this: take this woman off for a motorbike ride and leave her partner ashen-faced. Why had she brought him?

'You're *what*?'

'Does she have a helmet?'

'She can use yours.'

Eddy stood. 'Where are you going?'

'Little ride,' Romy threw back over her shoulder, already out the front door.

Eddy followed them out. 'Great machine, Fan. I'd be interested to check out the engine when you get back. I have a small bit of knowledge about motors, nothing really extensive, but ...' His trailing words could be heard through the open window, the warm night.

The chainsaw roar of a motorbike sliced through his words, and a picture fell from the wall of the lounge room. The glass cracked.

Eddy stood out on the verandah and peered into the night. They had been gone over an hour. He stared and stared, but it was pointless; he would hear the motorbike returning from two suburbs away if it came, the ugly damn thing was so loud. Did it have any safety features, or were there no such things for motorbikes? The velvet box in his pocket had been rubbed and rolled, over and over, until the nap, once comforting and thrilling, had become a sensation linked with sickening dread, and its touch only heightened the toxicity of his panic. He hated this place now, these people who had witnessed his humiliation, this dusty verandah with its pile of uncared-for bikes leaning against the weatherboard, a child seat on the back of one. The orange foot of the seat had dropped off onto the ground, a while ago judging by the cobwebs nested within. He checked his watch, again, and peered into the darkness, again. The biker's friend appeared beside him, shaking her head.

'She wants to call the police.' Melody gestured her head in at the front door.

'Well of course she should!' Eddy strode back towards the door, his rage at Romy only too keen to be expelled upon a less-deserving subject. 'And why not? Does that man have something to hide? Oh, God. Oh please God, don't let him crash.'

'Van's a good rider.' Melody's voice was calm.

'He looks like a bit of risky business to me!' Eddy blustered. 'With that ... earring.' He sounded stiff and old-mannish to himself, and he braced for a smirk from this woman, some mockery. But there was none.

'You're right.' Melody picked a twig and snapped it carefully in half. 'Van is a risk-taker. He rides a motorbike. He lives a bit more ... well ... But he's never crashed that bike that I know of. She'll be safe.'

Eddy wished she'd go inside and leave him alone. He burned with indignant shame, to be left with these people, to have his doubts about Romy peeled open so he was exposed, just the rotten core of his needy, suspicious love on show.

He sat outside alone, for how long, he did not know. He checked the ABC news on his phone for Melbourne road accidents. He could hear the others talking inside. The children were toasting marshmallows. The night that had been about to end had somehow found a second wind on the back of his misery. Melody popped her head out again. 'Of course it's not *impossible* they could have an accident,' she speculated. 'Maybe we *should* call the police.'

'They haven't,' he blurted, leaning on the letterbox pillar and biting his tongue. Unknown to the others, he had called Romy's mobile. The dial tone had been interrupted by laughter at the other end; Romy's giggles, and a male murmur, before the unmistakable sound of someone fumbling to press the hang-up button. Eddy had held the disconnected line to his ear for a full minute. That had been not been the sound of a woman held hostage, or injured on the side of the road. And yet, strangely, it was a sound that made his heart dive into freefall.

What had Romy said recently? *This year will be my year of trying new things.*

'Oh! You got onto her, then?'

'No.' He put the phone back into his pocket. 'Well, I called her but there was no answer. But I just know ... that she's alright.' His gloom must be revealing it all. Such a despondent tone. 'I know she's not dead.'

'I guess you know these things. When you're close. As a couple. In a relationship.'

'We're very close.'

'You can see that.'

'We're practically engaged.'

'Oh, that's great!'

He took out the ring box and opened it. 'Argyle diamond.'

'Oh!' Melody took a step back and fanned herself. '*Shit.* Was that ...' She gestured, dismayed, out at the night and back at Eddy. 'Were you going to ... tonight ...?'

'I still am. I hope.'

'Absolutely! Absolutely! You know I think we should call the police ...'

'I thought you were worried about getting the police involved.' Eddy hadn't asked why this was so. Drugs, rape, murder, general hoondom, it went without saying just to look at the man. If Romy wanted to try new things, she had certainly found something new.

'I was. But you know what? I think it's more important we get your girlfriend back.' Melody narrowed her eyes. 'Van's a big boy.'

Eddy kicked some leaves into a pile, fear stabbing his heart. He dialed again, but the phone had been switched off.

'Is your kid asleep?'

Melody shook her head. 'Not yet. Will you come back in? It's nice by the fire.' She touched his arm lightly and walked inside the open front door, raising her hand again as if she had planted a line on him with her touch, and was now reeling him in.

Eddy cast one more despairing look into the darkness, but the line on his arm tugged him authoritatively. He reluctantly went back inside.

Years later Melody would wonder what might have happened had Romy and Eddy gone tidily home to their lives. The dinner party probably would have ended with them all saying goodbye at the earliest polite point. Some lives might not have ended in the way they did. Others might not have begun at all. Certainly she would not have bothered seeing Grace again, outside kindergarten. Even if Eddy had left for home after Romy left with Van, things might have been different. But he did not. He let himself be led back inside in front of the fire, and once there he began to weep. Horrible, cough-like sobs, water spraying from his face. Grace and Melody exchanged looks of alarm. Somehow the brittle shell of the whole night cracked and peeled off, and beneath it was a gentler world, with more of their real selves in it. They sat very late by the funny little woodburner with its clover-leaf wrought-iron door, toasting bread and lighting clove cigarettes on glowing embers. Eddy had a cigarette and coughed violently, and it sounded like he might start crying again, until Tom poured him a straight scotch and he laughed bitterly instead. Grace told them stories about her sadistic boss and did an imitation of her, and she was actually quite funny. Tom told a story about having to take Lotte into a board meeting at work where he gave a presentation with her winding around his legs until she interrupted his PowerPoint display by tipping lemonade into the $2000 projector. Melody told them about Tuntable Falls, about the enchanted blue-moon parties and the all-night dancing, the strange and marvelous faces and hair sculptures and clothes concocted of leaves and vines and curtain scraps. About the mad people who had eaten too many magic mushrooms, and the ultramarine lobsters in the Tuntable Creek, and the teenagers fleeing their greying, wrinkly, rainbow-clad parents for Sydney as soon as they were old enough, to become merchant bankers and real estate brokers, and to run internet startups.

Finally they were all talked out and dawn birds chattered outside. They stared into the dying fire. Romy and Van had not returned. The children slept on the floor, a blanket tossed over them, facing each other with lips pursed as if they shared secrets with each even, sleeping breath.

Eddy looked at his watch. 'Well,' he said, and climbed to his feet. 'I should go.'

'Maybe you'll find her at home.' Melody cupped Skipper's cheek in her hand.

'Maybe. Can I give you a lift?' he said.

'There's sleeping bags, you can crash here.' Tom spoke

sleepily. Melody slipped under the blankets which covered Skip, and laid her head behind his on the pillow. Grace rested sleepily on Tom's shoulder, but hastily opened her eyes and climbed to her feet. 'Bye! Thanks for coming! It's been so great. Really. So much better than I ...'

Tom clapped Eddy on the shoulder. 'Give us a call. Keep us posted. We want to know if she comes back.'

'*When* she comes back,' said Grace.

CHAPTER FIVE

Thin branches scratched the dark glass; pale twig fingers flashed in and out of sight. Drops trembled their way down the pane. A paperback sat on his lap, lit by lamplight. A comfortable home, his girlfriend had fled. Where was she on this rainy, rainy night?

He sighed, closed his book and dialed his parents' number.

'What's it been now, over a week? That girl was always going to go and join the circus,' his father growled.

'That's not fair, Dad. Romy never got over losing her parents.'

'We all lose our parents.'

'She was young.'

'She was an adult!' snapped his father. 'I was only a kid when we lost *our* parents.' A farmhouse fire, an older brother who drove the siblings away from the inferno that their parents stayed to fight, and to die in. Eddy could be surprised anew each time he remembered it, his father orphaned and small.

'You don't really know her the way I do.'

His father choked, as if on something unspeakable, and continued. 'Well, I'm sorry. But you'll meet someone else—'

'Don't say that! I don't want to meet someone else. And that's not the point. I'm worried about her. I want to know she's safe. And not ... in trouble.' Safety. Risk. Loss. A farmhouse in flame while a truck full of children bumped away to the rest of their parentless lives. How much of his own life as a risk analyst, a hedger of disaster, had been influenced by that image passed down by his father.

'Jesus, Eddy, of course she's in trouble. She's been in trouble since the moment you've met her. That's the only place she ever wanted to be ...' There were murmurs away from the phone; Merle's faint protests. Ray returned, grumbling. 'Well, that's just my opinion. No one wants to hear the truth these days.'

Eddy watched his reflection, passive in the rainy window. His father was wrong; Eddy did want to hear the truth. If he'd wanted soft-edged comfort, soothing nothings, he would have asked for his mother. But it was his gruff, angry father he needed now. If he could argue with his dad, he might have a hope of convincing himself. 'Should I call the police again?'

'Sure. Tell them to look out for a bloody vegetarian university drop-out who thinks she should be an actress. They can head up to Brunswick Street and bring you back a truckload of them.'

'Dad.'

'Joking.'

'Not very funny.'

'Well, you wait 'til you have a kid and you work like a dog to give him every opportunity, to raise him right, and then some hussy comes along and wipes her boots on him.'

'She didn't!' Eddy stared at the phone. What an awful

image. And what was Romy doing for cash? His own wallet was unnaturally full.

'Well, she didn't bother to say goodbye before she pissed off.'

'Maybe she's been kidnapped.'

'Then ring the police.'

He sighed. 'Yeah. Maybe. Gotta go, Dad.' Examination of Romy's wardrobe and toiletries after the dinner had revealed that she had probably stopped by and packed a small bag. He would not share this with his father, who would be so enraged on his behalf that Eddy would be sapped of his own indignation.

'Have you eaten? Why don't you come over here for dinner?' Behind the abrupt tone, Eddy could hear his father's worry, and his mother's murmuring *tell him ... but ... don't say that* in the background.

'I'm fine. See you.'

He sat and watched the window some more. He had been Romy's hero, her saviour. But saving her from what? Her own vulnerability, her orphaned loneliness, even while he uncomfortably sensed a steely underside to her, a lack of compassion. 'Damaged people are dangerous — they know they will survive,' she had quoted to him. He never believed her, always wondered whether a steady-enough love would stop the bouts of sobbing, the neediness, the despair. Had hoped his constantly applied warmth and kindness could thaw her occasional coldness. She was such a strange mix. She could maintain a silent rage for a week over something as small as running out of coconut milk, exhibiting an icy disdain worthy of a nineteenth-century headmistress. And then he could find her in the garden under the moon, singing in the dew, eating a whole box of ice cream. An artistic temperament, without the art.

Eddy went to bed, got up in the morning, made a tea and returned to his window. He didn't bother getting out of his pyjamas. He had spent the past ten days in them, and nothing had been lost. The world had kept turning. Outside, now, his neighbour walked briskly east along the street, his tie flapping over the shoulder of his white business shirt as if waving Eddy farewell. The man and his tie were heading off to catch the 8.08 city-bound train from Meadowview Station. Eddy double-checked his watch: no doubt about that, the man was definitely aiming for the 8.08. It was 8.01 now and it was about an eight-minute walk to the station. He, personally, would have left nine minutes for the walk, and always did, but he knew that his neighbour, the father of a baby and a toddler, was a man who arrived running and breathless at the station platform each morning, often with the stain of creamy baby-sick on his left suit shoulder, sometimes too late and only seen looking desperate on the wrong side of the window as the train pulled away. Why don't you leave two minutes earlier, he felt like suggesting to the man: George was his name. Your whole life might change. And yet George was married with children, an achievement, it now appeared, beyond Eddy. If *you* had only stayed two minutes later each day, George might say back to Eddy, if you had only lavished those milligrams of extra attention, if you had only sometimes missed a train, if you had made more mistakes, if you had been more fun, and less *you* …

Eddy studied branches of trees. Surprising, the little things that changed from day to day, if you spent long enough just sitting, and looking. This was what it must be like to be old. Maybe he was old. He watched a black bird with a long black beak, and a more delicate grey one with yellow wattles under a yellow beak. After a long pause, where his mind went pleasantly blank, the school children started wandering past, with backpacks that yawned open like clowns' mouths, holding mothers' hands and chattering up to the sky where their mothers' ears were: *and then we ... and then she ... what's your favourite ... but why?* The child traffic dwindled away and there was the faintest chime of a bell. Eddy had rarely, in all his years of living in this house with Romy, heard the local school bell. After another pause the mothers reappeared, walking past on their way home, some in happy clumps, swinging bags and laughing and waving; others grimly tapping on mobiles while they half-walked, half-ran. Things to do. Nobody busier than a working mother, they all knew that. Pillar of the nation. Unlike him, sitting there in his pyjamas, in a daze.

He roused himself. Maybe Romy's departure was not a spontaneous thing; maybe it had been coming for weeks, and he, obsessed with getting the right ring and making the right proposal, had missed the signs. Eddy carefully sent his mind scurrying back through the weekend before The Dinner, the last weekend he had spent with Romy before her dramatic departure.

It had been a long weekend, a public holiday. They had gone to the country, a place called Ten Mile, with Romy's friends. Eddy had been leaning back, quietly looking at the stars, before his folding chair broke. The sky, as he leaned back and gazed, seemed more like a dome than an infinite space, so closely massed were the stars. You forgot about stars, living in the city, or you started to believe those paltry few sparkles spotted through the night-time smog, around the tops of chimneys and at the tops of alleyways, were all there was. Then you came out to Ten Mile, and you remembered. He had carried the diamond in his pocket, as if he had plucked one of those blossoms from the night sky and mounted it on a ring, ready to present to his girl. He remembered hearing something about Mars being visible that night, a big red star, apparently, and he leaned back a little further to look for it. The beauty of the night sky, the roaring fire, the guitar, the singing of Romy and her friends, the ring in his pocket, all combined in a moment of quiet joy. Then he leaned too far back and the chair broke.

There were hoots, screams of laughter, wild applause, cries of 'Taxi!' He laughed along with the crowd, hoping they thought he was drunk. Not likely, they knew him too well. He could sit on a single can all night, and surreptitiously pour out the remains behind a tree at the end. 'Do it again, Eddy!' He clowned around for a while, dragging himself to his feet with a piece of chair in either hand, pretending to puzzle over fitting them back together, like a stupid giant. He mocked himself for the requisite amount of time until their attention waned and he could escape into the darkness. At last the singing started up again and he felt his way to the trampoline at the end of the garden, rubbing his arse. Ow. That really hurt.

'Are you alright?' Mary, Andy's wife, lay stretched on the trampoline staring up at the stars.

'My chair broke.'

'I heard. You wouldn't want sympathy from that lot, would you?'

'Landed right on my coccyx.'

'Ouch. Here.' She rolled onto her side, leaving him room, and he crawled gingerly onto the screen, feeling the rolling motion of the web that held he and Mary, and the give of the steel springs. Her eyes gleamed in the darkness. 'Can I do anything?'

'No thanks.'

'Rub your coccyx?' Was she teasing? He couldn't tell. Surely not Mary, too; he spent enough time feeling like the rest of these guys were privately laughing at him.

'Uh, no thanks.'

'Get some ice?'

'No, no.' Maybe she was actually caring, but he wanted nothing that would draw the mob's attention again. 'God, they're so pissed.' Romy's voice sang high above the others. The guitars played fast and wild, catching the songs' shapes rather than the notes.

'Oh, they're pathetic.' Mary waved her hand, its outline blocking out the stars. 'They get together down here and they regress to sixteen years old. I'll never get Andy back to the motel tonight. He'll be passed out around the fire.'

'Romy's the same. She always comes home from here so restless and grumpy.' How had he forgotten this about Ten Mile? Why on earth had he thought that this might be a good place to propose? It was the worst place in the world. Or no, he could have taken her back to London and out the front of the theatre where she had narrowly missed making her acting debut, robbed by her parents' death. That would possibly be a worse place.

'I know. How long does it take to get sixteen out of your system? I couldn't wait to get out of my teens. Seems like Andy never wanted to leave.'

'Maybe they just had a better time than us.' Romy's friends had bonded in high school, and taken to hitchhiking down here every available weekend to camp. It was a circle knit close with histories of drunken adventures in the hills and valleys now around them; unusual in a time when most of their peers were seeing out their adolescence in the local shopping mall. One member had bought an old farmhouse and moved down here to raise a large family, drawing back all the old gang again in a regular festival of nostalgia. Some of these adults had children of their own, and these offspring were now doing laps around the farmhouse, a mad tribe brandishing light sabers and running through stars, falling in long grass, city kids dizzy with so much space and freedom. From the trampoline, Eddy could hear shrieks and see gashes of torchlight bumping through the night.

Mary said: 'Do you think you and Romy will have kids?'

'I hope so.' He felt in his pocket for the velvet-coated box holding the ring. 'My mother would love a grandchild.'

There was a pause from Mary at this, something that went unsaid. Then she spoke. 'Romy's so lucky to have you.'

'Why, cos I'm a bloke who wants a kid?'

'Cos you're a bloke who thinks about his mum, and about what she wants.'

He exhaled, a little indignant, not sure whether to be flattered or feel silly. 'Right.'

'Hope my girls find men like you.'

'Mary! I'm not that good.'

'Yes, you are. You're better.'

Blushing in the dark, he squeezed the ring box tight; imagined losing it, in this wilderness of long grass and fruit trees; a pastoral island barely marked out by wire in a sea of bush. You might never see it again; a month's salary trampled into the cow dung.

'Getting cold. Might head back.'

He returned to the fire and stood close to Romy. She wore a jacket of synthetic fur and she slipped her arm through his.

'Where have you been?'

'On the trampoline.'

'Ah.'

'Want to go for a walk? Look at the stars?' He rolled the velvet box around the tips of his fingers, out of sight.

'No, thanks.' She sipped a can of beer and looked across the fire to where Alison and Peter were deep in discussion about agents and publicists. One was a writer, one was a painter, and they were both embarrassingly earnest about their success. Romy grew stiff and silent now as she listened. She let go of Eddy's arm and moved closer to them.

'So when's your exhibition, Peter?'

'Next month. And you? Any auditions coming up?'

'I just did the one for the photocopy paper ad,' Romy said, with studied offhandedness. 'But you know how they are. They always want some blonde bimbo.' The photocopy audition had been three months ago now, and Eddy remembered Romy had already told Peter about it, and had already made the dig at the blonde who had won the job. But Peter acted like he hadn't heard the story before. He expressed sympathy, again, and Eddy liked him a little better for it.

'Bastards.'

'Daddy.' A small figure appeared in the doorway of the farmhouse, clutching a blanket. Only Eddy heard her above the noise. Her father, Thomas, had his hand immersed in an esky of ice, a circle of blokes around him counting the seconds as he sought to break the night's record.

Eddy went over to the child.

'Are you okay, Ella?'

'It's too noisy.' She rubbed her eyes and glanced back inside, where sleeping babies and toddlers were scattered on cushions and crumpled blankets, their closed eyes all facing the television screen, like corpses circling a dried-up billabong. A finished DVD played its menu screen in ghostly rotation.

'Come on, I'll take you back to bed.'

Inside, Eddy picked his way carefully amongst small bodies to the vacant spot on the couch, still warm. The girl tried to curl up on his lap, a move he deftly dodged, telling her she was too heavy. He sat her beside him, put a blanket over her and tucked her in.

'Can you tell me a story?' she asked.

He glanced outside; the child's father had now yielded his place at the esky and was chanting along another contender. No real reason to bother him.

'Uh. Once upon a time a man loved a lady very much. So much, that he wanted to ask her to marry him.'

'Was she a princess?'

'Well, to him she was. Anyway ...'

'Was she a *real* princess?'

'A suburban princess, let's say. Anyway, he wondered how to go about this task ...'

'He has to get a ring.' At their feet, a baby moaned and jabbed some unseen monster with a chubby fist before rolling over.

'Exactly. So he went off to the shop and got a ring.' He tugged a blanket up over a curly blond boy, and pushed a pillow away from a sleeping toddler's face. Ella watched him until he sat down again.

'And he has to do a mission,' she told him.

He stared at her. 'What?' This may have been the wrong topic to choose; Ella's eyes were wide with opinion, and her wakefulness seemed to be gently sweeping the room. One toddler made a short, unintelligible but distinctly formal speech in his sleep, another kissed the air longingly and began to whimper. Eddy spotted a nearby dummy and hastily reinserted it.

'You know, if she's a princess, he has to do a mission —

like kill a dragon, or find a riddle that makes the sad king laugh ...'

Eddy thought about bungy-jumping in New Zealand, which Romy had wanted them to do, and which he had wriggled out of. God, could you imagine the risk ranking matrix on that? The insurance premiums those people must pay ... 'Well, maybe he went to the king and the king didn't need him to do a mission.'

'They *always* need to do a mission.'

'Who's telling this story?'

She stared at him doubtfully. Man, little girls were being born hard-wired to want more, more, more. What was it, some genetic selection programme? Now that a diamond ring, the ability to vacuum and a willingness to take family leave when the kids were sick were commonplace, the next generation would want all this plus a dragon slain, to say nothing of an act of undergraduate stupidity involving a steep drop and a massive rubber band. He pressed on.

'Okay then, the king said you must go and speak to every frog in the land ...'

'Are you and Romy going to get married?' Like a flute, that little voice.

'Maybe. Keep your voice down a bit.'

'Well, are you?'

He blinked and consulted his empty hands. 'Er, maybe. No. Well I don't know.'

'Can I see the ring?'

Eddy regarded her. She stared back at him. She was scary. She could read minds. She had x-ray vision. It was time he left this nursery; went and did man things.

'That's enough. Go to sleep.'

Next morning the air in his tent smelt stale and alcoholic, and he wrenched open the zipped door, gasping for oxygen. He fell back and stared at the polyester roof, tracing the lines of the seams, and finally Romy stirred and opened her eyes.

'My head.'

He kissed her forehead and got up alone, the ring still in his pocket. He would make her a coffee. But out in the eucalyptus morning, where sun kissed dewdrops on every glittering green surface and the air was sweet, dirty urchins drifted upon him like a polluted tide.

'I'm hungry.'

'I'm thirsty.'

'Can we have breakfast?'

'Don't you have parents?' he muttered, as he built a fire, boiled water and crossly washed bowls still caked with the previous night's dessert. He dried them and laid them out in a row. He found some Weetbix and rationed them out. Raided someone's esky and used up almost all their milk, saving the last centimetre for Romy's coffee. Washed spoons and then handed out a bowl of Weetbix and milk to each child.

'Sugar?' A little one held her bowl up to him, baby legs bare below a too-big jumper. She belonged in a seventeenth-century orphanage.

'Rots your teeth.'

Back in the tent, Romy sat with her head in her hands. She accepted the coffee and huddled over it.

'There's no sugar?'

'Romy. You could say thank you. I did have to wash up and feed half a dozen children out there before I could even get to the coffee.'

'Thank you.' She sipped sadly. 'You're not having a good time, are you? You don't like these guys.'

'That's not true. They're okay, it's just their parenting skills leave a bit to be ...' He lowered his voice to a whisper. 'I mean, if they're going to bring their kids, it might be nice if they actually looked after them.'

'Mmm.'

'They're fine, they're fine, these people. They're your friends, I know. It's just ... you get different around them. You're not you.'

Romy put down the coffee and stared thoughtfully out of the tent's flaps. 'I feel like I *am*. Sometimes I feel I'm more *me* with these guys than anyone. And then I go home and I wonder just *who* I've become? Who *am* I?'

Eddy sighed. They would drive home today, and Romy would be deflated. 'You'd be a better mother than any of them.'

She made a face. 'I don't know about children.'

He smoothed her hair, and cupped her jaw. 'We could make one, you know. I've heard it's quite easy.'

Romy put her forehead between her fingers and rubbed desperately. 'I think I'm going to be sick.'

There was a knock at the front door, startling Eddy from his memories. He inhaled sharply; he would not answer. He checked that his pale blue pyjama top was buttoned. He rolled the navy piping that edged the jacket between his fingers. He froze; there was the ghost of a face in the window. He stared at it for a full half a minute before realising that it was his own reflection. He was losing it. More knocking. Who was it? He could not speak to anyone, he felt too close to weeping. Real men didn't weep. Was it his mother, maybe bearing a plate of hot roast? He was kind of hungry. But he wanted to see no one except for Romy, and Romy would not knock. This was her home. Or was it, in her eyes? Maybe it *was* her, maybe the knocking was an apologetic overture, an acknowledgement that she had betrayed him. He stood and reached the door in giant steps, his heart bursting for terror that she would creep away again, into the mysterious world of Missing.

He threw open the door, but it was not Romy. A man stood before him. The little girl's father. From the road accident. From the dinner. Tom. He was momentarily unrecognisable in a navy suit and white shirt, although he had loosened his tie and was holding a six-pack.

'G'day, brought some beers. Wanna drink?'

Eddy looked down as if feigning surprise to find himself in sleepwear. 'Uh. Okay.' At this time of morning? But then he saw the time: it was well after lunch.

Tom had flowed inwards by now, like a liquid. Eddy could not remember whether he had gestured his guest inside or not, but Tom roamed through the house swigging his beer and checking out the décor. Patches of mud and grass stuck to the back of Tom, on what looked like a good-quality suit, but Eddy decided not to mention it. He did not really think Tom would care. Was he drunk? Not very. The school children would walk past again soon. He felt ridiculously sad at the prospect of missing them, and anxious to return to his window. 'Shall we sit in the front room?'

'Here in the kitchen's fine.'

'But I need to … it's nicer up there … this way …'

'Sure. Are you sick?'

'No.' Eddy declined to offer any reason for why he was wearing pyjamas at three in the afternoon. 'And you? Not at work?'

'Nope.' Tom offered no excuse either, and so the two

men sat in harmony at the front window, cautiously free of explanations, and drank beer. The women drifted back along the street, their faces ambivalent as they left behind the private pleasures of the day and took on their mother-selves again. Eddy looked at Tom nervously; his own isolation had given him a queer, dislocated feeling, as if he was speaking through fifty layers of soundproof glass.

'She hasn't come back,' he said, too loudly. And then he shrank back from himself; all wrong, all wrong. Being human was too difficult.

Tom nodded as if he knew. He took out a newspaper, and flicked through it, then folded it and held it before Eddy. 'Seen this?'

Eddy read it reluctantly, without touching it. He did not like this particular newspaper, and had not read it in ten years. Big pictures, small articles, lots of supermarket specials and erectile dysfunction ads. Tom pointed at a large blurry picture, a stock-standard image of a security camera's perspective on a store robbery. Eddy had seen similar pictures a hundred times. The caption of this one indicated it had taken place in the early hours of the day before. A small grocery store, with the shadow of petrol pumps in the corner, and rows of chocolate bars and advertisements. A slim hand reached from one side of the picture, behind the cash register, offering — one could almost see the tremble of the fingers — a bundle of cash. Clear also were the two thieves, one close to the counter and one a step behind, darker images against the tinsel and glitter of busy rows full of products.

And what was that on the robbers' faces?

Pirate and Cat get the Cream in 7/11 Hold-Up

Two thieves believed to have robbed a series of petrol stations in the eastern and northern suburbs have been dubbed Pirate and Cat, due to their unusual disguises.

Police are hunting a man and woman believed to be in their thirties who have gleaned close to $55,000 in cash from grocery hold-ups. Security cameras show the woman wearing a cat mask and the man in a balaclava with a red patch on one eye, and a tricorner hat. The woman is estimated to be 170 centimetres tall, of medium build with dark hair and olive skin. The man is possibly part Asian in appearance, estimated 190 centimetres tall and of muscular build, police say. Both have Australian accents, and left the scene of each crime together on a motorbike.

Members of the public are asked to contact police with information.

Eddy's eyes moved on to another article below it, about giant feral cats that had been sighted in some national park; maybe this was what Tom had meant him to read? But then Tom's finger jabbed the robber picture again, making Eddy jump. 'You see it?'

'See what?' Eddy felt shaky and irritable. He wanted to be alone. He hardly knew this man, Tom. But then his eyes, drifting over the page, suddenly locked on the female thief.

Tom said, 'The crims.'

The woman rose from the page at Eddy, even while remaining flat. The picture was impressionistic, made from the giant pixels of a poor-quality camera, but even so you could make out the cartoon cat expression on the mask, which curled around the side of her face. Oh God. It couldn't be. The robber's hair was not short, as he had first thought, but tied up at the back — you could make out one long tendril, falling over her shoulder. Like the pirate, she held a very large gun, a fact which made him momentarily check his rising horror — but then he looked at the way her shoulders were raised. Romy always did that when she was nervous — and the way her jeans flared over her shoes, and the way she leaned her head, cat mask and all, on one side. But, oh, it was more than all these things, it was a certain shiver in the air around her, a displacement of the pixels that he recognised.

'Look familiar?' said Tom.

'No.'

Tom nodded, watching him. He half-grinned, as if it might be funny, but he was hedging his bets in case it wasn't.

Eddy breathed fast and deeply. He could not believe this. What a ridiculous thought. 'Fuck,' he said. 'Fucking hell.' His head hurt.

Tom stopped smiling. 'Are you—' But then his mobile rang. He took it out, looked at it and swore, before he answered. 'Hi, darl! Yeah, working, just out getting some supplies. Some transmitters. Then back to a three-hour meeting. Tricky client ... I did? Oh, I did, that's right. Miss Laura rang me from kindy. Some issue about Lotte she wanted to talk to us about ... Can you? That would be great. I'm just hectic all this week.'

And he hung up and twisted off another bottle top. Eddy's breathing finally slowed, although he kept staring at the newspaper picture. Tom talked a bit about robotics and asked him things about risk analysis, which seemed like a far-off life now to Eddy, although he surprised himself by managing to find the words to talk about it, and by sustaining a possibly normal-sounding conversation. They talked about footy. Eddy didn't ask Tom why he was lying to his wife about being at work, and Tom didn't ask Eddy how he felt about his crazy girlfriend who had become a robber. Finally the conversation fell silent, and just as Eddy was feeling that it had been an uncomfortably long period without a word, he looked over at Tom and saw that he had fallen asleep in his chair. Relieved, Eddy relaxed back into his own chair and watched until his neighbour ran past on his way home from work, his tie still flapping. Finally, Tom woke, alarmed at the time, and Eddy pointed out the grassy mud chunks that were still inexplicably on Tom's pants, although now redistributing themselves onto Eddy's carpet, and Tom brushed more of them off onto the carpet without apologising, and left to go home.

Eddy sat in the gathering dark with his newspaper and his disbelief, until finally he came to with a start of anger and hunger, and ordered a delivery pizza. The girl on the phone recognised his voice, or his phone number, and asked if he wanted the usual — gluten-free, thin-based vegetarian delight with extra rocket — and he reflected for a moment and told her that, actually, he really, really did not. He would have a meatlovers with the lot, thick wheat base, and he didn't want to see a shred of anything green.

CHAPTER SIX

'They what?' spluttered Grace. She had been surprised to find Melody also waiting to see Miss Laura at kindy, and then dismayed when the teacher ushered both mothers into her office. God, can I never get away from this woman? Grace had wondered, trying not to meet Melody's calm blue eyes. The kindy teacher had sat them down and made it clear: There Was A Problem.

'They are very good friends,' said Miss Laura. She was attractive in a strong sort of way: thick eyebrows and rosy cheeks and generous breasts and hips. Her eyes crinkled from long days of smiling down at children.

'But?' demanded Grace.

'They are excluding other children from their games.'

'Are there that many who want to play with them?' Skipper was new, after all. And Grace's understanding from three-year-old kinder the year before was that Lotte had repelled most of the other children by now, and was generally left to her regal solitude.

'Well, there's little boys who want to play with ...' Miss Laura trailed off and glanced at Melody. Ah. It was clear now. There were little boys who wanted to play with Skipper. Of course. Her dysfunctional daughter was holding back the other child's social chances.

Melody blinked. 'Does it matter?' she said, coolly.

'Well, it's more than that actually.' Miss Laura smiled apologetically. 'I keep catching them in the toilet together.'

Grace reeled. 'Doing *what*?'

Miss Laura shrugged. 'Number ones. Twos. But they are insisting on being with each other when they do it. Or, well, Lotte—'

'Oh God,' snapped Grace. 'Can't you just stop them?'

'We can, of course. But you are their parents. It's right you should know. Maybe you can say something.'

As they left the kindergarten shortly after, Grace's face burning, Melody put her hand on her arm. 'I don't see anything wrong with it. They're four years old. They're just curious.'

'Of course!' Grace nodded, tearful with relief. 'Well, I'm off to do some shopping.'

'Can Lotte come to the park for a play on Saturday?'

'Yes!'

Grace watched Melody go, and then she furtively crossed the street and entered a coffee shop. She settled herself at a table with three other women, mothers from the local kindy. She knew Verity, a stay-at-home-mother, from mothers' group. There was Nina, an elfin-looking lawyer, whom she knew from three-year-old kinder, and Anna Trapper, Grace's mother-of-four neighbour down the road with the wannabe actor/director husband.

'How is Lotte's leg?' Verity had been appalled by the accident, and couldn't seem to stop talking about it.

'Getting better,' Grace said crisply, and she hoped, discouragingly. She knew it was all her fault. A failure of the parent on duty. Any other job, you'd be sacked.

'Will there be any lasting effect?'

'She looks just fine to me,' said Anna smoothly, sipping the froth off a coffee.

'But will—'

'She does seem fine, doesn't she?' Grace hastily agreed, nodding at Anna. 'And Damien: how did his job interview go?' Damien Trapper wanted to direct movies, and had spent the past two years not working, and trying to get film projects up and running. Anna did both waitressing and telephone sales shifts so the family could meet the rent and eat. Grace was secretly horrified by Damien, all the more during the year that her own husband had started to resemble him, tinkering away on his own personal R2-D2 out the back while their savings shrank.

Anna was calm. 'Just a chat about a possible movie later this year. How's Tom's new job?'

Grace nodded. 'Great. We'll both work for a while to save some money, and then I'll take maternity leave and we'll have another baby.'

'Well, if we can help with picking up Lotte at all, just say. Clare would love to have a play with her anytime.'

Grace could not miss the generosity of this; the even-tempered and popular Clare had little patience for Lotte's princess-like tantrums and could have expressed no such wishes about her neighbour. 'Thank you.'

'No, really. Since my sister left her husband, we don't see as much of the cousins. Clare's missing them.'

'Lotte really seems to have hit it off with the new boy,'

Verity interjected. 'You know, the one whose mother saved Lotte in the accident.'

Grace was also baffled by the strength of her daughter's attachment to Skip. Lotte had not really had a friend before. She had had competitors for toys, people to dominate, obstacles to her will, but not someone you would call friend. Playing with Lotte was not something other children clamoured to do. Nor had she ever been very interested in other children, until now. But Skipper! Lotte drew pictures of them together, she talked about him, she ran to him when they arrived at kindy. Lord above, she apparently defecated with him. Could it get any more intimate, at age four?

'She does seem to have found a kindred spirit,' she said.

'And the going to the toilet together! How funny!' Verity whispered. Great, so the whole kindy knew about it already. 'I had a friend whose daughter did that. With her neighbour's kid. Would hold on until he was around.'

'Oh?' Maybe it was normal.

'Not anymore, though. Child psychologist helped.' Ah, apparently not normal.

'They're kids, for God's sake,' said Anna. 'Lucky Grace isn't the type to stress over something so perfectly natural.'

'Of course not,' said Grace.

'Apparently the mother lives on a commune,' Nina said. 'And the father? Separated?'

'Lives on a commune?'

'I think that's what they said on the TV show, isn't it? When they screened the accident?'

'Yes,' confirmed Nina. 'Commune.'

'But ... no.' Grace felt the unease she generally did when talking about Melody. 'She's in one of those one-bedroom apartments on Chawton Street, the crappy brown brick ones.

She *used* to live on a commune, up north. The TV show got it wrong.'

'So are you guys friends now, too?'

'Noo, although we did have her for dinner. To say thank you. But not really. We're very different.'

'*Very* different!' Nina rolled her eyes meaningfully, and Verity and she cackled in a way that indicated that this conversation, about to be rolled out for further consumption right now, had begun in private elsewhere. 'She's—'

'No, I think they're very similar,' said Anna, gathering up her bag. The statement was so astounding that everyone stared at her.

'Who?' said Verity.

'Grace and Melody, of course. Very alike. Gotta grab some groceries before kindy, I'll see you at pick-up.'

Grace turned back to the other two, eager to hear their opinions on Melody, but they had been derailed by Anna's departure and were now remembering errands they also had to run before pick-up. Grace found herself suddenly alone with their empty coffee cups, the froth hardened on the edges in a thousand expired milk bubbles, and the dregs of an abandoned conversation. What on earth did she have in common with Melody?

Melody meditated. She knew people who envisioned white lights, who recited chants. She, however, just tried to empty her mind. Every time a thought passed through her, she sponged it away with those very words: empty your mind. Those kindy mums who had gone for a coffee without her, glimpsed through the plate-glass window of Café Romanos? Empty Your Mind. Including Grace, who she had thought might become a friend, especially after the dinner-party bonding? Empty Your Mind. Even though Melody had saved her child's life, and Skipper and the child seemed to have hit it off, oh Grace was all gratitude one minute and then the next all pretending she was off to go shopping when she was sneaking out with the other mums ... Empty Your Mind! Shut up Already!

This beautiful world. A basket of sun-dried, folded washing. A loaf of freshly baked bread. The smell of her son's hair. She breathed out, and relaxed. She felt the backs of her hands resting lightly on her inner thighs, her legs crossed. She heard a far-off bird, and a train. She was a daughter of the universe, and the universe would provide. It always did.

The doorbell rang and she opened her eyes. Who was that? An hour until she was due back at kindy to collect Skip. She needed to get on the laptop and look for jobs. She already had an interview lined up for a job putting letterbox numbers into packaging, about which she was hopeful, in a reluctant sort of way. There was no way around it, she could be thrown off the single mother's benefit any day now. She needed work.

Melody ran down the stairs and opened the door. It was Van.

She peered around him; he was alone. He didn't look good. His face was flushed, his jaw covered in stubble, and the whites of his eyes were red. He glanced furtively behind himself. She led him in and made him a cup of coffee.

'So, how's your new girlfriend?'

He didn't meet her eyes. 'We're staying at a friend's. Just for tonight, and then we're heading up to a party in the Talna Valley.'

'And Romy's there?'

He shrugged. 'Maybe.'

'Has she rung her fella?'

'How would I know?'

He smelled stale. She was glad Skipper wasn't here to see him like this. 'So, what brings you here?'

'Wanted to give you something.'

'Oh! Well.' She watched as he brought out a fat white envelope. Her smile faded. 'What's this?'

'Some cash to get you by.'

She took it, and pressed it between her thumb and forefinger. About two centimetres thick. She could smell it; ink and paper and the sweaty hands of commerce; the residue of a thousand different cash registers. Grace had shown her the newspaper picture, and she thought of it now. The blurry figure holding the gun, his posture so familiar, his face hidden. The female form beside him.

'Lucky you didn't shoot the checkout boy.'

He laughed without smiling, and surveyed her for a moment. He looked exhausted. 'It wasn't *luck*. I'm not that much of an arsehole.'

'Poor kid's had to quit his job and get counselling. Post-traumatic stress disorder. His parents are completely freaked out, can't sleep. His little sister's stopped going to school, scared of men with guns.'

He snorted. 'How would you know that?'

She shrugged coolly. She had made it up. 'Read it in the paper.'

'Well, it *must* be true then.'

She pinched the envelope again, rattled it close to her ear with a playful smile. 'Fifties?'

'Hundreds.'

She whistled, but something trembled inside her. Her will, maybe. 'Could pay for a lot of counselling for that boy. Could help cover a job he might never be able to do again.'

Van's face went cold. He stood up. 'I thought you had money trouble. Sorry for giving a shit.'

The trembling thing stilled inside her, and became stone. Skip. How much dirty money was this? How much danger could this draw to them? 'I don't have money trouble. I just don't have money. Give me *this* and I'll have trouble. Cop trouble.'

'I don't care about robbing some multinational. They rob us blind all the time.'

'Ah. An eye for an eye.'

'So when did you get all full of virtue?'

She sighed, thought of Esme and softened. 'Are you hungry? I could heat some lentils.'

'Are you going to take my present or what?'

She laughed. 'Van. Van, Van, Van. At least you've come back. I haven't seen you since, hmm, since Grace and Tom's dinner. Since you left me stranded for a lift home.'

'Oh, is that what this is all about? You had to walk home? On your little feety-weety?'

She didn't like him like this. She wanted him gone. 'Oh, please. Give me some credit. But now that you mention it, you did turn out to be a hell of a dinner date. You sort of stole the show when you took off with another guy's girlfriend and vanished for a month.'

He laughed nastily at the thought of it. 'Melbourne people. Easy to shake them up, isn't it? With their bloody dinner parties. Man.'

'It was mean.'

He stared at her and she shrugged. 'He's brokenhearted. Eddy. Her boyfriend.'

'Oh, puh! Give a fuck! Not my problem. So are you going to take this money? It will keep you living well for another good six months, at least. *Very* well. Or not so well, for twelve.'

She looked at him, and at the envelope. Six months. Maybe twelve. It was a tempting stretch of time. She thought about the job she'd just applied for, parceling up letterbox numbers. She thought about the kindy mothers who had not invited her out to coffee.

She thought of Skip.

'Nah. I'll get by.'

His face fell and she did not like the look in his eyes. But she had never been scared of Van, and she wasn't now.

'What if I don't give it to you? What if I give it to Skipper?'

She pursed her lips and began to clear away the cups. 'And why would you do that?'

'Well, *you* tell *me*.'

She stared for a long time into the sink, where she ran her finger around the rim of a saucer. Then she turned around and dried her hands on a tea towel. 'Look at the time. I have to pick Skip up from kindy.'

'I'm leaving this money for him. I have a right.'

'You think.'

'I do.'

Why didn't he just ask her outright? *Am I Skip's father?* Maybe he didn't want to know, for sure. Oh, one drunken night. What a fool she had been. She took the envelope and pushed it back towards his chest. She raised her eyes and stared at him with all the authority she possessed. She jingled her keys with the other hand and moved towards the door. 'You don't, actually. Have a right. Now I must go.'

'I'll wait.'

'Please don't.'

Van sighed and walked towards the door, the movement

seeming to loosen him once again. 'You're crazy, Melody. I know you've got no money.'

'The universe will provide.'

'You are such a fucking old space-cadet, you know that?'

'Go and tell your girlfriend to phone home. To do the decent thing and stop everyone worrying about her.'

'The *decent thing*? My, my. Listen to you.' They were outside now, in front of his motorbike. 'And she's not my *girlfriend*.'

'No?'

'Why are you so stubborn? Why do you stay so ... alone?'

'I'm not alone. I have Skip.'

'Maybe that's not enough. For Skip.'

Melody picked up her backpack and averted her eyes, keeping her breathing steady. She let that comment sail freely over her head, until it was safely in the past, and she suppressed the urge to laugh. Such a thing would not even be safe, at this moment.

He spoke gently. 'Can I see you after pick-up?'

'No. We're going out. Seeya.' She kissed him quickly on the cheek, and their eyes met before she turned away. Pain and hurt were in his eyes, and she and wished she had not looked. The angry roar of his motorbike cut through the air as she walked, and she breathed more deeply and hastened towards her boy.

In at kindergarten, she pinned up a sign on the noticeboard. *Worried about the future? Need advice? Come to a qualified fortune teller. Experienced to the ninth level, Certificate from the Lismore Community Centre; can do tarot as well. Special packages available. Melody.* And a phone number.

Grace stood beside her and read it.

'I'll do *you* an *extra*-special rate,' said Melody.

Grace considered it. 'I don't know that I really want to know my future. At the moment.'

'Maybe that's wise.'

'Oh! Well!' Grace looked hurt and moved on to read a flier about a first aid course. Melody read the laundry roster. She had offended Grace, she could see. But it was true. There was a colour around Grace, something ominous heading her way. It was always difficult to be the bearer of bad news.

'But the universe provides. Always.'

Grace rolled her eyes. Provides what? 'Any word from Eddy? On his girlfriend?' She laughed falsely. 'Maybe you can see *those* things in the cards?'

'She's still not back.'

'How do you know?'

'Eddy rang me. He wanted Van's number.'

'Did you give it to him?'

'Of course.'

'Oh, okay. I just thought maybe you might want to, I don't know, protect his privacy.'

'God, no.' Melody shook her head. 'I take the guy out for dinner and he nicks off with someone else's girlfriend. He gets no protection from me.' She took a pen and wrote her laundry duty date on the pale skin inside her arm.

Grace nodded. Over in the home corner, Lotte and Skip had set up a table and were playing dinner parties. 'Some potatoes?' trilled Lotte, fussing over Skip like a waitress. 'Sushi?' Little Clare Trapper came to sit and join Skip at his lonely table, and Lotte screamed at her. 'No! No! *You're* not playing!' And pushed her off the chair and onto the floor, where she kicked her in the ribs.

Grace took a deep breath and closed her eyes. At this moment she really did not want to see into the future.

Grace arrived at work late. With a heavy heart, she sat down to begin work on the Good Works grant application. There was no question, the loss of the more lucrative federal grant was an unmitigated disaster for the association, and finding new funds would be essential for its survival. This was work she did feel was worthwhile, far more so than getting Barbara into the papers for her moment of glory. And Grace knew her writing skills were truly valuable here; she could persuade, she could cajole, she could mount a good argument and fill in pedantic paperwork as well as anybody. They were lucky to have her. She worked for an hour on the grant, and then went online to find a reference to mental health projects the association had worked on in the past.

Somewhere searching in the dusty library shelves of cyberspace, she started worrying about Lotte and her outburst at kindy that morning. Lotte had always had a difficult temperament, and Grace was gloomily familiar with the silent and watchful gazes of other mothers as she remonstrated and pleaded with Lotte over some public assertion of irrational will, or worse, like today, some childish act of violence. That morning Lotte had been wildly determined to keep Skip for herself, and to push away anyone who wanted to join in the play.

Privately, Grace shared a kernel of understanding for her daughter; if women were having a one-on-one in a coffee shop, it wasn't like they were obliged to include everyone in the entire café. Imagine it: now everyone, including you, secretive post-Pilates ladies in the corner, and you, book-group baby-boomers by the window, pull your tables together. Let's all go through each other's handbags for interesting items, and then we'll swap phones and read each other's texts. There would be a riot. However, kindergarten world demanded absolute inclusiveness, and tolerance of Everyone, All The Time.

Grace looked at various childhood conditions that could be loosely connected to Lotte — ADHD, autism spectrum? — and suddenly realised forty precious minutes had passed. She needed lunch.

She was standing at the side of the road, watching a tram, when she realised she was doing it again. That thing she did, that thing that was a sign. It started as a fantasy, a small film clip unravelling in her mind, where she stepped out in front of the tram and it hit her. Then she was dead. In her fantasy. Which, to be honest, didn't make her feel as bad as it should have, although, being fantasy, it probably lacked a few elements, such as physical sensation. It was a pretty tempting prospect, actually. Like a sweet release, a black-hole-esque absence of stress, release from mortgage anxiety and job boredom, of the sheer juggle of working mother-ness. This fantasy of near-death came in various forms; once in chest pains which she had — it was summer and the news was full of stories of midlife executives on holidays dropping dead from the cardiac stress of back yard cricket and negotiating with teenagers — anyway, she had attributed her chest twinges to pending or in-progress heart attack, and had proceeded hopefully to an emergency ward where scans had found nothing.

'Really?' she had said, from the cool nest of the crisp white bed where she had dreamed of spending weeks and weeks, reading a pile of library books while kind nurses stroked her forehead.

'You sound disappointed,' the doctor said, his fingertips on the pulse in her wrist. "No, that heart rate feels nice and steady. Your blood pressure's normal. ECG's perfect.'

'I would have to leave my job, if I'd had a heart attack, wouldn't I?'

'No, no, no! Goodness, we wouldn't have an executive left in this city if that was the case. Every corporate board would be deserted.'

'But ideally—'

'You don't need a heart attack to leave a job, you know. If you don't like it you can just, you know, leave.'

'Oh, I know *that*!'

Of course she knew that.

CHAPTER SEVEN

The days cooled, the leaves fell, and Grace took out the cool-weather work clothes she had packed away last year. Like old friends from another time; the light wool cardigans, the leggings and boots that would turn summer clothes into autumn ones. She looked at her heavy coat and put it back. Not yet. She walked to work through the city's parklands and breathed in the scent of autumnal trees, and crunched her boots through drifts of dry leaves along the path.

One day she arrived at the office to find anxious faces. An email had gone around: the chairman of the board would visit that afternoon to congratulate the team on their recent winning of the state Good Works grant, and to meet the people behind the 'really impressive work on the Teenagers Attack Depression campaign'.

This was immediately interpreted as the announcement of pending redundancies. Grace's colleague Josh pulled her into the kitchen.

'Do you think it will be me?'

'Not at all,' lied Grace, deeply sympathetic. The lost

federal grant had specifically funded project workers, and had underlined Josh's existence in the place. Josh was the best project worker they had; the most efficient and compassionate, and it stood to reason that in an organisation run by Barbara Boiler, privately dubbed throughout the office as the Bunny, good people like Josh would be the first to go.

'I hope it is. I want a redundancy.'

Grace was shocked. 'You want to lose your job?'

'I want to get a payout. I've been here 12 years. It might be enough for me to take some time off, do things I've never been able to.'

'Like what?'

'I don't know. Pottery. Train for marathons.'

'But what about money? To live?'

'I've paid off the mortgage.'

Grace could not imagine such freedom. She trailed disconsolately back to her desk, where the Bunny was waiting to announce she had finally graduated from her PhD. This was in something or other — perpetuating mental illness in the workplace, or pathological vanity, Grace had hardly paid any attention. Until now.

'My thesis was on modern day electro-convulsive therapy for manic depressives,' Barbara explained, flapping a piece of parchment. 'And I'm prepared to offer myself for interview on this topic, and on the new research my team came up with.'

'Oh! Interview. Right.'

'With *all* three major metro daily newspapers.'

'But—'

'No buts, Grace! This is a sensational story we're handing them on a plate. Hop to it!'

Grace sighed. She had had a tough morning getting

Lotte to kindy. Skip was home sick, and without Skip, kindy was pointless for Lotte. She had just received a text message from Miss Laura: *Lotte says feels sick wants go home.* It was not the day for the Bunny's vanity to reach its Everestial peak. 'We can't give it to all three newspapers and call it an exclusive. Why don't I ring Jen Craigson at *The National Daily*?' she said calmly. 'She writes some good features.'

'I don't want it buried in the health supplement. I think they could get a feature *and* a news piece out of it!'

'Do you?' Oh, Lord. Greece looked set to be thrown out of the EU and the Bunny thought it might make the news that she had finished her PhD.

She slipped back out to her desk and rang Tom's mobile. Disconnected, as usual. Why did they pay for a mobile, when the man never turned the thing on? She rang his desk phone, which was picked up by a colleague, someone Grace didn't know.

'Ah yes, the boy genius.'

Grace paused at the unmistakable sneering. 'I'm just trying to track him down,' she said politely.

'So is his boss. He never turned up today. He missed a meeting with a client. A *big* one.'

Big meeting? Big client? Grace gritted her teeth, and did not ask. In that sardonic, unknown voice on the phone she could hear exactly how it was at Tom's workplace, without even setting foot in the building. If Tom got sacked, if he wriggled out of his working life down that passive-aggressive pathway ... surely not. But right now, she had to get someone to pick up Lotte.

She rang Verity at home, the only person she really felt she could ask who wasn't working. Verity was out playing tennis and said gaily that she wouldn't be home for another two hours. No problem, said Grace grimly, envisioning a life of tennis and happy lunches. She dialed and left a message for Jen Craigson.

Her phone rang as soon as she put it down, and she snatched it back up. Maybe it could be this easy, maybe it was a slow domestic news day, despite Greece, and Jen Craigson might gobble up an incendiary interview with Dr Bunny and Grace could race off early.

But it was Miss Laura from kindy.

'Grace? Just wondering how you're going there. Lotte's temperature is up to 39 degrees and, well ...' Laura paused. 'She's complaining of a sore foot. The one she hurt in the crash.'

'Oh dear, thanks for letting me know.' Grace silently uttered every profane word she knew. 'Well, I guess I'll come pick her up as soon as I can.' She hung up.

Dammit, where *was* Tom? Grace would have to go, if she couldn't find him. But maybe she could strike it lucky, and shop this story before she left, and handle the rest by phone. What the hell was Barbara's doctorate in again? Electro-convulsive therapy for wilful employees? For men who wanted to slink away from their jobs? Grace couldn't read her own writing. She glanced over at Barbara's office. It was empty. Her newly minted PhD would be lying somewhere around there, in her office. Surely Grace could just find it herself in half a minute?

Inside the office, she guiltily scanned two desks and a shelf, all bearing piles of varying heights of reports, envelopes and documents. Her manager was not a neat worker, and Grace later reflected that it was amazing that she had somehow focused through the chaos onto the one place that bore her own name: a fat yellow envelope. Labelled, *Grace Ellison*.

It looked so official! A pay rise, maybe, some

commendation for good service? But then her blood froze. She crossed the room and turned the envelope over. Unsealed. She slid her fingers inside.

A letter of termination. Regrettable. No reflection on. Commendable work. A page of figures that were incomprehensible. It could not be. She was dreaming. She heard a noise and hastily slid the page back in the envelope and tossed it on the desk, her heart racing. An identical letter for Josh Papps. He would be pleased. Grace quickly returned to her desk, seized her pen and drew triangles all over her notepad, so deeply that the page tore in places. She breathed fast and hard, and kept drawing triangles until her vision cleared.

Finally, she packed the contents of her desk into a box, emailed all her personal files to herself, and checked her handbag one last time. Then she wrote an email.

Dear Dr Boiler,
My little girl is sick at her kindergarten and I have had to leave immediately.
Grace

Out at the taxi rank, her heart raced. She felt the city sharp and new around her, as if a fog had lifted from her vision. A woman in a skirt, sunglasses and bike helmet, directly over the road from her, leaned her thighs into a parked bicycle and wriggled her fingers into gloves. A labourer pushed a wheelbarrow into a construction site, making his way through city workers in expensive suits. How old a tool was the wheelbarrow, this ancient device? A stiff-legged man on a mobile phone marched back and forth across the pavement, while a woman on a phone nearby stood still and smiled, a waterfall of curves, the phone raised to her ear like a cup. A weathered woman with purple hair stared at Grace and held out her hand.

'Gotta dollar?'

Grace carefully counted out three, as a taxi pulled up beside her. She put them into the woman's claw, and then she climbed into the back seat. She wasn't sure she had enough to reach the kindy now, and she may regret her generosity at the other end. And the woman hadn't even said thank you. But somehow Grace needed at this moment to believe— what was it Melody had said? — that the universe would provide.

Eddy felt the tears sliding down his face and let them fall. Who cared if he was on a peak-hour train, with weary commuters in shades of grey filing on all around him, setting off from Flinders Street. No one was looking at him anyway; he was just another nondescript middle-aged man, holding a briefcase. There were dozens of him everywhere; he was a clone, except for the tears. No one would ever look at him again for the rest of his life. He looked over the shoulder of a mature woman with a tortured perm, who had opened her briefcase and was scribbling down a list. *Washing x 3. Tell kids: no Wii til homework done. Cake for fête. Call Tracy re: breast cancer, how is??? Flowers. Tape Farmer Meets Wife. Mum: call re dr 5pm Friday. Set mouse traps!!* (This last underlined angrily.) *Call Geoff, tell him—*

Eddy waited, his tears drying on his cheeks as he gazed absently around the carriage at people taking out newspapers, jabbing fingers at phones. Tell Geoff what? Still nothing. Another woman pulled a tangle of headphones out of her handbag, accidentally dragging a lipstick lid and a receipt and a tampon out as she did, grabbing at the receipt with a look of shock and swearing under her breath at it. A nearby man inserted two fingers into his chest jacket pocket and slid out a circular box. He opened it to reveal earphones perfectly coiled around a pair of pegs custom-designed for the purpose. He unwound the thin white cord slowly, with no tangles, and then planted the clean ear buds in his hairless ears. Eddy sighed, a little comforted by such homage to order and hygiene. Everywhere, people were inserting headphones. One man held his mobile face-up, and ran his forefinger around the surface like he was drawing lines in sand. Eddy waited a couple of minutes and then risked another glance down at his neighbour's list. *Call Geoff, tell him—*

The woman gazed out of the window now, her fingers slack around the pen. She stared unseeingly out at the city buildings; rows of rectangles stacked up on their sides, cars snaking between them all below. Then suddenly they were in a tunnel and the window went black and Eddy's reflection, a man in a suit, stared back at him, and the air rushed out of him at how ordinary he was, how boring, just one of a million amoebas crawling the Earth. No wonder Romy had fled. How long had she been dreaming of doing so? He wanted to flee from himself, too.

The train stopped and a seat became vacant. He glanced at the bulbous belly of a pregnant woman swaying near him. He gestured towards his seat.

'Please. Before it goes.'

The woman sank into the seat and smiled gratefully, but he could do nothing to acknowledge her. He would never smile again. He maneuvered awkwardly through the commuters to get away from her, before she too realised how boring and awful he was. Someone plucked at his sleeve and he turned.

'Eddy!'

'Tom.'

'You've left the house.'

'Dentist.' Even in his grief, Eddy could not miss his six-monthly check-up. The receptionist had called three days earlier to remind him, and like a robot he was obeying the call. He had put on a suit because that was what he always wore to the city. It had been weeks since anyone had asked him to go anywhere, except for his parents.

'Watching the game Saturday night?' In Tom's recent visits the two men had discovered a shared love of rugby union, which could divert the conversation from unwelcome topics. They could talk about the new team lineup, and who was favoured to win the Bledisloe Cup, and then they could slide into the past, to great moments like Stirling Mortlock's legendary try of the England Australia World Cup of 2002, when the great man streaked up the field and did the impossible. Not unlike Melody's magical rescue of all those months ago, he sometimes reflected.

'If I can get out to a pub.'

Eddy mused. 'Maybe I should just bite the bullet and get pay TV.' Romy had been opposed to it, but hey. She had not been seen for three months, except in the media wearing a cat mask. If that counted.

'Yeah. I'd come watch it.'

'How's the job going?'

'Great,' said Tom. 'I work with morons. I do moronic work. I get paid my super by morons. I catch the train in and out, with—' A man nearby glared and Tom lowered his voice. 'It was a mistake to let myself get sucked back into it.

I'm really getting somewhere with the solar roof. But I need time to iron out the glitches. I just wish Grace would be a little more supportive.'

Eddy nodded. He had heard the story before. It looked to him like Tom had it all whatever he did; lovely wife, sweet child, house, maybe even another little baby along the way one day. 'Bummer,' he offered.

'My mate, who's been working on his tree-lopping robot for ten years, he got a huge contract yesterday. Eleven point five million dollars.' Tom stared at Eddy, who blinked.

'Really?'

Tom nodded. 'Max doesn't have a family. So he's been able to get it over the line. Bastard. While I have to go be a wage slave.'

'But it's been Grace who's been the wage slave, hasn't it?'

Tom shrugged and leaned towards the taller man, helped by the swaying of the train as it journeyed through the inner suburbs. 'Anyway, guess what? I've written my letter of resignation. I left it on the boss's desk tonight. They'll try and make me stay. Throw more money at me. But I won't take it. I'll tell Grace tonight. She'll *have* to give me another year.'

'You've resigned? Without telling Grace?'

'Yup.' The train stopped and people poured out. Tom and Eddy sat down, freed now to peer out the windows at the spread of suburbia, the far-off Macedon Ranges, the city skyline in the other direction growing larger.

'Well, that will surprise her.' Someone's phone was ringing. People started patting their pockets.

'Sometimes you've got to do these things. Fortune favours the bold, and all that. Put the bit between your teeth and—. Hang on, is that my phone? Ooh, bet it's my boss.

Here we go! Game on! Hello? Tom Ellison, here ... Oh, it's you.'

From Tom's disappointed tone, Eddy guessed it was Grace. Tom peered unseeingly out the window while his phone chattered away tinnily at him. Grace was in full flight about something, and Tom companionably rolled his eyes at Eddy and momentarily held the phone away from his ear, in the universal signal of mad spouse, before resuming the conversation.

'She finished her what? Oh, she's such a cow ... Oh I don't know how you put up with her ... And then what did you say?'

His eyes widened and his voice turned to ice.

'Sorry, did you say ... Gosh I thought you said *redundant* then!' He laughed breathlessly. 'Redundant ... You *did* say redundant? Oh Jesus. Are you serious?'

More squeaking. Two commuters sitting in his sightlines edged away from him.

'Oh shit, Grace. That's terrible ... No, it's terrible. More terrible than you can imagine ... My job ... lucky we've got ... Ah yes. Lucky we've got my job. I heard you that time. Sorry, you're cutting out now ... tunnel ... breaking up ...'

A long silence, and then the angry chirping on the phone broke out anew and reached a crescendo of noise. Tom lowered the phone, grimaced at it and then very carefully, with the precision of a surgeon, used the tip of his forefinger to touch the hang-up key. The sound abruptly halted. Tom slumped back in his seat, pale and breathing fast. The train had stopped and he stared out the window, his breathing shallow, his face distorted in distress.

'Well, that's it,' he said finally. 'She can't argue any longer. We will have to sell the house.'

CHAPTER EIGHT

Grace would marvel later that splitting up with Tom had begun with something so small. Sure, there had been the unfortunate conjunction of her redundancy and his ill-considered resignation, which his firm seemed only too delighted to accept; in fact, they refused to reverse it 24 hours later. These were not small things, and these were the things their friends and family used to explain the breakup. 'She was made redundant and on the very same day his work told him they were letting him go! Or he resigned! Or something! Just a bad coincidence! Who would believe it? And then ...' And then burble burble burble, the narrator would finish with something like '... financial pressures, fighting, all just fell apart ...' The punchline was always: 'Then the marriage broke up.'

It was The Story, and, exhausted with answering questions and lying to her daughter and splitting up possessions, Grace herself would sometimes revert to The Story. It was an easy shorthand, to fob people off. The wiser among her listeners would frown and say 'But ...' as if realising there was a great chunk missing from The Story; for example, the thread that linked the job losses with the breakup, which was as frail as cobweb. Because couples endured such things, without ending marriages. But usually even the more astute of her listeners held back from asking too many questions. Because really, as everyone murmurs when filling in the sometimes vast gaps in relationship breakup stories, whoever knows what goes on in a marriage?

Grace would have agreed. Who the hell knew? She hadn't known what was going on in her own marriage, apparently. Of all the things she had worried about — babies, money, mortgages, leaking taps — she had never worried about Tom leaving. Maybe *that* was the problem. A bit of worry might have done the trick, headed it off.

Her own private breakup tale went like this. On the day after the mutual job losses, many angry words were said, but things in Marriage Land were still not destined to go any particular way. And then Grace, staring at the blue sky, saw a tiny thread hanging from it, a blue thread, of course, because it was the sky, and, being a picky type, she gave it a little tug to see what would happen. What happened was that the sky around the thread unraveled like a woolly jumper, gradually leaving a ragged rip, through which she could see another world. It was a very different world, a frosty, dark world, with music that sounded more like a piano falling through the air than real music, threaded with the sound of, say, a drum kit falling off the back of a truck. There were people in it whom she knew, but with angry expressions, and a smell that made her stomach knot with fear. But she pulled Tom over to show him this world, sneeringly triumphant that she had discovered it, and, full of her own power, she used it to menace him.

She threatened him with leaving, with an end to their marriage. She didn't really mean it. But in doing so she pulled the thread again, and the hole in the sky grew bigger, and bigger, and suddenly Grace couldn't work out how to stop her own dear, tender world from unravelling, and this continued quite quickly until the world as she knew it was gone. It sat at her feet for a while like a spaghetti pile of unpicked yarn, and she grabbed handfuls of it and tried to put it back in the sky, but it didn't work, not at all. Then, then they were all totally in the cold, sad, new world; Lotte, too, poor little Lotte who had never wanted to be there. Grace had no idea how to get back into the beloved old world — and only now did she realise how beloved it had been — and with a sick feeling in her stomach, she realised that that place was gone forever.

The house seemed bigger without Tom, and noises were louder, and his absence was everywhere. Tom would not even tell her where he was living now. In the new world there were many things they did not tell each other, although, sometimes unfortunately, there were things they did. While she loved Tom and wanted him back, she was also not sure she would ever be able to forgive or forget some of the things he had said to her in recent weeks, as the world unraveled. In the new world, words were sharp and dangerous and history was always being re-written. *You never really believed in me. You wanted so bloody much. You're mercenary. Shallow. Selfish. You don't know what it is to have a dream. You're small-minded. All you can think about is yourself. What about that time six years ago, in that caravan park in that place with the ducks, when you ...* While she had wept and pleaded to talk with Tom in the early days, a few new-world conversations with him had cured her of that. Enough had been said. Texting was fine.

It was time to pick up Lotte from kindy. There were very few threads of continuity in the new world, but kindergarten was one of them. And, of course, Lotte was one. Grace was crouching like a one-woman army over Lotte, prepared to do battle for her child, but as yet the battlefield was empty. Tom saw Lotte every week, but seemed too busy with his new life to demand much time with his daughter. For Grace, unemployed for the first time in fifteen years, life revolved around kindy. She spent an hour dressing for pick-up or drop-off. She arrived twenty minutes early. She let Lotte play as long extra as she wanted. She thanked Miss Laura for any small task the teacher granted her; washing hand towels, sewing on name tags, covering books with clear plastic. Other than this, she shopped for one day's food at a time. She wrote out figures on pieces of paper and reflected on her looming penury. She stared into space for long periods, like someone waiting to be struck by an idea, one which never arrived. For the first time in years, she did not know what came next.

Melody poured the saucepan of milk into the jar, Skip and Lotte watching as the milk rose up the sides. White steam swirled through the glass mouth, until Melody put the tin lid on and screwed it shut.

'There.'

'Can I have some?' Lotte jumped.

'By tomorrow morning it will be yoghurt. You can have some then. Now,' Melody turned and pretended to consult her list, while actually checking Grace's expression. The other woman had not moved to look at the yoghurt-making; she just stared vacantly out the window, into the bare black branches of a persimmon tree. The orange fruit hung like lanterns against a grey sky, and Grace seemed overwhelmed by them. She chewed her bottom lip and gazed out into the world.

Melody summoned some energy into her voice. 'Let's make laundry detergent!'

'Yay!' shouted Lotte.

Grace's gaze shifted momentarily to her daughter, and she studied her for a long second, like an almost-dead mountain climber might have contemplated the Himalayas.

Melody had come with a list of things to make from scratch. She brought yoghurt-starter and Borax and rolled oats and seedlings. She had been frightened at the tone of Grace's voice on the phone the night before. It was a dead voice, like the zombies had moved in. Grace was barely conscious with grief; couldn't sleep, couldn't eat, her voice a limp whisper. The money was draining away, she said; her redundancy vanishing into the mortgage repayments and takeaway food. She and Tom had no job between them now; there was only the single mother's benefit, yet to arrive.

'That's what I'm living on,' said Melody.

'How?' Grace had asked, without much interest.

'I'll show you,' Melody had said. And here she was.

She found a big soup saucepan and filled it with soap flakes and water, and boiled it until the soap had all melted. She stirred in washing soda and Borax, and then carried it to the laundry and poured it into a big plastic bucket with a lid, and added cold water. In an hour it would cool to a slimy sludge and Skip and Lotte could take turns stirring it, squeezing it through their fingers. Grace reluctantly came to see.

'Oh.' Grace folded her arms and squeezed them against herself.

'Ten litres of washing liquid, for less than a dollar,' said Melody triumphantly.

'Oh.'

Melody sighed. 'Grace, you've got to get a grip. Tom might come back, or he might not, but in the meantime you've got to ... survive. Be a mum. Keep a house going.

Grace's eyes filled with tears. 'I feel so useless. Thank you.'

'Don't thank me. Just help. Next we're making muesli.'

Grace had a photo of herself on a top bunk bed, hunched over in thick brown glasses with lank brown hair. She had once scratched the surface of the picture, over her face, a deliberate vandalism. It was a photo of her first-year school camp and she was in a room with her three best girlfriends, who had decided for that week, as teenage girls can, that they hated her.

There was lots to hate. Her quick answers to questions in class. Her mounting insecurity, her hunched shoulders. She couldn't remember the details of the camp. Time had mercifully scratched away most of it, like her nails had done to her face in the photograph, but she could remember enough. It was at a place called, fittingly, Nhill, on the edge of the Little Desert in northwest Victoria, and her memories of red sand, sharp black desert plants and flaming sunsets over endless horizons were tinged with aching loneliness and dissatisfaction with herself. Maybe those girls hung around in a group of three and left her out, maybe they mocked her in front of the others. Maybe she ate alone. Maybe they spat on her, left a urine-soaked towel in her bed, maybe she spent a night in a tent with the teachers because of this, she simply couldn't remember. But in that photo, sitting on her top bunk, she knew she was feeling the misery of not just being truly *hated*, but having to *sleep* in a room with the people who hated you.

Tom had loved this vandalised photo, even before she told him how sad she was in it. He loved it with a furious protectiveness, as if he was reaching one strong, muscular arm back through the years and putting it around those puny, thirteen-year-old-girl shoulders. She had imagined him striding through time to give them all a piece of his mind, and somehow removing the scratches from that photo until she was whole again.

Once, that was how much he had loved her.

Grace's hand shook as she applied lipstick and tears ran down her face. Her lips were chapped and the colour left tiny crusts where it gathered on the flaky skin, in lines that went out from her mouth. She looked about sixty. Maybe now Tom could see what it was that those girls hadn't liked. Like in that photo, she was once again truly alone.

But a jarring clatter of slamming drawers disrupted her coma of self-pity. She was not actually tragically alone at all. No, there was Melody, taking her biggest bowl and filling it with oats, seeds and bran, and drizzling honey over it all. Melody handed the bowl to Grace, with a wooden spoon.

'Stir,' she instructed.

Grace stirred dully, turning her thousand-mile stare deep into the oats. Melody watched as the other woman feebly pushed the wooden spoon against the oaty mountain range below her, honey glistening gold on the peaks. The effort seemed to weary Grace, to make her expel air in little puffs, as she lifted the spoon from its bog and stabbed it back into the mixture.

Melody had seen this before, had felt it herself, a spiritual giving up. Strange to see Grace in this tranquillized state, instead of her usual highly-strung anxiety. Melody gently took the bowl and spoon from her, stirred the mixture herself, and found a baking tray to spread the mixture out on. She opened the door of the warm oven, slipped in the tray and closed the door. Outside, Skip and Lotte did karate, a sort of chopping, kicking dance where they circled each other and yelled Hah! Yah! Lotte kicked Skip in the tummy, predictably, and he folded over, crying. Lotte crouched to observe him, and after a few minutes they resumed rolling and laughing in the grass.

Melody made Grace a cup of coffee, and peeled the tea towel off a bowl, revealing the bread dough she had left to rise earlier in the day. She floured the wooden table, Grace appearing not to notice, and she tipped out the ball of dough, dusty with flour, and began to knead. Dough bubbles sighed and popped, and the dough shriveled into itself. She stretched it, took a sharp knife and sliced it into three pieces. She rolled each piece into a mini loaf, and covered the three pale hills with a clean tea towel. Still no response from Grace.

Was this neurotic woman her problem? Grace had chosen to test her husband's love for her, against his love for a dream. And what was a man without a dream, anyway — was he even worth having? Melody had spent the past five years in a world where everyone had dreams, and no one had money. Where ways of living — vegan, communal, freecycle, Montessori — were daily topics of fierce discussion and debate. The one point of agreement amongst the rainforest tribes of the north had been that chasing money was no way to live. All were refugees from that soul-destroying treadmill. And yet they were essentially non-believers, outsiders, and could believe in nothing for very long. People hated drugs, and then they started growing marijuana. Buddhists let go of meditation and dabbled in meat-eating, just like any dime-a-dozen lapsed Catholic, and then suddenly a baby was dead and the police were crawling all over paradise, sniffing at all the pot plants in the little school and pulling apart solar panels on ramshackle roofs. Where did they bury the baby? She wondered. What was happening up there? Had the druggies taken over? Had the co-op owners finally thrown them out? Who had gone to jail? All she had cared about in the end was getting Skip out of there before the Department started vetting all the families and breaking them up. She could not lose Skip. And anyway, it got so she could not sleep one more night in the valley that had been her home for so long; where the ghost wails of a baby drifted through the lantana and she woke shuddering from dreams where she almost saved the baby, where she ran to put a bottle into his whimpering mouth, only to find he was stone-cold and staring-eyed.

So here she was, back in Melbourne again. Her old life, idyllic though it had been, had finally not felt real, like a loaf of risen bread waiting to be punched down to reality. And now here she sat with a woman whose rubbish bin was full of McDonald's packaging, who had a daughter with more life in her than a sunrise, a woman with the saddest eyes in the world.

The children clattered in, full of accusations and recriminations. 'Skipper hit me!' Lotte glanced at her own mother, but seemed to realise she was non compis and redirected her complaint towards Melody.

'Is that true, Skip?'

'She wouldn't share the bike.'

'Skipper, you never punch. What do you say?'

Skipper kicked a chair. 'Sorree.'

Lotte flicked out a four-year-old hip. 'Well that's *two* times he's done it.'

Melody sat before them. 'Both of you know how to say sorry when you've done something wrong, don't you?'

'Yes.'

'But there's another part of sorry, and that's forgiving. It's like a two-step dance: I'm sorry and then I forgive you.'

'No.'

'It's very hard for some people to forgive. Even harder than saying sorry, sometimes. But you're young, so you can get good at it. If you practise every day.'

They stared at her doubtfully.

'So it goes like this. Skipper, you say "I'm sorry" to Lotte.'

'Sorry, Lotte.'

'And, Lotte, you tell Skipper you forgive him.'

'I for-GIVE you.' Lotte nodded patronisingly at Skip, her brown hair sliding forward, her little face suddenly lit with beneficent kindness.

'Now hug,' said Melody. They turned to each other and embraced stiffly at first, frozen still. Then Skipper squeezed Lotte around the waist and jumped, and they squealed and jumped like little frogs. She shooed them outside and closed the door. A tear rolled from Grace's eye.

All she wanted was to rewind the past, unsay the things she had said, and, please, bring on the robots, the plastic-bottle solar rubbish roof, if that was what it took. She felt lost without Tom, and even more lost without a job. What was Barbara Boiler doing without her? Was her replacement succeeding better than she had in promoting a cause that, despite Grace's cynicism, she knew to be worthwhile? Who was she without work, without a husband, without the money for the next mortgage repayment? Who was she now?

CHAPTER NINE

As Eddy's months of absence from the workplace grew, his employers began to fret. They needed him. To be honest, Eddy adored the world of risk management, and it loved him right back. His risk work the previous year had been impressive, with his tally of monies saved to companies worth millions. Spotting the fire risk in a processing plant where the fire protection was rated adequate, because the fire hoses reached all parts of the plant ... but there were no smoke detectors — potential $10 million. Realising that a major chocolate-making firm held all of its packaging artwork in a derelict printer's factory, risking loss of six months' production — potential $3 million. A blue-chip CEO lowering his manicured hand to sign contracts on a massive stretch of industrial land in outer Sydney, halted in the nick of time by Eddy when his investigations revealed a history of toxic waste — potential $50 million in ongoing management and treatment costs. Et cetera. There were, of course, things he and colleagues had missed, which made him wince. All industries must have them. The publishers who knocked back JK Rowling, the mining company that built the mine on the wrong site. The poor soul in Atlanta who simply forgot to get a sponsorship deal for the gas to fuel the Olympic flame. Human error — he and his small army were up against it, time and again, Murphy's Law engraved on all their hearts.

When Eddy had used up all his holiday leave and Risk, Routing and Co still could not persuade him to come back, they sent one of their best performers to make contact. Alf Tankhouse, corporate lawyer, was secretly known by Eddy as Alphamale, and had been the subject of a running private joke between him and Romy for years. He was as tough as Eddy was tender, and it was ironic that RRC had sent him of all people to rout out their AWOL employee. Ironic because Alpha's own marriage had crashed on the rocks just before Eddy's, and may, Eddy believed, have helped destabilise his own, as it turned out, perilously fragile relationship.

Born to hippy parents, Alf Tankhouse had become the most acquisitive, materialist, competitive bastard around. Eddy knew other alpha males, and some of them he liked; their energy, their overconfidence, their wild testosterone. Their aggressive need to pay for everything. Alphamale, however, he was wary of. The man had bred six children in six years, an unheard-of tribe in this day and age, and his redheaded, laughing-eyed and quick-tongued wife seemed to have spent all of the time Eddy had known her pregnant, like a moving monument to Alphamale's fertility. Alphamale was tall and broad, and would draw himself up even taller while talking, almost leaning over his opponent. He and Eddy had a mutual friend, who had told Eddy that Alf was notorious among his circle of friends for sleeping with his cousin's wife, an achievement as yet unrelayed to the cousin. He had a short temper and had once kicked in the car window of a driver who had leered at Alf's then girlfriend.

Eddy generally, knowing this story, tried to avoid him. However, once they had landed at the same workplace, they had had various conversations in the lift, as one must, and these generally revolved around Alphamale's chosen topics:

1. How much he was earning now.
2. The next triathlon he was training for.
3. What their mutual friend was up to. Their mutual friend had now quit his job to stay home and care for his baby and toddler while his banker wife worked, a decision which both fascinated and repulsed Alphamale, as if the man had stepped off a cliff. After a few conversations about this, Alphamale apparently had purged himself of topic 3; in fact, he appeared to detectibly shudder if the man's name was mentioned. This topic was then replaced on his list by:
4. How great his renovation was going to be. And:
5. What his house was worth. And:
6. Sex.

His wife, by contrast, appeared warm-hearted and kind, if understandably cranky. The few work events to invite family featured her shouting at the children, and yet the constancy of her shouting was not matched by any sense that she was close to losing control; the babies seemed happy in their eternal puppy scrum, growing up year by year. Alphamale came and went overseas on business trips, and talked importantly into his mobile a lot. The office seemed to breathe a little easier when he was away. Eddy speculated that his family might, too.

They were a constant on the periphery of Eddy's life, so

he was stunned one day when Alpha, a pale shadow of himself, told him that his wife had left him, taking all the kids.

Eddy got it at once, or thought he did. It was all he could do to stop himself rolling his eyes. This walking cliché of machismo had been discovered cheating. But somehow that seemed too small a thing to provoke all this. He couldn't imagine Ginger-haired Girl even caring. Maybe in true alpha style it was a compound crime, a girl in each port. 'What happened?'

'She's been fucking the kids' swimming teacher. Says she *loves* him. She's loved him for six months.'

Eddy blinked. 'Mate,' he said in dismay.

'Fucking should have noticed how excited she was when Lucia moved up to Crayfish. *So fantastic! Swimming way beyond her age!* He finished with a falsetto mimicry of womanhood.

'What?'

'Crayfish teacher. Uni student. Mature age.' He kicked a table leg.

Eddy shook his head, confused but profoundly sympathetic, and put his hand on the other's arm. 'I'm so sorry.'

Alf looked at Eddy's hand, wearily incapable of his usual derision, although he did twitch it off. 'She loves me, too. She says.'

'Well, there you go!'

'And she wants me to pay child maintenance.' He showed Eddy a legal letter, demanding an annual amount of money that was slightly more than Eddy's salary, and about two-thirds of what he last remembered Alf's salary to be. 'That's what I've got to come up with every year. While she gets the kids and fucks the Crayfish.'

While Eddy had been shocked, Romy had seemed pole-axed by the news. She couldn't stop talking about it, telling her friends on the phone about these distant acquaintances. It seemed Ginger was part of an epidemic, according to Romy. She and her friends devised elaborate theories about women turning forty, women having midlife crises, women reaching their sexual peak, women with poor body image, neglected by their husbands, vulnerable to the encouraging eyes and near-naked body of a fit young swimming teacher. *I'd like to discuss Lucia's backstroke with you, can you come back for coffee at my place and we can talk about ... strokes?* Women having affairs was the common theme, as far as Eddy could see. Women cheating on husbands.

'What if Alf had been the one having the affair,' he had asked Romy one day, after one of her marathon analytical phone sessions, during which he had begun to ponder whether, if Ginger Girl were a man, she would be crucified as a macho pig, a symptom of man's destructive and hateful tendencies toward his family, whereas because she was female, the sisterhood moved like a construction crew to start building the wall of justifications around her. 'If it was him and not her, how would you feel about it?'

Romy shrugged, pretending to give the matter thought for three seconds, before dismissing it. 'Let's face it, all those trips overseas. He probably *was* having an affair.'

'In which case maybe he was having a midlife crisis, or suffering poor body image ...'

'Oh, *please!* That poor woman at home with all those children! *She* was the one struggling here!'

Eddy felt doubtful about this. The redhead had always to him seemed cheekily, resoundingly, not like anyone's victim at all. It seemed a little unfair that she got to keep the children, the house, the renovation, the Crayfish, a very large chunk of the husband's income, *and* the sympathy and support of the sisterhood, if not the community at large. But he said nothing of his bizarre outbreak of fraternal loyalty to the extremely annoying Alf.

Romy had never really talked much to the woman before, but obviously there had been some connection there, with these people whom Eddy would have said were just like far-off trees in the geography of Romy's life. Because after marveling, wondering, cursing and pontificating over the gross injustice of what had happened, after seeking reason or motivation or guidance within Ginger's behaviour and reluctantly sympathising with Alf, whom she had always despised, Romy came home from a weekend yoga workshop with something to say, through gales of tears that rendered her unable to speak for a full half-hour. Eddy begged and pleaded; swore over and over, on his life, that whatever it was, he would think no less of her. Finally, she came clean.

'I ... I ... slept with the yo ... yo ... ga instructor,' she sobbed.

Eddy wondered how binding his promise was.

'How *could* you?' he said finally.

'I just ... My body took over. I couldn't stop myself.'

'Fuck. What is it with women and bloody exercise people?'

'I *know*.' She stared big-eyed at him, as if admitting to being caught in the grip of a national plague, over which she had no control.

Anyway. Fast-forward some months ahead to now, and the cuckolded Alf Tankhouse appeared at the front door of the cuckolded Eddy, bearing a bottle of whisky from one of the managing directors, and a plea to return to work.

'You gotta get over it, mate.' He squeezed past Eddy and down the hall. Did no one wait to be invited in anymore? 'Dave and Stanny sent this. Its good shit. Do you want some now?'

Dalmore Highland Whisky, 15 years old, read Eddy. *Matured in matusalem, apostoles and amoroso sherry casks, it proffers all those winter spice, orange zest and chocolate notes characteristic of Dalmore.* 'Where is Dalmore?'

'Fuck knows. You want to drink some?'

'They sent you to give me this, or to drink it with me?'

'I just figure, seeing as you've got it ...'

'It's 10.20. In the morning.'

'It's good shit. Over two hundred bucks in the shop.'

'Well if it's so great, maybe I'll save it for a special occasion. Instead of weekday morning tea with you.'

'Fair enough. Although now I think about it, I did hear Stanny say he got a box in duty-free. So maybe not two hundred bucks.'

'And what, he keeps a box for messed-up employees?' Eddy could remember riding his BMX around Bulleen, dropping resumés into shops and pleading for his first job. Incredible now that someone was sending him an expensive bottle of alcohol and pleading with him to get out of his pyjamas and return to work. He should be flattered. 'I don't deserve this.'

'Well, you know. Employees market. Economy's gone crazy. All these recruitment agencies, they're always getting onto me through LinkedIn and asking me to go work for someone else. Let's me know what I'm worth. I've been to Dave three times in the past year to give me a raise, and he's said yes each time.'

Eddy was shocked. 'I've *never* asked for a raise. I mean, he raises my salary every year and it sort of embarrasses me, I wish he wouldn't, but ...'

'Well, there you go, a two-hundred-buck bottle of whisky to get you to go back is actually pretty stingy, if you look at it like that. Believe me, you could ask for a raise now! They're *desperate* to get you back. I mean, I could be charging out this time instead of sitting here in your kitchen.'

Eddy turned the whisky bottle over. 'They should be sacking me. I haven't turned up to work in months.'

'Yeah. But they're not. How about I pour?' Alf cracked open the bottle and found two Vegemite glasses in the cupboard. Eddy smelled the half-full cup placed before him and felt ill.

'I couldn't.'

'Dave and Stanny, they feel sorry for you. They've both been there. Wives left them. And me. You're part of the gang now, mate. Badge of honour.'

Eddy groaned and put his head in his hands. He would consider going to work right at this moment just to get away from Alf. He didn't want to be part of any gang Alf was in. Alf drained his glass and clanked it back on the table.

'Okay, I'm going to go back to them and say you'll come back if you get a ten per cent raise.'

'No!'

'Okay, okay. Fifteen. You tough guy, you.'

'Alf, I don't want a raise. I don't want to work right now. Maybe I should just resign.'

'Wow. I'll get you twenty per cent with that attitude. Hard ball.'

'No. I ...' I want my girlfriend to come back. 'I'm just not ready. Can they give me sick leave? Leave without pay?'

Alf refilled his cup and looked at Eddy primly. 'I'll do you a favour and pretend I didn't hear that.'

Eddy sighed, and looked at his glass. Despite himself, he was struck by the kindness of this gesture, this filthy-smelling alcohol sent to him from two overfed, maritally dysfunctional executives via their arrogant and highly paid lawyer. His eyes filled with tears, and, rather than reveal to Alf this embarrassing turn of events, he lifted his glass to his mouth and drank.

CHAPTER TEN

The one entertainment Grace could draw from her new status of abandoned wife was the way it shook the security of every married person in her world. She had at first mistaken the stricken looks and introspective silences from friends and acquaintances as sympathy. However, she gradually realised that they were not reflecting on her sorry state, as they sat dumbly, but rather on their own. They were scrutinising the state of their own marital nation and mulling over harsh words, long absences between sex, episodes of blame and neglect, resolutions for regular date nights that had gathered dust. *Am I next?* You could almost read the question across their foreheads, like a text ribbon of news running across the telly screen. Could people's unions be so delicate that the shattering of one threatened to chip and crack those around them?

It seemed so.

'But I can't believe it!' cried Verity at morning coffee, for the eleventh time.

'Why not?' said Grace wearily, although she still couldn't believe it either.

'I don't know. You guys seemed to me like the perfect couple.'

'Really?' Grace folded a serviette into squares, until it became a ball. 'Why do people say that?'

'*Do* lots of people say it?' Anna Trapper asked. Anna Trapper, who was now living a life Grace could only dream of.

'Well, some.' She heard it said a lot in general when people broke up, just like the way when people died they became all fabulous at their funeral. Although, come to think of it, she hadn't heard it a lot in her and Tom's case.

'Oh, I don't exactly mean that you were *perfect*,' Verity hastened to correct herself, and Grace felt a little sour. Why, exactly, hadn't they seemed perfect? Even a little? 'It's just that you guys seemed good enough. Getting by okay.'

'We were okay. But Tom was obsessed with his invention, he didn't want to earn a living in a normal way, and I ... well ... I guess I wanted him to change.'

'Oh.' Anna Trapper reached over and rubbed Grace's forearm, and Grace resisted an urge to collapse weeping into her arms.

'And I wanted a baby.' It was like confession: where was the priest? I wanted. I dreamed. And the greatest sin of all: I tried to change him.

Verity looked aghast. 'But I feel like that, too, with Stephen! Not about a baby, cos you know, two girls are enough and what are the chances we'd get a boy next time, but, you know, other things. Like the way he hangs out my shirts so I get peg marks on my nipples! Jesus! And the way I have to write all the thank-you notes to his relatives, cos he'd never bother, and, you know, the *snoring*, which is not his fault but, shit, it's so pig-like. I married a farm animal! Sometimes I think, Jesus, get me out of here. There was this moment about a week ago, where I asked him to fill in a school excursion form for Poppy, and he was doing it and he asked me *when Poppy's birthday was*. Can you believe! I mean, I carry all that stuff in my head like four hundred unwinding reels of cotton, and he drifts in and out like a tourist. And I had this dream of leaving him — that passed in a minute, but it freaked me out. Because maybe if I think it, I could do it. Maybe that's the start of it.'

'We think all sorts of things,' said Anna comfortingly. 'That's what I tell the kids. Just because an idea occurs to you, it doesn't mean you follow it. Things blow across our minds like, I don't know, like leaves on a windy day. Most of them mean nothing.'

Grace thought of that blue thread, hanging from the sky. Anna would have let it go, she could see that now. She would have folded her hands and kept them neatly in her lap.

'You never think of leaving Damien?' said Verity.

'Oh, never seriously. Just like I say, like a leaf blowing across a field. And now he's such a big deal in the movies, I'd be mad to leave him, wouldn't I?' She laughed uproariously.

Grace studied her. 'Damien got work?' She was ashamed to note her heart sinking at the possibility of good news for this kind friend and neighbour. What was wrong with her? Bad human.

'A one-year contract with Fox, as a casting assistant. It doesn't earn much, but it's a foot in the door.'

Grace was amazed. 'That's fantastic. Go, Damien! Why didn't you tell us before? You must be ecstatic.'

Anna shrugged. 'It's good.'

'But aren't you rapt? I mean, all these years of him waiting for a break. Will you work less?'

Anna seemed coolly resistant to euphoria, just as she had

been immune to despair. 'Hmm? Oh, actually, yes. I'll probably quit one of my jobs. He was trying to get me to quit both, but I quite enjoy the call-centre one. The girls there are nice.'

Grace could hardly absorb this. Damien, rocking on the verandah singing songs to his children, her low-water-mark for a useless husband, was now employed. While she no longer even had a husband. 'Well, it's a credit to you. You believed in him all these years, you encouraged him to keep trying.' Her own words stabbed her in the heart as she uttered them. Tom. The Oldbot, the solar roof, dreams once as dear to her as that of another child. Dreams which she had, Judas-like, betrayed.

Anna rubbed at a spot on the table. 'Oh, I had my moments, believe me.' But she would say no more on the subject, suddenly preoccupied with her phone.

Dissatisfied, Verity turned to Nina. 'What about you? Do you ever think of ... you know ... with Brian?'

'Leaving him? Sure. And since these guys broke up ...' Nina nodded towards Grace and lowered her voice to a whisper, 'I can't stop worrying about it. But I'm mostly terrified he's thinking about leaving *me*! I mean if Grace didn't see it coming, maybe I wouldn't either. And it would kill me! The money! The kids, the psychological damage. Leaving my house. What my parents would say! And watching him get with someone else ... Oh Grace.' She squeezed her hand. 'You must be devastated.'

Grace nodded, undoubtedly numb with pain, and yet feeling somehow robbed of something by this conversation. Maybe her future. Oh, Christ. *Watching him get with someone else ...* Would that happen? And did every dire implication really need to be pointed out to her? 'Yes. No. I don't know. I guess ... he might come back.'

There was a tragic silence, into which Anna spoke. 'I think there's a good chance he will.'

'You do?' God, if she could just crawl into Anna's lap and have a good sob, she would feel a lot better. If only her own mother could be so kind.

'He adores you. You can see it.'

Grace blinked hard and pulled out tissues. She never went anywhere without tissues anymore.

'But didn't you throw him out?' Verity again, eager for more.

Grace pressed a tissue to her eyes. She did not like to think of this, but yes, she had told him to choose between his plastic bottles or her. It was a foolish thing to have said. He was a fairly literal-minded man. And why should anyone have to choose? And why hadn't she said his bottles or his family, which would have been a harder decision for him? 'I didn't really mean it,' she said forlornly.

'Oh God, of course you didn't; I say stuff like that every day,' said Nina. 'Well, I mean I did. Until this. But nobody means it. He should know that. Were you premenstrual?'

'Um. No.'

'Still. He should know. It's just something you say.'

'Exactly. He's using it as an excuse. I've asked him to come back. Over and over. I've apologised. I've begged him.'

'And where is he living?'

Grace now knew this. 'In a squat. With some artists. Friends of Melody's.'

Eyebrows shot up around the table. '*Oh*. That was ... *nice* of her. To help him.'

Grace pressed her lips closed and made a grumbling sound in the base of her throat, which was correctly interpreted by all her companions, two of whom leaned forward in eager conspiracy.

'Oh, dear. She's a funny one, isn't she?'

'She's such a ... I don't know ... such a ...'

'Hippy,' said Grace.

'Exactly! So dreamy and strange-looking and uncompromising. And I mean, hippies are so over, really.'

'She did save Lotte's life,' Grace said, resentfully.

'That reminds me,' said Anna. 'Damian had some telly friends over the other day, people he went to film school with who work at that current affairs show — what is it? *Round Up* — and they were asking all about Melody. Heaps of questions.'

'Why?'

'I think they want to get her back on the telly.'

Grace was dismayed. 'Would they do something *else* on it? On Lotte's accident?'

'I got the sense it was just Melody they wanted.'

'Why can't they leave her alone?'

'She's so attractive. So unusual-looking. The camera loved her. That's what they said, anyway.'

There was silent consideration of this. 'She's like a wild animal. Like something that just crawled out of the jungle and has to learn how to live a normal life,' said Grace slowly.

'It's interesting you guys have hit it off.'

Grace blinked. Had she and Melody hit it off? It had all been so out of the blue. One moment Melody had been an odd-looking character on a sidewalk, and months later she was a part of her life. Grace had even been thinking the past few days of asking her and Skipper to come live with them, at least until Tom came back. Why not? It would be cheaper for them both, and the kids would love it. The house was too big with Tom gone. And Melody seemed so out of place in that little box flat, whereas she always looked at Grace's scrappy back yard with longing. 'She's different than you'd think,' Grace said slowly, thinking of Melody making their detergent and bread and yoghurt; of how she had pointed out where to plant herbs and veggies, of the elegant simplicity with which she lived on very little, like a musician making a beautiful song out of only a couple of notes. 'She's actually quite practical. Certainly more than Tom.' Which did sound odd, she realised now, comparing Melody to her former husband. But the girls switched in a heartbeat back to the subject of Tom.

'Oh, God, I still can't believe it! You guys were the perfect couple! And was there anything leading up to this, to make you expect it?'

'Nothing.' Why had she mentioned Tom? It was exhausting, this probing of the wound, and she reflected that this was another thing that drew her to Melody; her lack of interest in the marriage breakdown. Melody rarely talked about the past, or speculated on the future. She just lived for the day, helping Skip with kindy, and making her soap and her bread and her lentils. She was a still pool.

The others shivered with fear again, and fell silent, doing mental stocktakes of their lovers. Even Anna pinched her bottom lip between her fingers and stared into middle distance.

'But why? Why?' asked Grace's mother, a pained if sturdy-looking woman named Dawn.

'Mum, I don't know more than I'm telling you. I wanted another baby, Tom wanted to sell our home and quit his job and make solar tiles from recycled bottles. It was — what do they say? — irreconcilable differences.'

'Well, why on earth did you want another baby?' her

mother snapped. 'I mean what have you achieved by wanting that! You're not going to get another baby now without a husband, are you? And why would you want another baby anyway?'

'Because I just did! I'm not that unusual. I mean Lotte is four, I think we've left it a long time as it is.'

'Exactly, there's no point having another baby now — they wouldn't play together with this sort of age gap. I don't know why you were so fixated on ...'

'Mum! I don't need this sort of judgment, thanks very much.'

'Don't come all high and mighty with me, young lady. What about all my friends who gave you wedding presents, who set you up in a home ...?'

'We'd already been living together for two years. They didn't—'

'The Simondsons, who spent so much on that Sunbeam electric frypan, far too expensive, I told them—'

'Well, I never used it; it's still in the box. You can give it back to them if you like.'

But her mother was weeping, stray phrases audible through the sobs. '... do this to me ... after all I've been through ... but as I told the golf women, oh well, what's one more burden for this old back to bear ...'

Grace also had to face her mother-in-law, who was stiff and angry on the phone. 'Tom needs to see a psychiatrist. I've told him so. I just want to, on behalf of the whole Ellison family, to *apologise* to you for what he's done.'

'Oh, well, thank you, Maureen, but really, you've got nothing to—'

'No. I mean it. This runs through the family. We're riddled with it! More from my husband's side than mine, although ... Well never mind. I'm sorry we never told you. I told Tom to tell you before you got married. It was his duty, I said, but he just laughed at me.'

'Riddled with it? Sorry? With what?'

'Madness. Psychiatric disorders. This bottle foolishness.'

'Oh!'

'Again, once again, I would like to state that I. Am. Sorry. On behalf of—'

'In all fairness Maureen, Tom has had some good ideas for inventions. I mean, people have to invent all the amazing things we use, don't they? They're not all mad. And he's quite well progressed on the Solarbottle. It's not impossible, he could one day ...' Oh God, she was defending Tom. Had Maureen engineered this on purpose?

'Oh, no, it's the family malady. Invent a solar-paneled roof out of water bottles, he reckoned?' She gave a sinister laugh. 'Classic sign. Did he ever tell you about Uncle Adam, who believed he could win the Masters Golf Tournament?"

'Uh, no. But I guess someone wins it, don't they? Was Uncle Adam a golf player? Ambitious maybe?'

'He only had one arm!' crowed Maureen. 'He went on naked, carrying a cricket bat.'

'Oh. Well, Tom is a programmer. Good at computers. He's pretty smart—' Dammit, no! Stop!

'And there was Aunty Rita, who cried all day, every day. My second cousin Donald, older than me, sleeps in trees, that's his thing. Says he can see what's coming that way. Even my younger sister Amy, who was a big-time barrister, had to give it up because she hears voices in her head. She was in court making no sense at all, talking one moment to the judge and the next to the voices.'

'Oh dear.' It was indeed a little strange that she had not heard of these characters in Tom's extended family; she could only assume he had been completely uninterested or unaware of the common thread linking them. It would not be like Tom to neglect any opportunity for a laugh at his family's expense, but then again, had she ever really known Tom? Maybe he *was* crazy. Grace thought uneasily of her eccentric daughter. Oh dear.

'This is what I'm saying, right through the family. We must get Tom to a psychiatrist as soon as we can. There's a good one I know of out your way.'

'I really don't think I could persuade him to do anything right now.'

'You must try. In sickness and in health, remember. In the meantime, why don't you let Lotte come here and stay with us for a few days? We'd love it. We'll take good care of her.'

'I think I need her close to me right now, Maureen.' Now that you've declared your insanity credentials, thanks all the same.

'How about next week?'

'I, er, I've lost my job. I don't have a lot to do. And Lotte needs me at the moment.'

'You let her come soon then, alright? Little girls need their nannas at times like this. And while she's with us, you can talk some sense into Tom. And have some time for yourself. Get yourself a nice haircut. Get the greys dyed over. Try out some different clothes. Just because you're married, it doesn't mean you can't still show you're a woman. You don't have to look like a prostitute, but you could still look a little … You know what I mean.'

Grace contemplated lying on the floor with her face down. She might never get up again. Just when you thought the world had humbled you completely, it had one more go.

'I'll think about it, Maureen. Thank you so much for calling.'

CHAPTER ELEVEN

Eddy went to Bunnings and brought home a big old pinboard; white with a narrow pine frame. Inside, he used a handheld device to locate studs in the kitchen wall, and made chalk marks where the light on the device flickered red. He was just wondering how he would hold up the board while he drilled it in, when there was activity at the front door and Tom walked in with pizza. Tom never knocked anymore, and a trail of wet leaves marked his passage along the carpet. But whatever. Eddy welcomed company. He had finally returned to work and Melbourne winter was at its depth, wet leaves feeling obliged to wrap around your ankles as you walked to the train, and icy winds cutting through the crowds on the station, flattening out the women's hair and making them screw up their faces into scowls. He hoped Romy was somewhere warm. She couldn't stand the cold.

Tom obligingly steadied the pinboard while Eddy used the drill to push screws through the soft cork and plaster, and then into the hard studs beneath.

'What's it for?' said Tom, flipping open the pizza box. Salami- and olive-flavoured steam rose.

Eddy tapped a pile of newspaper cuttings with one finger.

'Ah,' said Tom. 'The criminal ex-girlfriend. Bit chilly in here, mate. What's with the plastic?' Eddy had hung a sheet of plastic between the ceiling and the kitchen bench, blocking out the lounge room.

'Keeps the heat in.'

'You're like the reverse of all those renovation people doing the open-plan living area, aren't you? Closed-plan living.'

Eddy shrugged. The plastic was opaque, turning the lounge furniture beyond into a watercolour of indistinguishable shapes and smears.

'I like smaller spaces in a house. You get an earthquake, you can close part of it off more easily. Barricade doors.'

'In Melbourne?'

'We get four point sevens, five point twos, every few years.'

'Oh. What day is it?' Tom had asked this every time he came, since leaving his job.

'Friday.'

Eddy's mobile rang and he answered it.

'Hey there, it's Bella here. Romy's agent.'

'Oh. Well, she's not here.'

'I've been emailing her about an audition and she hasn't gotten back.'

'Okay. She's not here.'

'Do you have a mobile for her?'

Eddy recited the number. Romy would be appalled to hear that Bella had not had her mobile number; she had been waiting for Bella to call for months.

'I really want to get in touch with her,' Bella added.

Eddy would not add: that makes two of us. He had some

pride. 'Try that number' was all he said, a little stiffly. It didn't appear to answer to *him*, anymore, but Bella may be different.

He hung up and returned to his board.

Tom asked: 'Is your heating broken?'

Eddy shook his head. 'I've turned it off. I live mostly in the kitchen, anyway. And if I keep the oven going it stays warm.'

'Ah. Handy. You can bake at the same time.'

'I don't really bake.'

Tom rolled his eyes and looked momentarily affectionate. 'Yeah, I'd sort of noticed. Want some pizza?'

'Later.'

'Are you eating?'

'Yeah. I'm alive, aren't I?'

'You're skinny. How's work?'

'It's work.'

While Tom ate pizza, Eddy took out a new box of thumb tacks and carefully pinned up his articles. There were eight. He studied the headlines as he pinned.

Pirate and Cat get the Cream in 7/11 Hold-Up

Fancy-dress Robbers Terrorise Eastern Suburbs in Small Hours

Extra Night Security for Besieged Convenience Stores

Pirate and Catwoman no Bonnie and Clyde, Say Armed Robbery Squad

Pirate and Catwoman Get Own Facebook Page

Pirate/Cat Combo Highly Dangerous, Warn Police

Police 'Being Played Like Mice' Say Opposition, as Catwoman and Pirate Lead a Merry Dance

Reward Offered

'For any information leading to the arrest of notorious armed robbers connected to the recent spate of convenience store robberies,' read Tom, through a mouthful of meatlovers. He raised his eyebrows. 'Tempted?'

'Save me a piece. I prefer it cold.'

'No, dickhead, I mean are you tempted by the reward?'

Eddy looked at him, offended. 'I don't know where they are!'

'But you know Catwoman's name. That's more than our mighty men in blue. Useless bastards.'

Eddy shook his head. He was surprised his own father hadn't yet rung on the sly and dobbed Romy in. He studied the layout of the articles; he liked it very much. And only half the board was covered.

'I think you're proud of her,' said Tom.

Eddy sighed. Was he? He had pored over every grainy photograph, to read Romy's body language. In the first few, she seemed hesitant, a little frightened. No one but he would have been able to tell. Moving on, the next picture was the first one where she stood straight, threw her shoulders back, held the gun with a new confidence. That self-conscious poise was there in subsequent pictures, too, although it had morphed into something closer to arrogance. And today's picture was a wonder. She stood with her chin tipped up, her back long and straight, the gun raised to her eye and one hip cocked. She could have been on *Charlie's Angels*. Eddy shook his head and couldn't hold back a smile. Romy was acting now. She had read the newspaper stories, she had seen the television footage, she had thrilled to hear herself described as a modern day Bonnie to Van's Clyde, and then she had, with the last gasp of her ambition, taken on that role as determinedly as Elizabeth Taylor took on Cleopatra. She might die fulfilling it, or go to jail, but she would go down being a somebody, not just a waitress.

'In a crazy way, I think I *am* proud of her.'

Tom cast him a wary look over the steaming pizza. Since he and Grace had broken up, he was here almost every two or three nights with pizza, or chicken and chips. He was cheerful and didn't speak of Grace, or where he was staying. Sometimes he talked about his bottle roof, as if it were a troublesome but beloved girlfriend. They talked of rugby. They watched the news. They speculated over Romy and Van, as if it were an ongoing TV series. Eddy had wondered at first whether Grace and Tom would get back together, but weeks and months passed and Eddy looked back at the night of the thank-you dinner and felt he must have misunderstood appearances that night. The perfect young couple, with a mortgage and a child. But now look.

So, Tom and Eddy played darts. The pizza boxes piled up in the corner. Tom never suggested removing the pizza boxes, or cleaning up the disgusting pit that was Eddy's home these days. He never brought healthy food, or asked Eddy to talk about his feelings. Eddy liked that.

Later, Eddy found a roll of red ribbon in one of Romy's drawers, and he measured it to the length of the sides of the board, and cut it and pinned it on, making a border of red around the edges of the board. He also pinned up a colour photograph of Romy; his favourite. It was the day he had met her, at her parents' funeral. It wasn't a picture she liked — she looked pale and weepy, with swollen eyes — so it had never been up in the house before, but hey. He could like her in any way he wanted now.

His father dropped by and frowned at the board.

'What's this?' He stared at the pictures and then slid his eyes sideways to his son, his toothbrush eyebrows making waves, his expression one of alarm.

'The article. I told you about it. That's Romy, see ...' He moved to point Romy out to his father, but Ray brushed his son's pointed finger away.

'I know it's bloody Romy. I mean, what's it doing on your wall? The girl's a lunatic, my boy. She's a selfish ... she's everything that's wrong with modern women. She's like a — what do you call it? — a ...' Ted stabbed a finger at his son. 'I feel sorry for men of your generation. Truly, I do. You're lost.'

Eddy gazed at the picture, not sure what to say. *Well, I reckon I've had sex with more women than you?* Sounded a bit nyah nyah nyah. And possibly not true; he had the sense his father might have been a bit of man-about-town in his youth. But then women those days, reputations and all. Probably true, but all the same. What about: *I like a smart woman, not just a domestic servant?* Could be construed as insulting his mother. Which would be awful. 'We're okay,' he said feebly, on behalf of his generation.

Ray lifted a corner of the board, discovered the point at which it was attached to the wall and began to prise it off. 'Do yourself a favour, boy, and ...'

'No!' Eddy gripped the board with both hands, his elbow almost hitting his father in the face as he did. He forced it back to the wall, turned and eyeballed his father. Ray's arms resisted for a moment, but his face was already stunned; Eddy had never shown any physical resistance to him. Eddy's arms across his father's field of vision were muscly and strong. Ray let go, his hair whiter and his face more lined than it had been the year before. His head shook, his mouth pursed with the bottled-up anger of an old man convinced of the next generation's stupidity, but faced with its dominance.

'Do what you like!' he said, and left.

Finally, one Saturday, Eddy woke with a rare ray of winter sun falling across his eyes. Outside, the world looked unusually good. He felt frail and cleansed, as if emerging from a long illness. He looked at the leftover pizza which he usually ate for breakfast, and shut the fridge door. He put on his coat and scarf and snow beanie, and walked to the nearest café, ignoring the happy couples, and the frazzled families, and he spread the business section right across his table, and ordered fried eggs and bacon and mushroom and baked beans and hash browns, orange juice and a coffee. He ate and read, glancing sometimes over the top of the paper at a couple nearby, slightly older than he and Romy. The man, greying at the temples, spoke gently, encouragingly to his partner. The woman, with black-framed glasses and pale skin, sulked. The man leaned over, touched the back of her hand. She sat back in her chair, crossing her arms and staring, purse-mouthed, at a baby nearby in one of those spaceship strollers. Eddy couldn't see the whole baby, just a leg clad in one of those onesie suits, as it occasionally kicked above the upholstered edges. After breakfast, Eddy left the couple to work it out, and walked home the longest way he could think of, because he needed some exercise, and because there was still a large piece of the day to fill in. And as soon as he let himself in the front door, he realised there was someone in the house.

Tom?

Romy. He smelled her before he saw her. It wouldn't have taken a detective. Her bag sat in the hallway, the heater hummed and the back door was wide open. She stood in the kitchen before the pinboard, reading the newspaper articles. She turned to him.

'Hi.' A small smile, maybe resignation, maybe shame. A plea for forgiveness. Like she'd never left. He resisted the urge to cross the room and gather her up in his arms. My girl. He felt like he was exhaling properly for the first time in months.

'Jesus, Romy. You scared me.'

'Sorry about letting myself in.'

'Well, it is your house.'

'I know, but ...'

'So, here you are.'

She shrugged helplessly, gave him an apologetic glance. 'I just ... I don't know what came over me, Eddy.'

He held out his hands, and let them fall. 'I've been out of my mind. Why couldn't you call me?'

Romy stared at the floor, and folded her arms. She reminded him of a child; when in trouble, she would turn inwards and not speak. Like a spaceship closing all its panels and powering down, as if trying to become an inanimate object. He was familiar with the aim of the exercise; invisibility. Only a tear streaked down Romy's cheek and she squeaked.

'What?' He stepped closer, smelt her spicy girl smell, resisted the urge to slip his hands under her arms, along the side of her generous olive-skinned breasts, the tops of which were hinted at through a black dress. God, had she even changed clothes since the night of the dinner party, five months ago?

'I don't know what came over me,' she said, in a high, near-tears voice. 'I can't believe I just got up and went off with him. That man. It was like I was bewitched.' Eddy was reminded of the yoga teacher; another time Romy had been in the grip of something larger than herself, as if aliens had made a habit of holding and brainwashing her.

'But what have you been doing all this time? I mean besides robbing shops.'

She stared aghast into space. 'It was the anniversary. The five-year anniversary of their deaths. It really got to me. Made me crazy.' She gazed at him, waiting for him to understand.

'Your parents' death.'

She nodded, unable to speak. Her eyes filled with tears. He opened his arms. In a moment they were back in their old, comforting roles: she the victim of tragedy, he the great comforter. She leaned against him and wept, a little wet patch seeping through to his chest.

'Your agent's been trying to get onto you.

'I know!' She pulled away, nodding emphatically. He recognised the spark of excitement in her eyes, and his heart died a little. That was why she was back. 'And?'

'I have to be out in Heidelberg by three this afternoon for the filming of an ad. I've got the address here.' She smiled through her tears and he stared at her. He was dazed, disbelieving. The touch of her, her smell, his injured pride, his pathetic need, his overwhelming relief, it was all too much. He could see the board of news cuttings over the top of her head. She was indeed a wanted criminal, but he pushed that aside for now. That brazen Catwoman of the press could not be this sparkly, soft kitten. It was all a bad dream that would melt away in the heat of long-awaited acting success. They had not caught her yet, they would surely just give up.

Every part of his body felt bruised, but it would heal. His sullen, angry heart would pick itself up off the ground. Her parents' death, the five-year anniversary. Well, that would knock anyone around.

'The police are after you. What if you're recognised?'

'Hard to recognise Catwoman without her mask, I think.'

'Can I drive you there?'

She smiled at him lovingly. 'Sure,' she whispered, and everything was alright. 'I'll just go and get dressed.'

Hours later, Romy the Rabbit emerged surly and depressed from a retail outlet called Rabbit Photos. The promise of a TV ad had been a little exaggerated; in fact, she had spent two hours in front of the shop dressed in a rabbit suit and handing out brochures, a free glare with each one. A CCTV inside the shop had indeed broadcast her image to those within, browsing amongst the frames, but in the main the gift of her presence had been bestowed upon adolescent boys trying to touch up her fur.

'Oh, sweetie.' Eddy grimaced at her furious face and opened the car door for her.

'I'm going to rip that bloody agent's head off,' snarled Romy, her inked-on whiskers twitching as she scowled.

Driving home, Eddy could hardly concentrate for his fear. Would she leave him again? He didn't think he could bear it. Distracted, he cut across the path of a semi-trailer, forcing it to brake sharply.

Suddenly, the semi was bearing down on them, blasting

its horn. The driver wore a look of fury in the vast windscreen of his vehicle; his mouth an open snarl of rage. Eddy's mirror was full of truck, his ears were full of the high-pitched yet resigned whine of a truck gearing down.

'Aargh!' Beside him, Romy sat still dressed as a rabbit, in a grey and white onesie with high heels. She clutched a set of bunny ears and bent them in fear as she stared behind. They were going to die.

Eddy controlled his breathing and glanced back at the truck driver in the mirror again. The truck driver waved a fist at him, as if wanting to punch this piece-of-shit small vehicle that was blocking his ability to drive at two hundred kilometres an hour down a suburban street.

'Shit!' He muttered. 'Lean over! Get in the brace position!'

'The what?'

'Brace yourself!'

The driver sped up behind him, and Eddy couldn't change lanes at this speed, so he was forced to accelerate further.

'Slow *down*!'

'I can't!' But finally he dared to brake, praying the mad truckie might glimpse his brake lights, although he was so close to their car he would probably miss them. Eddy braked slowly, terrified with each moment that the truck would run right over them, but there was nothing else he could do. He couldn't maintain this speed on these streets; he had to pull off the road. He got the car down to about ninety kilometres, then indicated left and pulled off the road. There was a clip as the truck grazed the back of his car, and then it was over.

'Are you alright?'

'Did he hit the car?'

'It's minor, I think. Insurance will cover it. Are you okay?'

'What a maniac. Did he stop?'

'No.' Eddy looked up to verify this fact, and was faced with the truck, reversing up to them. 'Shit. He did.' This guy was obviously off his face on whatever uppers truckies took to survive their long-haul lives. 'Oh, *shit*. He's getting out. Lock your door.' He hastily pressed down his own lock.

'*Lock your door?*' Romy sat up and gave him a look of such withering scorn he was momentarily diverted from the threat approaching down the road's verge, wearing King Gees and a high-vis vest. '*Lock your door?*'

'What?'

'Can you hear yourself? What sort of a man are you?'

'Quick, Romy, he's coming.'

'Fuck you, and fuck locking my door. Fuck everything.'

'Jesus, Romy, what the hell are you doing—' But she was climbing out of the car. Even as the meathead driver was leaning over and pounding on Eddy's window, looking like he might be preparing to eat man flesh for dinner, Romy had swung out and slammed her own door with a force that made the driver look up, his expression momentarily wary as he reassessed the situation. Which was that a voluptuous woman dressed as a rabbit, in a furry onesie with high heels, was striding around the car towards him, her pom-pom jiggling with every furious step. Eddy's jaw fell open as the two met in front of his car, framed by his windscreen. Romy jabbed her forefinger into the man's chest. He had gone from deranged fury to being bewildered and defensive, inching backwards even as he gestured towards his truck.

'... taken out my front sidelight ...'

'... driving like a GODFORSAKEN maniac!' screamed

Romy the Rabbit. The driver's glance slid down the length of her and back towards Eddy.

'... didn't realise I was tailgating ...'

'... like HELL you didn't ...' Romy actually slapped his left shoulder and then his right. He backed off like a whipped dog. Eddy was part frozen, part reasoning that Romy had the moral supremacy of a woman, as well as the ambush advantage of a giant rabbit. If he stepped out to defend her, which there seemed no apparent need to do at this point, he would only upset the march on power she had taken, and it would become a thing between men, which he would inevitably lose. As it was, there were pens out, and notepads, and pieces of paper being exchanged, and apologetic retreating by the driver, before the truck moved off, and then the return of glowering Romy the Rabbit. Who seemed to have absorbed all the threat previously manifested by the truckie.

Eddy watched her do up her seatbelt, and he started the car. It was a full five minutes before he dared speak to her. He began to ask 'Are you alright?', but it seemed a little obsolete. The truck driver was more likely at this moment to be patting at tears and touching up his makeup on the side of the road somewhere behind them.

'What's on the piece of paper?' He changed gear and coasted through traffic. His body was still flooded with adrenalin, he wanted only to get out of the car and stop driving.

'His insurance details.' She flung them at him.

'You ... He's going to pay?'

'Of course he will.' Dripping with scorn.

'You were amazing, Romy. I think you scared him to death.'

'Well, *someone* had to face up to him.'

'What are you saying? *I* didn't ...'

'That's exactly what I'm saying, Eddy. *You* didn't. You never do. You're scared of living. Scared of everything.' Romy hurled her rabbit ears at him. They bounced down to the floor at his feet, where they tangled hazardously with the pedals.

'What the— Romy, I know you're upset about the work today. It was disappointing, not what you expected, but it's a start. Better work will come ...' He tried to lower himself down to disentangle the rabbit ears from his brake pedal, all while continuing to negotiate the car.

'Oh shut up, will you! Stop being so bloody ... caring! Stop being such a marshmallow, just reacting to life with the least possible intrusion on the world you can! Why don't you own your life, why don't you get out there and take a risk? Don't you want to really live, instead of just cowering around the edges?'

He stared at her, amazed, hurt. Too caring? But that was his role with Romy; that was what she had always wanted him to be. That was the contract they had signed at the start, in fact they had renewed it just that morning. She, the fragile tearaway made vulnerable by the loss of her parents; he, the patch on her wounds. They were a couple based on caring, and being cared for, and surely that was what love was all about.

'Romy, don't take your bad mood out on me. That's really hurtful.'

She looked at him, her eyes bare with something he flinched before. 'When we got together, Eddy, I was hurt from the loss of my parents. I was broken.'

'I know that.'

'You were the right person for me, then, but I'm not broken anymore, Eddy. I'm strong. And I want to stay strong, I don't want to always be your project, like some pampered baby. I want to live. I want adventure.'

'With Van.' Pampered baby! Project! He pulled up in his driveway.

'Yes.'

'You're in a relationship with Van, now.'

She smiled, not at him, but at some thought out beyond the neighbour's Sulo bin. 'Van doesn't do relationships, Eddy. Van is his own man. But he'll let me hang around him, and that's what I want for a while, Eddy, that's what I need. To not be ... cosseted.'

'And me? Us? After all these years, you're just ... ending it?'

Confusion crossed her face. 'I don't know. But I know I just need to follow my heart for a while. Who knows, my heart might lead back to you.' She took his hand comfortingly between the bucket seats. He felt her touch, and his body went into meltdown at the sensation. He was one big ball of pain, and the person who would have once comforted him and made the pain a little better was the person causing it. His tears fell down on his arm.

'I hope it does, Romy. I'll be waiting here, just in case.'

An expression crossed her face, something between revulsion and exasperation. 'Maybe you shouldn't wait for me, Eddy. Maybe you should go and find a nice girl, and have a real relationship.'

'After all we've been through together, you want to end it?'

She sighed wearily. 'I told you, I'm not certain of anything.'

'Then I'll be here.'

'Oh, God. Of course you will be. Well, then, that's it. I'm ending it. It's over. You're dumped.'

She shook her head, sighed and climbed out of the car. The pink pom-pom that had been her bunny's tail was flattened now. Eddy fished the rabbit ears off the floor between his feet and watched Romy go inside their house. He stroked the ears and wiped his forearm across his eyes.

CHAPTER TWELVE

Options.

- *Keep paying mortgage on house*
- *Rent out house, keep paying mortgage*
- *Sell house*

Grace pushed the list across to Tom. They were sitting in possibly Melbourne's worst café, barely a step up from a truck stop. The front window shook with the force of six lanes of passing traffic outside. Dead flies trembled in the corners. The table was wobbly, and she suspected that a rip in the vinyl of her chair had already sunk its ragged teeth into the delicate knit of her sexiest skirt. Tom had been oblivious to the skirt, anyway. He drew two quick lines on the list and she leaned over to see, hastily withdrawing her hand from a sticky patch on the table. Her mouth fell open.

'Sell. You really want to sell the house.'

'Yes,' he said.

'Tom. This is a separation, isn't it? Not a divorce. We want to keep our options open. We might ...'

'Get back together?'

Her heart warmed a little. He had said it. It was at the top of his mind, too. Her entire body relaxed.

'Yes.' She smiled, kindly. Not too kindly, she knew he needed his space, and to feel alone for a while. When he came back, it would have to come from him, it wouldn't work if he felt pressured to come back. She couldn't gloat, or be vengeful. She would just be quietly waiting for him, not demanding anything, a purer and simpler version of her former self, until he finally realised ...

'No,' he said coldly. 'I want to sell. As soon as possible.'

She gaped at him. 'Tom, this is crazy.' At the back of the café, a torn shower curtain hung open, revealing a galley kitchen where the waiter leaned towards a mirror and trimmed his nose hairs with kitchen shears. 'You really want to burn all your bridges like this?'

'Like what?'

'It's one thing for us to have a little time apart. But selling the house, that's irr-e-vers-i-ble. That's—' She stopped and panted for a few seconds. Some creature had reached up a hand from her heart and was choking her. She stroked her throat frantically, trying to relax it, and speech returned. 'That's burning all your bridges.'

He gave her a funny look. 'Is it?'

'Well, isn't it?'

'Only if, like you, you feel married to a person and a house. Instead of a person.'

He wasn't making sense. She ran through the words again; nope, still no sense. 'What are you talking about?'

'Nothing. Here's the agent's card. She can get the auction happening next month.'

'Next month!' She gazed out the streaked window of Melbourne's worst café, towards where some of the city's worst weather, infamous throughout the nation, was on display. Rain lashed the road in drops so big they could bruise, while trees bent sideways in gale-force winds. 'Where will Lotte and I live?'

'You can find somewhere to rent. Like I'm doing.'

She tried another tack. 'Isn't there no auctions at this time of year?'

'It will be spring before our house gets to auction.'

Our house. 'That leak in the lounge room will put off buyers.'

'I'll fix it.'

Like you could have done last winter? Grace didn't say. 'It's too soon to sell.'

'I asked you to sell it a few months ago, even before we broke up.'

She tried again. 'The market's low. We'll lose money.'

'We'll lose the house if we *don't* sell. The bank will foreclose.'

'Can't we ask our families for help?' She scanned his face for something, anything. He looked slightly puzzled.

'No. Because we've *split up*. Don't you get this? So why would we borrow more money from our families to pay for a house we're not going to live in together?'

She sighed. The waiter, with freshly trimmed nose hair, brought Tom's coffee and her pot of tea. 'You like a biscuit?' he said. 'We open new packet.'

'No, thanks,' said Tom, smiling kindly. Okay, so he did have some warmth left in him, just not for her. He was apparently saving it all for strangers.

'Tom, why don't we—'

'Biscuit?' The waiter barked at her.

Grace jumped, startled. 'No, thank you.' The waiter looked her over suspiciously and went back through the shower curtain.

Tom stirred his coffee. 'Or you can buy me out of the house if you want.' His face was expressionless, he was zombie man. He had left his feelings at the front door of this rancid place, and they were pawing at the glass, saying Tom! You forgot us! Let us in! We like Grace! 'We get the house valued, you give me half, and it's done.'

'You know I can't do that. I have nothing, and I have no job.'

He put his hands on his gorgeous, denim-clad thighs and shrugged his broad shoulders. 'Precisely. Neither do I. We've used up your redundancy. I can't meet the next repayment. We have to sell.'

Something he had said earlier started working its way through her brain then, like a hot ember that takes a while to finally start burning carpet. She had asked him if he really wanted to burn all his bridges, and he had said *Is it?* And *Only if you feel married to a person and a house.* And maybe that was it. He just wanted to force this sale. He was pushing them to the brink of their marriage to get his way on selling the house. It was a test, to see if she loved him more than the house, or separately from the house. If she passed the test, he'd take her back. For a moment she was furious; the lengths he would go to in order to win an argument! Putting her through all this misery! And then she remembered that she had no income, and nor did he, and, for whatever reason he had done it, they simply could not pay the mortgage.

It was awful, yet it gave her a ray of hope.

'Okay.'

'Okay what?'

'Okay, let's sell the house then.' She waited for a flicker

of warmth, some moment of gratitude. He had won, he had got his way. But zombie man just blinked and nodded his stony, handsome face and rose to his feet, abandoning his coffee. Apparently, he couldn't bear to be in her company for a second more than he had to. He was already focused on the rain outside, and on leaving.

'Good. I'll call the agent, and let you know you the date.'

Grace forced herself to nod, from her still-seated position. 'Okey-doke. Well, see you.'

'You sure?' He hesitated. 'You changed your mind very suddenly.'

'No, no. I just see your point now.'

He looked at her a little suspiciously. 'Well. Bye.'

Grace watched him leave. She hadn't touched her tea. Gingerly, she tipped the stainless-steel pot, and hot water poured down its side, pooling over the tabletop. She halfheartedly dropped a serviette into the steaming slick of water, and watched the paper darken around the edges, and in growing spots in the middle. She paid the waiter and told him to keep the change, preferring to carry nothing else away from that terrible place, nothing more than the rock placed upon her heart.

A week later, the *For Auction* sign was hammered up out the front. Grace had hoped to conceal this calamitous and gossip-fuelling turn of events from the kindy mothers, but the three-metre high sign meant the jig was up. *Shape this Snug First Home to Your Dreams, or Demolish and Develop as Investment Opportunity (STCA)* it read. *Three Cosy Bedrooms ... Baltic pine floor boards ... Original kitchen ...* She wanted to mock the real estate speak (how was the originality of the kitchen an asset?! God, they should have left the outdoor toilet in place, or maybe there was a cave on the block that Neanderthals had once used), but her heart wasn't in it. It truly had been a Snug First Home, and it had fulfilled many of her dreams, she thought sadly.

A knock on the door sounded through the house like a gunshot. Grace let in her mother, there to help her clean up for house inspections. Dawn had thought to bring a packet of extra-strength garbage bags and a bootful of cardboard boxes, which was more than Grace had done. She had also brought a plastic container with a freshly baked sponge cake. The kindness of it reduced Grace to immediate tears.

'Mum!' Lotte had gone to spend the day with her father and Grace was free to fall apart.

'Shush, shush, there, there.'

'I don't want to sell this house.'

'No. Well. Life serves up some pretty poor meals sometimes.'

'It's all so awful!'

'There, there. Your marriage has failed, you've lost your job.'

Grace snuffled into Dawn's shoulder, and waited for more. Where was the encouragement?'

'I didn't ... I haven't ...'

'No, no, you're right. You're a penniless single mother, abandoned by your husband, without a means of support, your career in tatters. That's what I told the golf ladies. It's terrible. Terrible.'

Grace stepped away from her mother and wiped her face dry, suddenly embarrassed. Jesus, was that the best her mother could do? She had been a junior primary teacher for over twenty-five years, so there were probably entire generations of children still in counselling to recover from their first year at school as five-year-olds. *No, Dianne, you can't read. Nor can you tie your laces or drive a car, like any normal human being. Pretty doomed state of affairs if you ask me.*

'Right, well, I thought we'd start on Lotte's room,' Grace said briskly.

'What? Did I say something?' Her mother followed her.

'No, nothing, really, I just wanted to get going on it.'

'I said something wrong, didn't I? I hurt your feelings.'

'Not at all, Mum.'

'I just like to tell it how it is. I don't like to butter both sides of the bread — you know me.'

'What on earth does that mean? Butter ...'

'You know. Blow smoke up your—'

'Mum! It's fine. Really. And you were so kind to bring the cake, and to come to help. Really.' She hastily gave instructions for Dawn to pack away Lotte's toys and fled to the back garden.

The shed door hung open. Grace peeked inside, her eyes needing a moment to adjust to the dim light. The roof was, of course, clad with the opaque plastic tiles that doubled as mini solar panels, but they had been installed at an early stage of Tom's research, and didn't work, beyond letting in a little natural light. But then she realised her eyes were fine, that there was just nothing inside. Not the workbench, or the tools, or the pile of scraps of metal, screws, brackets. Tom had taken it all. The shed looked enormous. Grace closed the door shut and wrestled the lock across. She crouched under her clothesline and studied the back of her home. Her mother passed inside like a shadow across the window and disappeared again. The weatherboards flaked and rotted at the edges. A piece of guttering sagged. A pot of rosemary grew beside the door, and a little garden bed held a pool of dry leaves, in the same space in which Lotte's flower seedlings grew last spring. Buds were bursting out of bare branches, sunlight bathed the grass. The arrival of spring in Melbourne always felt slightly miraculous, as if someone had brought you a holiday and left it kindly on your doorstep.

She could hear the neighbour from two houses away, talking to her grandchild, so brimful of tender affection that Grace had to resentfully smile. 'Peek A *BOO!* I *SEE* you!'

To sell this house, it would feel like cutting off parts of her body. The way light fell in a certain room, and had illuminated the face of a new baby. The way leaf-shadow played on a wall, and Lotte had watched it. The way the key sounded in the lock when Tom was coming home to her. Grace knew the entire house with not just her eyes but her hands. For the past ten years, since buying the house straight after their wedding, she had got up once a night to go to the toilet. She could make her way around in the dark, knowing every creak and the feel of every surface.

Grace remembered a friend's grandmother, who had declined with dementia until she had to be moved out of her knick-knack-filled home and into a bare-walled nursing home. The woman had lost all of her remaining memories almost instantly; something Grace understood. Your home was full of placeholders for memories. Tom did not realise that this was irreversible. He just couldn't.

'The sale's in a month?' said her mother, stepping out the back. She peeled off plastic gloves and tucked her hair back off her face. 'You should get a bit of money for it.'

Oh well done, Mum. A positive. 'Most will go to the bank. To pay back the mortgage.'

'All of it?'

Grace forced herself to consider it, and did the sums. 'No. Some will go to the real estate agent for commission, advertising, auctioneering, that sort of thing.'

'But surely something for you? You've been paying this mortgage for ten years.'

'Maybe,' said Grace, daring to dream about it. That much? Or even, *that* much? Enough to put a deposit on a small flat? But no, Tom would come back to her, so she wouldn't do that. Invest in shares? Start a business? 'Or maybe not.'

Her mother shook her head like one who's just had bad news. 'All those mortgage repayments for nothing,' she said, patting Grace's shoulder. 'Fifteen years in that job and you might as well have stayed home.'

'Yeah. Right. Jesus, Mum …'

'You can always come and live with me, you know. There's space for you and Lotte. I won't get in your way.'

'Thanks. But I'll find a new place, and we'll start afresh,' she said.

'You sure now? I'd love to have Lotte.'

'And me.' Grace prompted.

'Well, of course. And you. I'd love you both to live with me.'

'Thanks, Mum.' Hell would freeze over first, she silently resolved.

CHAPTER THIRTEEN

Melody took the spray can from her bike basket and shook it, the inner pebble knocking inside a full tin. Prussian Blue. Destined for a pale orange wall, visible from an inner-city rail station. The spring full moon had already risen above the northeastern suburbs, most of its ghostly arc ahead, yet to be completed. As was her task.

'You right?' she whispered back to Eddy Plenty, on a bike behind her. Some shiny new forty-speed number, straight from the box. He had called her earlier, angry and wanting to contact Van and punch his lights out. There had been more news stories in the papers in the past week, and one on the news, about the city's celebrity thieves, Cat and Pirate. Melody had gone to visit him. She saw from his pale face and the state of his house that he was not doing well. It was a pity Romy had dropped back in, just long enough to break his heart all over again, by the look of it. But Melody already knew Eddy's weakness: he loved to help. She had cooked him dinner, and coaxed him out into the dark night, on their bikes.

Risk Being Alive. How nice to have this angry man, so

straight he had probably waited for the green man all his life, as her apprentice on this mission. *Risk Being Alive.* A little present she was planning, for the half-dead commuters of the Fairview rail line. She leaned around her son, traffic lights reflected in his eyes, and nodded at Eddy. 'You right?' she repeated.

He walked his bike up alongside her, holding his legs apart as if the bike were on fire. 'Where are we going?' he whispered. God, don't let him bail on her now, timorous soul that he was. Imagine him thinking he could punch Van's lights out. Ha! She'd probably saved his life by stopping him trying. Whatever rage burned in Eddy, it was a dead match compared to the blaze in Van, whose switch could flick from languorous to insane in an instant.

She looked ahead into the darkness and then back at him. So many people, they just had to know everything up front. 'It's a surprise,' she said. 'Trust me.'

Eddy settled his backside on the seat of his bike, folded his arms and looked at her warily. He was pleasant-looking, in a straight sort of way. 'Surprise' might have been the wrong thing to say to him. 'Okayyy.'

He was the good-with-kids-and-animals type. A listener. She stepped onto the pedal and launched down a side street, down roads of mostly darkened houses. Ah, suburban Melbourne, all those millions of souls, sleeping at precisely the same time. She could feel their deep breaths, sense the loosening of their muscles, smell the enchanted forest of so many dreams, spooling like serpent-entwined smoke from the ashes of the day's purpose and drive, winding their miasmic ways around the driveways and For Sale signs, the council rubbish bins and the empty cans in the gutters. Knitting the world together again, for the new day ahead.

She pulled up at Victoria Park railway station and parked

her bike at the foot of the grassy slope that led up to a factory, its pale orange wall facing the rail bridge high above. The trains wouldn't start again until 5am; she had a clear couple of hours. She lifted the hood on her son's head and studied his vacant, sleeping face. Perfect. She scooped him out of the bike seat and waited for Eddy Plenty to catch up, his face a mixture of curiosity and alarm.

'Here.' She thrust the sleeping child at him and he let his spanking-new bike crash to the ground as he hurriedly held out his arms and took Skipper. He sat them down on a low wall, under a street light, and Melody knew her boy was safe. She turned to climb a narrow maintenance ladder, to take herself up to the trestle bridge far above. 'What ... what are you doing?' whispered Eddy, looking angrily aghast, his arms full of sleeping child. She climbed. At the top of the ladder she hopped out onto the empty tracks; two sets, one heading east, one west. There would be no trains for a couple of hours, she hoped.

Below were the drab shop faces of the hardware store, a baby-wear shop, a petrol station. She picked her way along the track, shaking her can, hearing the quiet squeaking of fruit bats and the leathery flap of their wings in the sleeping, city night. She stood before the factory wall and reached high for the first letter, and worked her way through them: *R, I, S, K ...* She stepped back after each one to regain her perspective. Once, she stepped back a little too far and fell over the girders of the track, almost falling off the ten-metre-high bridge. She crawled back from the edge, trembling, a sole car passing underneath, maybe someone going home from shiftwork. She went on through the letters, her heart beating too fast. *RISK BEING ALIVE.* By the time the moon had moved to centre stage, right above her, the job was done. A train hooted, far away. Sometime tomorrow she would feel the true satisfaction of it, but, for now, she just wanted to smell the neck of her child, to feel the inky night air as she rode her bicycle into it, to go home, put on the kettle and have a cup of tea. She lowered herself onto the ladder and climbed down, one rung at a time, to the dark shadow figure below.

'Why the hell did you do that?' said Eddy. 'You could have killed yourself.'

'Well, here I am safe.'

'What if the police catch you?'

'Well, they won't now.'

'What does it mean?'

'What?'

'Risk being alive.'

'Just ... be alive. Take risks. Don't press the pause button on living.'

He looked appalled. 'You're crazy.'

'Do you really think that?'

'Well, not literally, but—'

'Hey, it's Grace and Tom's auction tomorrow,' she said, swiftly changing the topic.

'I know. Tom's in a state.'

'I thought I'd go. Wanna come?'

'Ahh ...' Eddy shifted the little boy back into her arms.

'I reckon Tom could use your help.'

'Oh?' Eddy looked surprised.

'They both could. Grace, too.'

'Oh. Well. Maybe.'

She settled Skip back into the bike seat and wrapped a sarong around him, binding his sleep-floppy limbs to the seat back. Then, climbing aboard, she looked over at Eddy for a minute. In the shadows he looked quite dark and dangerous. Could she shag him? A thank-you shag? Maybe not.

'I'm going to go. To the auction.'

'To help Grace?' said Eddy.

'Maybe.' They rode off into the night together, speaking quietly, sailing through the meagre patches of light cast by street lamps and the longer patches of dark shielded by trees and sleeping houses.

'I'm a bit surprised they broke up. They didn't seem ...' His wheels squeaked and the night air felt cool on Melody's skin.

'... at the dinner.'

'I know.'

'Grace thinks it's because of the accident.'

'What?'

'The breakup. It gave them both a fright. Made them assess their lives, shake everything up.'

'Oh.'

'These things happen for a reason.'

'You think?'

'I do. So, do you want to come to the auction tomorrow? I can ride past and pick you up.'

'Can I really help? I might be intruding.'

'We'll help.'

'Does Grace really think the breakup is because of the accident?'

'Well, you know Grace.'

'That would make it my fault. Sort of. And that's why Romy met Van, too.'

'It's no one's fault. It's just the pick-up-sticks of the universe, falling in a certain way. Now we look at what's there and work out how to make the best of it.'

The bikes creaked as they pulled up out the front of his

house. Melody yawned, and Eddy looked reluctantly at his front door and sighed deeply.

'Do you want to come in for a hot drink?'

She smiled. 'I'd better get Skip home. I'll come past tomorrow?'

'Okay. Actually, I might take the car, and take some tools, just in case. Can I pick *you* two up? About ten?'

'Sure.'

Grace should have known how bad auction day would be, she thought later. The fact that she and Tom couldn't agree on a reserve price for the house could have given her an inkling. (She wanted higher; he wanted to practically give it away.) Nor could they agree on whether to spend some money on the house first, on things like clawing the garden back from its wilderness, and getting the windows washed, and the roof fixed. (She wanted these things done; he refused.) On the morning of the auction they nearly had a standup fight over who would park in the driveway, until the agent came over and said that it would be better if the driveway was left clear. They had both come with their mothers, in their mothers' cars — Dawn a crumbling Volvo, Maureen a red Commodore with *Doncaster Holden* stickers on the back. Dawn and Maureen each sat behind their respective steering wheels ignoring each other while their children fought it out on the nature strip. Dawn cried while Lotte patted her shoulder, and Maureen read a *New Idea* with shaking hands. As if divorce wasn't bad enough — Grace noted that Tom had gone from calling it their separation to their divorce — there was the enforced return to the company of their mothers. She knew she should be grateful for the help of her mother, but accepting her help was so humiliating she had to hold back her rage. Her only comfort was that she could see that Tom was in the same boat, and that his abrasive, opinionated mother was even more annoying than her own gloomy and frequently weeping parent.

Right now, standing out on the footpath, she could see that down the side of the house Tom appeared to be in an argument with his mother. Maureen rested her hand on her fat hip and waved her right hand expressively, one moment towards the house (with a disgusted flick of her fingers) and then the next towards Tom, chopping the air in front his chest as if she were demonstrating how to slice bread. Lotte stood between them, and Grace urgently beckoned her daughter over to her.

'Sweetie! Are Daddy and Nanna having a little argument?' she whispered.

'I don't know.'

'What are they saying?'

'I don't know.'

'Of course you don't.' Grace straightened up. She kicked the ground casually and tried desperately to eavesdrop on the argument. She couldn't hear anything, but after a few seconds she got it, by some effort of wilful osmosis and reading of body language. Maureen was agreeing with Grace; they should set the reserve higher, hang out for more money rather than cave in for a low price.

'Maybe it's possible, maybe we will get a decent amount,' Grace murmured to her mother.

Dawn looked worried. 'Ooh, I hope so, love.'

'Lotte and I could take a little holiday. Maybe Bali.' They could do their hair in silly braids and buy fake watches and lie on sun-loungers.

'Ooh, not there, love. Terrorists.'

A car pulled up, and Melody and Eddy climbed out. Grace stared at them. Had they come to watch the misery of it all? To gloat? They hadn't seemed the types. Lotte ran to extract Skip from the car.

'It's still early,' Grace said. 'Another half-hour before they start letting people through.'

'You know the gutter,' said Eddy awkwardly. He rubbed his nose and waved toward the guttering that had fallen down over the western window.

Grace looked at it. 'Tom and I couldn't agree on whether to pay someone to fix it.' They had fought just the day before over that very gutter, shouting for almost an hour.

'Would you mind if I ...?' He waved again towards it. 'It would only take a ...' He shrugged, to indicate that it would be little more than a minute's work.

As in fact it was. Eddy sort of streamed up a tree, Melody handed him tools and the guttering, and the whole thing was fixed while Grace stared. Then the two of them grabbed a rake and clippers and in ten minutes' work the garden had gone from bedraggled to presentable. The real estate agent was almost prostrate with gratitude at Eddy's feet. Melody persuaded the agent to let her in the house, and she took out a small bag with an oil burner, and lit some essential oil that Grace had never encountered in her life, with a smell she could not have described. A smell of warmth, and welcome, and some faraway place and time which Grace could not remember, but which had been the best time of her life, whenever it was. By the time people arrived to start inspecting the house — mostly neighbours and kindy mothers — the smell had wafted through every room and the first thing everyone said was 'Mmm! What is that divine *smell*?'

Grace went outside to sit in the car and let her hopes rise, as more and more people arrived. She had been applying for jobs for two months now, and had received approximately zero responses, except occasionally from computer-generated emails. Even they were negative. *We have received your application along with six million others,* they warned. *We will not be able to contact all applicants personally, so if you have not heard from us in a period of time, please consider yourself unsuccessful.* She would steal a march on them and consider herself unsuccessful already, she figured. All the marketing ads now wanted a knowledge of SEO and HTTP and an embrace of social media, including obscure things she had never heard of and was not convinced anybody used. (*I am excited about the potential of pintagram*, she had written to one, only realising after mailing the application that she had fused two forms of social media into one that did not exist.) She had thought the fact she had a Facebook account which she checked monthly meant she was on-trend with new media, but apparently not. A windfall from this auction could be fantastic.

Over an hour later she was settled inside the lounge room, able to peek from the side of a curtain at the possibly two hundred people who had arrived. The auctioneer had never seen such a crowd in this area, he marveled. He was outside now, delivering a long speech about the merits of the house, the area, the land, the street, the spring sunshine, which apparently came with the house, to hear him speak.

'Maybe we'll have a future,' Grace whispered to Lotte, who was running between Grace and the kitchen where Tom was sitting with his mother. 'Mummy might start a business! Or maybe I could go back and study! Buy us some nice clothes!' Maybe getting out of this huge housing debt and having some money to play with would help she and Tom relax, help them sort things out. Maybe Tom could come to Bali.

Finally, the agent threw open the bidding, in the horse-racing tone of an auctioneer. 'Hut! Now! What Am I Bid! Let's start at eight hundred! Eighthundred-eighthundred-eighthundred! Hut! Who's got an opening bid for me? Eight! Hundred! Thousand!' He postured and pointed his rolled-up catalogue in several directions in quick succession, and people twisted and turned to see who was bidding.

No one, it soon became apparent.

Graced silently prayed for the bidding impulse to strike someone, anyone, as she stared anxiously at the crowds through the window. Her mother sat beside her, covering her eyes. Grace wrung her hands until her fingers hurt. 'Why does no one bid?' Maybe they were waiting, as people did. It was a pulsing, heaving crowd, most of them craning to look for a bidder. Like some terrible, adult game of hide-and-seek.

The agent went back to his speech about the virtues of his house, and then he tested the waters again. 'Hut! Give me seven-fifty! Bargain-basement price for this renovator's delight!'

Nothing.

Were the buyers foxing? The agent seemed to think so, too. 'With no buyers, the house will be taken off the market,' he warned. Grace flinched: how *embarrassing*. 'That's what is about to happen, people: this house will be going off the market in three.' He hit his palm with the rolled-up catalogue. 'In two. Chance of a lifetime people. In—'

There was a rustle in the crowd. Someone had spoken. Thank God! The agent leaned forward to hear, and then reared back in horror. '*Six hundred and fifty*! Well, it's good to hear an offer, but let's have a serious one, good people.'

But there was nothing. The agent finally came in, and

everyone clustered in the lounge room. The agent sagged, looking exhausted. 'Wow. It's brutal out there.'

'I want to take it,' said Tom. 'That offer.'

'No, you will not!' snapped his mother. 'You'd be crazy.'

Tom's father had turned up, and he agreed. 'Take it off the market, son,' he urged heavily.

'Well it's Grace's house, too,' said Tom. 'What do you think, Grace?'

Grace felt weepy with gratitude to hear Tom even say her name. She suddenly thought she couldn't bear the whole thing to go on a minute longer. The shame of taking it off the market. The dreariness of having to keep discussing it with Tom, having every discussion they had be about this house, which she could see he had grown to hate. It had become a millstone around his neck. It represented the strangling of all his creative dreams, the choice of a mortgage over life's purpose. It represented the end of their marriage. She should have realised it earlier. And she had a sense that after this rollercoaster of losing her marriage and her job, maybe, maybe if she could lose her house, too, she would hit rock bottom, and stop falling.

'I'm with Tom,' she said bravely. 'Sell it.'

Outside in the crowd, with the news delivered, a man punched the air in triumph, and then he hugged a pregnant woman who was weeping with joy. Grace let the curtain fall back and pressed her fingers into her eyes. Lotte ran back in the room, wriggled onto Grace's lap and prised back her fingers.

'Daddy says to say thank you, thank you, thank you.'

CHAPTER FOURTEEN

Melody took a train ride into town the next day after the auction, and Skip chattered the whole way in, announcing the arrival of tunnels and bridges with delight. People stole glances at him as he swung his feet and peered out the window. Every station name was discussed with grave interest.

'Westgarth,' Melody said.

'West — GARF,' he repeated, eyes comically wide. 'West-GARF!' An old man harumphed into his hand, eyes amused, and hid himself behind a newspaper. His wife watched Skipper with unashamed longing. Melody's graffiti flashed past while she was watching her son and she didn't even remember to look until it was too late — she liked seeing her graffiti around town, reminding her of late-night adventures. But suddenly she didn't really care about seeing it: what did it matter? She realised it would be her last big graffiti, and that, like the commune, that stage of her life was passing, and leaving. Really, so much of what she had cared about for all these years was falling away from her, she was not sure if anything would be left. Only Skip.

She wondered how Grace was feeling this morning. She had seen Tom leaving after the auction with an elderly couple who must be his parents, both of them hissing and remonstrating with him. She knew the house had been sold very cheaply, although to her it seemed like a fortune. More than half a million! Melody had turned to see Lotte watching, her face impassive.

'How's Mum?' she asked the child.

'She's crying,' Lotte said tonelessly, staring into the middle distance. Melody had stroked the child's silky brown head and Lotte did not pull away. Children's shoulders were so absurdly small, one could be cupped in each palm. Too small for adult burdens.

A man on the train vocalised his haunted thoughts, while passengers glanced at him, embarrassed, fascinated. 'Look at me when you speak!' he barked into thin air. 'Look at me when you speak!' As if it was the last thing heard before he snapped. Something a mother might say, or a father. And yet maybe those words weren't the cause of his malaise, maybe his psyche was trying to recreate the last time he had felt protected and safe. Melody squeezed Skip so hard he squeaked; she might never let him go. Maybe she would home-school him.

At Flinders Street station, Melody and Skipper held hands and she let him put the ticket in the slot at the gate. They walked over the bridge, peering through the gilt-painted slots at the river below, and slowly made their way to the little tent where the circus show would be. After the show, all trapeze artistry, and silliness in pyjamas, they walked up to the gallery, to put their hands on the water wall, and lie on the floor of the Great Hall and look at the colours. They bought a babycino from the kiosk and rode the elevator up and down a few times. Then Melody brought out the Vegemite sandwich she had packed. Skipper had been allowed to choose a one-dollar picture postcard from the gallery shop, and he had chosen a picture of four cherubs blowing trumpets. They looked not unlike himself, really, except for the wings.

The reverence of these days. Melody felt a love between them so perfect and pure, she wanted to capture it, pin it on a butterfly board and have it forever. She felt a wondrous and frightening certainty that these were the very best days of her life.

Stopping by the Hare Krishna restaurant, she picked up a flier for an Aboriginal dreaming camp, at the end of the year. A week in the country in teepees, Aboriginal elders, dreamtime tales, sacred rituals. She knew the group that were organising it, and she would know some of the people going, she was sure. There might even be some refugees from the commune, with children Skip knew. It would be late spring, when the weather was coming good. Skip would love it. Something to look forward to. She folded the flier carefully and tucked it down her shirt.

They rode the train home and once again she just missed out on seeing her graffiti, although she did look up in time to see it reflected as a blue flash in the windows opposite, and to see a few passengers' faces arrested in the direction of it, reading silently. At home, she and her boy lay at opposite ends of the couch, their legs entwined, and watched each other, Skipper eventually falling asleep. Such tenderness, in this grotty apartment. Heaven could be no more than this.

Grace sat that night with Lotte, and ate the meal Melody had dropped over. It was a lentil curry, flavoured with sweet potato and sultanas, gently spiced enough that Lotte, finally bored with chips and takeaways, stirred it through her basmati rice and ate a few mouthfuls, and Grace, suddenly starving, wolfed down three helpings.

For a moment after the auction, when Lotte had brought the string of thank-yous from Tom, beloved Tom, Grace had thought that this was it. They would make up; he would forgive her. The cost had been the house sale, as she had thought. She hoped it tearily, even as she suppressed a flash of rage: how manipulative of you Tom! But then, after all the paperwork had been signed, she heard him leave the house, saw him arguing with his angry parents, and then he drove away. Grace had spent the next twenty-four hours in bed, only getting up to answer the door and find Melody's steaming curry in a chipped pot on the doorstep. Melody was already sailing off on her bike, Skip on the back, and she lifted an arm and waved before she vanished around the corner. Grace had crouched, lifted the lid on the pot and blinked away tears at such kindness.

They watched television as they ate; *Round Up*, the current affairs show that had screened Lotte's accident. And suddenly, she realised she was watching the accident footage again.

'Mummy!' squeaked Lotte, wide eyed. 'That's when I hurt my leg! That's Skip's mummy!'

There it was. The blistering hot day last summer, the ice-cream shop, Melody in her green dress amid the hot metal cars, snatching Lotte in her white dress, saving her from death. Grace stopped breathing for a few moments, only exhaling when Lotte, screen Lotte, was safe. She reached for her daughter, squeezed her tight.

But then there was new footage. The same day, she could tell — there was Mel in the green dress, Skip in his flapping shirt. They were in the supermarket. Melody reached for a bottle of something, reached into her handbag and her hand returned: empty.

Was she ... stealing?

'Mummy it's Melody! What's she doing?'

'Shh! I don't know. Listen.'

'... viewers hailed this woman a hero earlier this year, when she snatched a child from certain death in traffic. But, tonight we have footage here that shows her engaged in activity that is less than heroic. Melody Chase was caught on film stealing from this grocery store, and when confronted by the owner about the theft minutes before the accident, denied all. We want you, our viewers, to decide: saint or sinner? What do you think? We want to know. Ring now to cast your vote: 1800 899 000 to vote saint, and 1800 901 000 to vote sinner. Remember, calls cost ninety-nine cents. Later in the show we'll announce the verdict and we'll interview Australia's top forensic psychologist about why people shoplift. Come back after the break ...'

No. Grace had been chewing a mouth full of food, which she suddenly found herself unable to swallow. She actually had to spit it back on her plate. Saint or sinner? Melody? Did she know she was being dragged onto television again; had she any idea? But of course not, she didn't even watch television.

Grace set her dinner aside. Something came over her for the first time in weeks: a cold fury, a bitter determination. Shame at her own ambivalence towards Melody. In her kitchen sat three loaves of bread, a pot of curry and another of rice that would feed them the next three nights. A forty-litre bucket of phlegmy goop that would apparently see them through laundry washes for the next year; a bucket of muesli, a vase of fresh herbs, and a bowl of green veggies harvested from Grace's own small wilderness of a garden, which she would never have noticed herself. A load of washing on the line. All contributed by a woman who was also living on a pittance.

Melody might be a little bit unusual, she might look slightly weird, despite her beauty, she might be friends with a man who was apparently a criminal, but she was not ... this. No. At worst, she was a woman stealing food to make ends meet on a single mother's pension. Okay, that was olive oil she was stealing, and it was admittedly an expensive cold-pressed extra virgin, but Grace could see her point: if you were going to steal something, why not the best? ... But how many viewers did this show have? It was one of the nation's most popular. This, this was a public crucifixion, of a single mother whose real crime was to be too beautiful for television to leave her alone, now it had discovered her.

Grace would not allow this. She would *not*. Suddenly filled with a righteous anger, she was on her feet, holding her phone and dialing. And with the smell of fresh bread and vegetable curry in the air, she dialed one number, over and over again. She sat there and dialed from her mobile for six hours, until voting closed. Damn the expense. For the first time in a long time, she was overwhelmed with an emotion unrelated to Tom.

In Eddy's house, a kilometre away, a man sitting before a television dialed a phone, again and again. He had the landline as well as his mobile, and he carefully juggled the two, to make the most calls per minute possible. He took a moment to text Tom, so he could get calling, too. Then he returned to his mobile, and called until his cheek grew warm.

The next morning, Melody delivered Skipper to kindy, and that was where she realised something was wrong. It began when she casually greeted another woman, a sort of interesting-looking type she thought she had hit it off with. And the woman didn't seem to hear her.

'Hi!' Melody said brightly, again. Skipper stood in the middle of the room, his backpack sliding off one shoulder to the floor. He looked around, searching for Lotte. Little bags were being placed on hooks, short people and tall people moved around at their different levels. Melody ducked her head to catch her new friend's eye. Had she had a bad morning?

The woman finally met her eye.

Melody froze.

It was A Look.

The woman finished delivery of The Look, and moved away. Melody stood in a pillar of salt, a zone of social shock. That had undoubtedly been, her own mother would have said, 'a Dirty Look'. Had Skipper done something to her child? Had some four-year-old social *faux pas* been carried out?

'Ah, Melody, the TV star,' said another woman, in a tone like she was sucking on a lemon. Melody moved aside so a child could access her coat hook, feeling her pillar of cold air expand a little wider.

But it had been months since the screening of Lotte's accident! And she had been the great hero anyway. She stared bewildered at the woman, as little raincoats rustled around at the level of her knees, and motherly heads bent to converse with children. Now she looked around, actually, those motherly heads seemed quite determinedly bent. When they were raised, their faces wore dreamy smiles, and they all looked straight ahead, no one meeting her eye. The air almost crackled with her sudden invisibility.

The door opened again and Lotte skipped in in her dress and sandals. Melody looked past her for Grace, and felt a sudden fear that this social chill would also have touched her, her one friend. Grace's eyes met her own and she paled. Melody froze.

Grace glanced quickly around at the other mothers, walked straight to Melody and put her arms around her.

Now Melody knew something was catastrophically wrong. She stood utterly still for a few bewildering moments, her cheek against the shorter woman's hair, her hands touching Grace's light cardigan. Her skin rose in goosebumps. Grace had never, ever hugged her. Grace did not hug.

Melody pulled back and stared at the other woman, baffled.

Grace studied her face and whispered. 'You don't know, do you? You didn't see the telly last night. No one's told you?' There was now apparently a stampede of mothers trying to escape the locker room.

'What?' Melody whispered back. 'Did they play the footage again?'

After a few minutes frantically whispering with Grace, Melody left the kindergarten and went straight to the local library, where she sat at a computer in the darkest corner, bathed now in the light of the screen as last night's current affairs show played before her. After the first couple of minutes, her heart sinking, she pulled the hood of her jacket up and over her distinctive hair, so she wouldn't be recognised, and she turned the sound down low. *Saint or sinner?* squeaked the screen. Vote now! Have your say! She clicked the arrow back to the start of its ribbon, and watched the evil, hateful supermarket manager's footage of her shoplifting, the lifting of the item, the casual searching in her bag, the withdrawal of her empty hand. She put in cans, olive oil, vitamins. Her on-screen face was calm and expressionless, except for one moment when her eyes slid sideways, checking she wasn't being observed. How shifty she looked, like some low-life-trash robber. And how stupid, not to sense she was being not only watched, but *filmed*. Melody thought of her little boy, up there in the tender, innocent world of kindergarten, alongside children who might know that his mummy was a thief, a robber, a bad lady on the television.

She could feel a thousand eyes watching her, although when she looked around there were only students focused solely on their computer screens. But she knew, when she walked out of this door, everyone would know her. She didn't deserve to have a little boy as beautiful as Skipper, with his invisible friends and his squishy hands and his total trust in her. What had she been thinking all these years, that shoplifting was some form of protest against capitalism, some expression of abundance from the universe ... Oh God, she was a fraud. Why on earth had she come down to Melbourne; just to endure this bitter lesson? Could the universe hate her so much? She had thought she lived by a policy of do no harm, but she may have harmed her son with this horror. Shamed him. She had harmed Eddy, by bringing Van into his life, Van who appeared to have turned to some life of petty theft; stealing fiancées, robbing shops. Not unlike herself, as it turned out.

She walked home, utterly lost. On the way she passed a café where a child's birthday party was underway, children blowing bubbles to float through the coffee-scented air, while toddlers clapped sticky palms. She passed a front garden where a ladder leaned on a tree, and a circle of stones sat on one big flat rock like a message, glistening black after the rain. Safe in her ugly kitchen, she re-read Skip's mother's day card, made at kindy. *My mum's favourite food is ... sauce. My mum loves to ... wash the dishes. I love my Mum because ... she has a beautiful love.* A photo of himself on the front wearing a Bob the Builder hooded towel, staring out grave and passive as a druid. She ripped open a letter from the real estate agent. He demanded she pay the three months' rent in arrears, or his agency would evict them.

She felt hot, and she ran to the toilet to throw up. It seemed a long time after that she stared into that bowl, at the disgusting insides of her disgusting self. She couldn't even climb to her feet to flush, she just turned on her hands and knees and crawled out to the lounge room, where she curled up in a ball on the carpet and shivered.

Melody woke to voices, to touch on her body. She was hot and dizzy, and still on the floor, but Skipper and Lotte crouched over her, as if casting spells, flying their imaginary planes over the terrain of her head, her shoulder, down the dunes of her thighs. She heard the quiet *brrroom* of the pretend engines, and the swooshing of wings, like enchanted creatures come to stitch her up with thread so fine that only a child's eyes could see the gossamer scar it left.

'What's the time?' She tried to sit up, pushing aside the hands. The world spun, and she crumbled down again. Her clothes sat damp on her skin, her breath stunk. Grace was in the kitchen setting out cups and saucers, spooning dandelion coffee into a cup. Melody closed her eyes, wishing the spinning would stop. 'Oh, no. Did I miss pick-up?'

Grace poured the boiling water. 'Don't worry. We waited a few minutes, and then I brought Skip here. You were sleeping.'

Melody lay back. 'Thanks.'

'You seem to be running a temperature.'

Melody shut her eyes, the whole sorry mess watching over her. 'I feel hot. Dizzy.' Dizzy with shame.

She listened to the sound of a teaspoon stirring, bumping in the sides of a coffee cup, and thought how much comfort that sound promised. The children had fetched the op-shop Prada bag with the red cross she had painted on it, and were playing doctors. Obediently, she submitted herself to the gravity and nurture of Dr Skipper, who was giving ejections with an empty syringe and poking his broken stethoscope into her breast. She held her breath and felt her own nurture coming back at her, through the divine medium of her son. He gave her a massage, his touch as gentle as a kitten's, his kind spirit flowing through his fingerpads. He squished her shirt against the flesh on her back.

Next time she woke, she climbed to her feet, catching her toe on the hem of her pants and stumbling against the wall. She felt them all watching as she righted herself and walked down the hall to the toilet, where she threw up again. Then she staggered to the room she shared with Skipper, and subsided onto her bed, crawling under a pile of sheets and blankets and books. She did not speak to Grace — and was that Eddy she had also seen? — and she registered that she may have been rude, but she had no choice. She was dying. Every muscle pumped poison, every bone groaned. She could feel her brain in her head, sloshing in some toxic coating. Her breathing was fast and shallow, and she was hungry for air, but too weak to gulp it properly. Her pillow was cold and dry and that was all she wanted.

It went on for two days and two nights of heat and sweat and shivering and pain. She held her face to her pillow as if telling it a secret, as if it might hold the recipe for health within its poly-foam depths. Skipper came and went, each time with Grace and Lotte, and once with Eddy. In the eye of her own cyclone, the mother in her registered that her precious boy was in the hands of kind people, and she was cautiously reassured, and sank back into dreams.

Melody woke once in the night and the bed was empty — no Skipper. She panicked, dragged herself up and along the hall to ring Grace. But when she turned on the lounge room light, there they were, Grace, Skipper and Lotte, asleep. Grace was on the couch, in an unfamiliar sleeping bag, Skipper and Lotte slept crossways on a foam mattress, their angel faces turned in the same direction. The lounge room was as fat and warm, with the gentle sound of their breathing, as her own room had been cold and terrifying in their absence. Grace opened her eyes.

'Sorry,' said Melody. 'I just wondered where Skip was.'

'How are you feeling?' said Grace. 'You really should drink something.'

But the effort of walking and talking had already exhausted Melody, and she just nodded weakly and turned off the light. Fell back into bed, bleached of all life.

The next day held more dreamy waking and sleeping, Grace and the children coming and going. Grace woke her twice and made her sit up and drink something sweet. Then Grace and the children were not there. Melody woke once to see Van and she nodded at him, or she thought she did, but then she woke later and he had gone, and maybe it had been a dream. She swam down to the place deep in her soul where she was troubled about Van, a place she rarely visited. Deep in this underworld yellow submarine land, everything was just as she left it. Her sister's funeral. Van's everyday presence after the death. Her decision to move up to the commune, his decision to follow. Or did he decide first? She could not remember. That night. That week. She touched all those old relics. She swam in one place for a while, staring at Van's love for Esme, and then Van's love for Melody herself. Was it real love, or mirror twin love? She had never been sure, and she pitied it, whatever it was, but she did not trust it. Then she stared for a while at the guilty fact of her non-love for him, swam around it a little as she had done so many times. Nup. There it was. Would have been much simpler otherwise, but whatever. Move on.

Melody swam to the surface and lay in cool sunlight for a while, dishes clanking from the kitchen, voices chirping. It was all dreamy and yet jerky, the way children grew up, it occurred to her. You looked at them one day and they'd grown two inches overnight. Or they suddenly came out with a phrase you'd never heard them say before. She remembered the jerkiness herself from childhood, when she realised she had changed all over again. The world was anew, and the dimensions and perspectives around her seemed abruptly different, as if a cartoon had morphed into a film, developing shadows, dimension, pores on skin, flyaway hair.

She dreamed about a party in the commune she had

been to the year before, a cold night not long after the Winter Solstice, a party to mark the burial of a child's placenta. Seven years old, the little girl was, and the question had not been fully answered, where had they been keeping the placenta these past seven years? She woke from this puzzle to find Skipper beside her, talking to Grace, telling her a long involved story about an UNO game he'd played the night before, apparently with Eddy. 'Then I put down collect four! Then he had to pick up *six*!'

Finally she woke again, and the world was flat, cleansed, new. She felt cool and clean. The sheets and blankets were no longer in a pile on top of her, but had been neatly folded and tucked around the mattress. Her hair was damp against her head. She barely had the energy to blink, but she was better. She lay and stared out at the powerlines, out at the sky, and a little plane passed by with a sound like a far-off lawnmower on a Sunday afternoon. She felt very, very grateful.

Grace came in and sat gently on the side of the bed. 'Better?'

Melody nodded. 'Thanks for looking after Skipper. I don't know what ...'

Grace shrugged it off. 'Forget it. You've been so sick.'

'And I think I was meant to do a reading for this guy ...'

'He came. I told him you were being rushed off your feet and I was your delegate.'

'You what?'

'I did the reading for him. Told him all good things. He's going to meet the love of his life. The money's on the kitchen bench.'

'Oh.'

'It's good money! You could really expand that business you know. Set up a website.'

'Yeah.'

'Guess what? I've got good news and bad news.'

'Oh.'

'The good news first. You were voted a saint! Overwhelmingly!'

Melody stared at her. The evil television show. 'Not a sinner?'

'Not a sinner.'

'People really voted?' Was the world mad?

'They did! *Thousands* voted. It was all on the telly the next night. You were sleeping.'

'Should I watch it?'

'Nup. Let it pass.'

'And the bad news?'

'Well, the bad news is that your real estate agent rang to say he's evicting you for not paying the rent.'

Melody sighed and laid her head back on the pillow. She was exhausted already, and yearned to return to the subterranean world of illness, where someone else took responsibility for her child. Was that the first time ever in Skip's life?

Grace folded the edge of a sheet into a fan shape and said 'Um ...' and 'Uh ...', and Melody waited for whatever it was she was trying to say.

'I just, well anyway, I was wondering, now the house is sold we have to leave next week, it's a quick settlement, and Lotte and I have looked at this really old place down the road, maybe you've seen the old blue one on the corner, well it's up for rent, and it's a dump, a total dump, someone should put a match to it, but for now it's okay, and they'd let us bring the cat, and there's plenty of room, enough for you and Skipper, too, and even though it's a dump I thought you might not care. I mean I don't mean it like that, but you're so good at making simple things better ... Anyway, have a think about it, we could, you know, live together, share the rent, share expenses.'

Melody shifted her thoughts sluggishly to the blue, condemned rental, which she walked past on the way to kindy, green things growing wild through every crack. Her heart lifted. And that Grace would ask her, that she really didn't think Melody was a thief. Or if she did, she didn't think she would contaminate Lotte. Somehow that was more reassuring than the forgiving vote of telly world.

'Could start a veggie patch,' she croaked. 'It's spring, perfect time for planting. The kids could share a room.'

'And,' said Grace, her eyes shining, 'if you want to do it, we will stop eating meat. And we will get rid of our telly. I know Skip's never lived with one.'

'You would do that?'

'Sure.'

'I mean you really don't have to, but—'

'No. I want to. It will do us good.' Grace appeared to be holding her breath, waiting.

'That's very generous of you.'

'Soo ... what do you think?'

'We'll do it.' Melody raised a limp hand to shake, and Grace beamed. Her handshake was so firm, she made Melody tired. She looked at the ceiling of her poky little flat, and thought, we're leaving this sterile box. She would have a patch of dirt again.

The children burst in the room screaming, leaping on the bed and landing on their little knees. 'Did she say yes? Did she say yes?'

CHAPTER FIFTEEN

Eddy Plenty stood beside the kindergarten teacher, in front of a square-and-triangle cubby house. He crouched and looked up to talk to Miss Laura, spreading his hands apart as he did, outlining some inaudible solution to the sagging window shutter, or the mossy eaves. From Melody's perspective on the far side of the kinder yard, they looked like a nursery-rhyme husband and wife, come home to find their house had shrunk. *But Hans, how do ve get in, now ze door iss ze height ov our goat?*

Melody and Skip had moved house that morning. Eddy-the-Kind had arrived at Melody's flat with croissants and coffee, and offers of help to move her possessions into the new-old house, to which Grace had already moved her things. Melody and Skip didn't have a lot of stuff, and in two car trips the job was done. Melody liked the run-down old house, although she could see Grace was appalled by it. The taps coughed and spluttered when you turned them on, as if shocked at such demanding behaviour. While there were two shabbily grand front rooms, the back was a series of lean-tos upon lean-tos, like a card house. Every floor, wall and ceiling was made of dark brown lining boards. These boards had shrunk over time, leaving gaps the wind blew through. Grace had said gloomily it was like living in a rabbit hutch, but for Melody it reminded her of the quirky home-made cottages up in the commune. Rose-patterned carpets were worn down to hessian in the high-traffic areas. Every gutter was full with wild green grass, circling the roof in a gaudy tiara of weeds. The floorboards had a trampoline-like feel to them, because the stumps beneath had rotted, and the parts of the floor which were solid were only so because they were sitting on dirt. It creaked with history, and memories of the living, and of the dead.

Then the women set off to the kindergarten working bee, which was on that day, and Eddy cleared his throat and offered to come help. He had brought a toolbox from the back of his car, and he looked more at home there than the real fathers. One of the dads, with a ponytail and a wispy growth, sat holding his head, wearing too-tight jeans and sunglasses, at the base of a downpipe, which he had been motionlessly studying now for about an hour, emitting a gentle scent of last night's alcohol. Another father, this one wearing a fine wool pullover, iron-pleat jeans and Bulgari glasses, pushed a wheelbarrow full of tanbark and asked Melody plaintively for the third time where Miss Laura was; it was possible he had been pushing the same barrow around the yard since early morning, stopping every few metres to check his mobile. Only Eddy Plenty looked like he had a purpose, and tools, and the ear of Miss Laura, the queen of proceedings.

Melody, fully recovered from her illness, was preparing to paint a mural on the ugly brown back wall of the kindergarten's garden. She dipped the brush in the pot of gold paint, steadied herself in a crouch, and made a long, confident, downward slash of gold. Some drops fell on the lavender ballgown she had chosen to wear to the kindy working bee. This dress would be spattered from top to bottom by the end of the day, which was just fine. It had cost her five dollars in a Brotherhood of St Laurence shop, a relic of her grandmother's era, when gorgeous dresses were being churned out of the local garment district in Flinders Lane. It would be all the better for a bit of paint. She stepped back to see her wall. She had brought rollers and a tray the day before and started by painting the whole thing white. Then today she had chalked out her whole design.

'Do you want to see the picture I've planned?' She handed the paper to Grace, who sat dully on a log wearing a pair of bib-and-brace overalls that featured such an authentic layer of dust and grime that they must have been Tom's.

'Uh ... yeah.' Grace seemed about to burst into tears. Melody said nothing. Whether it was the overalls, or the moving to a grotty house so soon after the auction, something had sunk Grace back down to an all-time low. But Melody was getting used to it. She looked over Grace's shoulder and admired her own work.

There was a mythical city on the left, chalked in all rising gold turrets and a wizened old queen beneath a flag, staring out into the distance. The city petered out to a stretch of land, which ended in a dark forest. Pools of light in the forest showed three scenes; a wolf tearing apart something unidentifiable on the ground, then further on a stern and tall fairy with a group of littler ones sitting around her, and the last grove revealed a tiny treasure box, emanating paint-swipe rays of light.

'We just have to fill it in.' Melody pointed over to the green paint and handed Grace a brush. 'Do you want to have a go at the forests or the plains?'

'I don't know. You can do the hard bits.' But then Grace only held the brush and stroked the bristles as if it were a live animal, her eyes staring unseeingly into the pot of deep green. Melody went back to her castle, blocking out the entirety with gold, planning how she would later do the bricks and the turrets. She stood back to get perspective. Grace still caressed her brush, bending the bristles of the cheap Chinese tool so hard that spikes flicked out. Over on the other side of the yard, two mothers whispered as they sieved sand in the sandpit, placing rogue leaves in a bucket. Melody returned to her lovely gold paint. There was a sob from Grace. It was no longer possible to ignore her.

'What's up?' She glanced over at Eddy as she crouched at Grace's feet. He was wearing a welding mask now, raised like a peak cap, and he listened as Miss Laura waved her arms vigorously. Maybe he would come help with Grace. He could rapidly become her go-to man, she reflected. Good for babysitting, moving furniture, mopping up tears.

'I'm so sad about losing our house. And I miss Tom.'

'I know.' Oh God, she hoped living with Grace wouldn't be too demanding.

'Do you? Do you really know?'

'Well, I understand.'

'Do you … have boyfriends?'

Melody exhaled. 'I don't have a boyfriend now.'

'But are you … you know?'

'No, I don't know. Am I what? Gay? Hetero?'

'Well. Yeah."

Melody shrugged. 'Not really. Not gay.'

'Oh.' Grace laughed a little. 'Er …'

'I like girls, though.'

'As friends, you mean.'

'No. I've had girlfriends.'

'*Oh!*'

'But I've had boyfriends, too.'

'Oh! I mean, okay. That's interesting. I hope you don't mind me asking. Everyone I know is, you know. Normal. So, you're ah … bi.'

'I'm just me.'

'So, if you don't mind me asking, who is Skipper's dad?'

'Me.'

'Ha ha. Is it Van?'

'Do you think he looks like Van?'

'I don't know.'

'Here we go. Gold, gold, gold.'

Melody lifted her brush and painted a nice long streak. She did love gold. Grace would learn, she could ask all the questions she liked. Melody had never felt a need to explain herself.

The late spring sunshine faded. Melody put a hoodie over her ballgown and returned to her painting. She would go to the Aboriginal dreaming workshop out at Ouyen in summer; she had paid the registration fee that morning. A week of living in teepees and studying the various dreamings, under the tutelage of a wise elder. Hopefully it would be warm by then. It would be great for Skipper to have some wild time again, to get back among people who were a bit more zen. This kindy was okay, but the recent freeze-out by the mothers had reminded Melody, you're not in Kansas anymore. You might not have belonged at the commune, in the end, but that's not to say you belong anywhere, yet. Go with your heart. Feel where you belong. But the dreaming camp would be like the old days, the good bits anyway.

'Hey,' said Grace, sidling close to her. 'Do you think I should ask Eddy out?'

'Out where?'

'You know. Out for dinner. On a date.'

Melody painted in the drawbridge. Where on earth had this come from? 'Do you like him?'

'Well, it would piss Tom off.'

'Oh.'

'I mean that's not the only reason! I mean, Eddy's not bad-looking. He's okay. And how *nice* is he, coming to this working bee when he doesn't even have a kid here. He's so *dependable*. Maybe he's more right for me anyway. Maybe I should have been with someone like him all along. Someone who would appreciate me. For. Who. I. Am.' Grace stabbed green onto the wall viciously.

'Okay, maybe keep the green a bit lower. Not higher than that line.'

'Do you think I should do it?'

'It's up to you. Just be a bit careful with the ... see how it's spotting over there ...'

'Imagine Tom, if he found out. He'd be *wild*. Bet he thinks I'm just sitting around crying.'

'Mm.'

Grace painted the same patch for the fourth time. Her tears were falling into the paint pot. 'Yeah. *Bet* he does.'

Melody turned her brush to the arched gate. Painting the vines would be fiddly, but she would just start with the slate bricks. 'I rang that woman from the current affairs show yesterday,' she said, mixing up grey with white, to get some variegated slate. 'Anthea Schulberg.'

Grace slid her brush into the green and slapped the excess onto the edge of the can, splashing flecks of green on her forearms. 'I hope you told her off. What a complete cow. You could have sued for defamation, if the vote hadn't gone your way.'

'Well, I only rang because she rang me first, and asked

me to call her. Although I did say to her, you know, lighten up, sister. Not very cool on the voting thing.' Melody hadn't really said that, but she sensed Grace needed to hear that she had.

'So why did she ring?'

'Actually, it was the weirdest thing.' Melody paused. She still couldn't quite believe it herself. 'She's asked me to come back into the studio.'

'For what? Another bloody episode?' Grace groaned. 'How many times are they going to remind the whole nation that I was the mother who let her daughter run into traffic?'

Melody blinked. She hadn't thought of it like that, had considered any subject of national humiliation to be herself, rather than Grace. 'Actually, it's not about that. She's been promoted to producer, and she remembered me.' *I couldn't get you out of my head*, was what Anthea Schulberg had actually said. *We did research on you; you have an incredible face, no viewer in our research group could turn you off.* 'She wants to start a horoscope section, once a week on the show. And she remembered I was a fortune teller. I told her I read futures through the hands, through *feeling* the soul, rather than, you know, global horoscopes, so I wouldn't be much good to her.'

'You said *what*? Shit, that's a *job*, a *great* job. Don't knock that back. We can make up horoscopes! You didn't say no, did you! It would be—'

'No, no, she hassled so much that I finally said I'd go in. Read a script, give it a go.'

'Couldn't you write horoscopes?'

'Maybe. Someone showed me once. I could try.'

'Jesus, *I* could write them for you if you like. We could just take a few women's mags and cut and paste.'

'Grace, I couldn't do that. That's totally dishonest.'

'Says the saint, or the sinner?'

'Stealing from a shop is much different to making up horoscopes. People make *decisions* based on these things. They can take steps that change their lives. It would have to be real, or I wouldn't do it.'

'And would they pay you?'

'For the audition? Probably not.'

'But if you got it?'

'Well, I guess so. I haven't asked. But I won't get it. It's ridiculous. People train at uni for these things. I have no experience at all.'

'God, it's telly. If you got a gig like that you'd ... you probably wouldn't need to live with me anymore.' Grace's face fell, and she looked like she might weep again.

'Oh, please,' Melody switched brushes and dabbed some brown tree trunk on the wall, feeling uncomfortable. 'As if I'd get it. And anyway, as if I'd move out, just when I've moved in. As if Skip would *let* me move out now.'

She was getting some weird looks from the women in the sandpit. No doubt they thought her lavender ballgown inappropriate attire for mural painting. You're the ones sieving dirty sand, sweethearts, she felt like calling out. Feel perfectly free to think my outfit's a little weird.

Back home the day after the working bee, Eddy watched out the window, where a man his own age, with long dirty blond hair, waited to cross the road. The man wore boardshorts, a Rip Curl hoodie and thongs, although the weather was mild. He stepped from foot to foot as he waited, a quick step-step accompanied by the shaking loose of his fingers. If it wasn't for that step-step, and the finger shaking, he might look like any old man of Eddy's generation who was either a surfer or had adopted that look to express his attitude to life. But the stepping told a different story, the shuffling inside the shell of his loose-fitting boardies and his T-shirt. He talked to himself. His thongs were worn to holes at the heels. Eddy's heart ached for him. When had it happened, what went wrong? Would the woman waiting on the other side of the crossing notice? Would she shun him as she passed? Did surfing help sustain him through whatever engine failure propelled this frantic fidgeting, or was he frozen in time there, waiting for a perfect wave to surf out of his malaise?

Eddy sighed and reflected that Sundays were too long. He looked around. His house disgusted him, but there was also a wild freedom in being able to cut his fingernails on the carpet, in letting the spray from his whiskers build up, shave after shave, on the vanity basin, in being able to fart with abandon, or reach down at any moment and do a thoughtful, caressing stocktake of his testicles.

His phone rang and he stepped across the lounge room to reach it, skidded on a pizza box and knocked last night's can of beer, luckily empty, off the table. 'Hello?' he said, sounding squeaky after his trip.

'Well, hello. Is this Eddy? A female voice, sexy, in a gentle way. Kindly sexy, if there were such a thing. Familiar. But not Romy.

He steadied himself, reached for a more manly note deep within. 'This is he.' He turned down the sports channel.

'It's Laura here. From the kindy, yesterday?'

'Oh!' He rescued the image from his mind; the young, nicely plump woman with dark, smiling eyes and dark hair. Had her voice been this sexy, and he just hadn't noticed? But this woman was a god to forty young children, and a figure of great respect to their parents. She could not be sexy. 'Oh, *Miss* Laura!'

'Well, you can call me Laura. It's really only the kids who call me Miss Laura. Makes them feel like they're in school.'

'Oh! Well, thanks.' Now he was thanking her for being promoted from pre-school. He was a buffoon.

'I hope you don't mind me calling. You did leave your number in case there was a problem with ... the cubby-house door.'

'Well I was a bit worried those hinges might be a trap for little fingers. You should really get some rubber to put around them. I mean sorry, I know I told you that, I don't want to go on about it ...'

'It's fine.' A trace of laughter in her voice. A flirtatious being had invaded the body of the kindergarten teacher. He should alert someone, this wasn't right. 'Actually, I hope you don't mind me calling you, but I'm just ... Well, I've discovered I've got nothing in the fridge ...'

'Oh no! Can I ...?' Maybe she was poor and hungry.

'Just too slack to shop, I'm afraid. I tend to eat out more than at home. Anyway, nothing in the fridge ...'

'Oh, me too! I mean, nothing in the fridge ... and love to eat out ...' Could she be asking him ...? No, surely not.

'... and I was thinking of going out for dinner and I was wondering whether ... I'm sorry, but Grace said you lived on your own ...'

'I do! I do!' He almost shouted. That much at least, he knew. Okay, he had an engagement ring, he hadn't completely given up on Romy, but no one, no one could deny the truth of the fact that he was not married, and he, now, lived alone. He started to face that reality with more anticipation than ever before. 'Would you ... maybe I could join you for dinner? I mean, we could go somewhere?' Oh God, had he got this all wrong?

'Have you eaten?' she said.

'I've had a really disgusting pizza, to be honest.' Oh no! Why had he said that! 'But I could fit in a little bit more. In fact, I'm still starving.' And then he burst out laughing, from sheer terror and hope. Who would have thought? Someone would ask him out. A woman. A nice woman. Asking him out.

'Well, great! Do you know the Italian joint, on Fairbrick Street?'

'Yes! I love it!' Oh, cool it, man, stop leaping down the phone at her.

'Seven o'clock.'

Eddy consciously lowered his tonal register, took a deep breath and slowed his voice. 'Great. See you there, Miss Laura.'

He hung up. Shit. Had he really called her Miss Laura again? Laura, Laura, Laura. He gazed around himself at the pizza boxes, the wobbly piles of DVDs, the beer cans. It all looked different from how it had a few minutes ago. It looked like an offence to his eyes. He had a date! A date! Back in business, he hummed, flinging clothes out of his wardrobe. He ran to the bathroom and turned on the shower, ran back to the bedroom again. Quirky op-shop shirt, nice-boy Pierre Cardin, no, maybe an open-necked business shirt with jeans. God he had to shave. Did kindergarten teachers do sex?

Eddy met Miss Laura in a small Italian restaurant, where she waited in her faded jeans and sneakers and a T-shirt. She was friendly in an uncomplicated way that unnerved him a little, and at the end of dinner she kissed him on the cheek and said 'Are you free Friday?' and he stuttered nervously 'Sure!', and she said 'I'll call you, we'll work something out', and then she smiled and turned to walk home. He watched her go, and he felt good. He was just about to walk away when she turned back and caught him looking, and she laughed in a way that told him she liked him looking. He smiled and waved. Back home, he glimpsed his face in the mirror; he was smiling, stupidly, at nothing. Jesus. He felt happy! He saw he had a text on his phone. From Grace, Tom's ex, Lotte's mum. Did she need more furniture moved? He hoped so. It was nice to be needed.

Hi Eddy, Wondering if you'd like to go out for dinner and a movie this Friday night, just you and me? Dressed For Success is on at the Nova. Let me know!!! xxx

He looked aghast at his phone and dropped it like it was hot. *Dressed For Success?* He'd never heard of it, but he hated it already. He could see women in power-suits and female solidarity and some hapless male who hadn't yet moved out of home, maybe being the subject of a makeover by the power-suits, and possibly there was a musical number involving Greek peasants. And, even more disturbing, *Grace?* Asking him out? Kiss kiss kiss? He hadn't felt the faintest pulse of sexual tension between them; in fact, he would have said she irritated her. He distinctly remembered she had crossly slapped a tissue box in front of him when he had sniffed too many times the other night. It was confounding. He wasn't sure he'd ever had a female advance that was unwelcome to him in his life. He certainly didn't think he'd ever had two dinner invitations from two women in the one night. Exhausted, he stripped off down to his jocks and went to bed.

The peal of the phone cut through his sleep later, and he dragged himself upright, and squinted at his clock. 2:43 am. Who on earth. Maybe Miss Laura? he thought hopefully. *Eddy, my body is on fire for you. Come over right now and peel my jeans off my hips and lift my T-shirt over my shoulders ...* He snatched up the phone.

'You never let me look after you.' A woman. Another woman! He was momentarily bewildered. But it was Romy's voice. Truly her! She must be speaking to someone else. Maybe she had accidentally pressed the automatic home-dial on her mobile phone. He was eavesdropping on a conversation. He sat up and switched on his bedside light. In the mirror opposite, he looked like some squinting old bum. He held his breath, hoping to hear more.

'Eddy?'

'Romy?'

'Why aren't you talking?'

'I wasn't sure you were actually talking to me.'

'Why not?'

He sighed and leaned back on the pillow. 'Well, you sort of skipped a few of the social niceties, like *Hi, Eddy, how are you? Sorry I haven't come home for the past nine months, except for one day when I had to be a rabbit, but I've been—*'

'You never let *me* look after *you*.' Was she crying?

'Romy, are you drunk? What are you talking about? Where the hell are you?'

She was either crying or breathing heavily.

'You always wanted to look after *me*, and I think I just got sick of being ... the hopeless one. The one who needed looking after.'

'That's ridiculous!'

'It's not. We felt closest when you were doing things for me, and the more of a wreck I became, the more you rescued me. But it was *bad* for me.' Romy gulped for air, and he sat naked on the edge of his bed and stared down at his bare thighs. She went on. 'I tried a few times to reverse the order, I tried to bring you tea and toast when *you* were sick. You'd say thanks and then you'd get up and get dressed and bring the tray back out and eat at the table. It just seemed to make us awkward.'

'Romy, are you somewhere safe?'

'When we came home from places, I couldn't even get my house key out before you. You would bring the shopping in before I could, you'd get to the steering wheel before I could. You were always the strong one. You disempowered me. You made me into a ... child.'

'Is that so ...' Eddy shook his head. He wasn't sure whether he should feel grateful she'd called, or affronted at these claims that he had been too, as far as he could understand, nice. 'Romy, you just take off, all your stuff is here ... Are you ever coming home? Can I come and pick you up from somewhere? I could come now?'

She was crying again, talking over him. 'Just once, just once I wished I could have held *you* while you cried, told *you* that everything was going to be alright. But you could never give me that, could you?'

'I'm sorry Romy ...' He was crying, his nose blocked, his eyes streaming, his body aching and feeling like he had swallowed a rock. Just as he suspected, it had all been his fault. He hadn't been lovable, had done everything wrong, he had made her run away. 'Romy ...' he wept, but she had gone; just a dial tone now in his ear. He put down the phone and curled up on his sheets, touched his forehead to his knees and cried.

The next morning he texted Grace and said tersely that he had a prior commitment that Friday night. He wasn't sure he had ever said no to a woman in his life.

'Librans, you may be feeling uninspired at present due to the weak position of your ruling planet. But this is an opportunity for you to think deeply about what it is you want. If love is your goal ...'

Melody glanced over at a monitor, and there was her reflected self, reading a script, a miniature figure in a long crimson dress. It was an Alannah Hill, the wardrobe woman had said, whoever that was. And this gorgeously fluid dress did feel like that mellifluous word: alannahill, yeah. They had spent forever getting her ready; twitching at the dress, pushing her pale breasts up to expose more of them in the low neck-line. 'Do ya mind if I just ...?' wardrobe had said, prodding at Melody's small cleavage as thoughtfully as an obstetrician checking for cancerous lumps. The hair man said 'Ooooh' when he saw Melody's dreads, and he had to try a few things, like a child with new play dough. Coiled up on her head? No, no, no. Part pulled to the back, princess-style? Impossible to evenly separate at the roots, Melody could have told him. Finally, he sprayed some pomegranate-scented mist to gloss them up, arranged them fussily around her shoulders, and propped a couple of plastic reflective stars on one side. Makeup lady muscled in and painted her up, wet brushes stroking over her cheeks, alongside her nose, gently pushing the skin. Melody remembered crouching with Skip in the Tuntable River, painting each other's faces with fingerfuls of wet ochre. Hair man hovered at the side, murmuring bits of advice to makeup lady, who sighed heavily each time he did and said 'Yes. Thank you, Kevin' in a louder voice than his. Behind her, a large screen was lit blue, and speckled with planets and moons.

Anthea Schulberg stepped forward to interrupt. The crew exhaled as one, turning away to check mobile phones, whisper among themselves and gaze longingly in the direction of the network canteen. Hair man leapt towards Melody's dreads and waited on alert.

Anthea smiled. 'Okay, we'll have a go on-camera now. See how you look in the great eye. Try using your hands a bit, maybe even pointing your finger for emphasis. Not aggressively, but just like you're persuading, or making a point. Like you really mean it.'

Melody nodded. This was one of the more surreal experiences of her life. *Round Up* had sent a limousine to bring her to the audition. Which was lucky, because she was short of cash to refill her train card and had calculated a ninety-minute walk to the studio.

'Like I really mean it. Sure.' There was something about Anthea she warmed to, despite everything. The woman had a golden, slightly fizzy aura, and the spiritual path before her gleamed. She had great karma; much bounty would fall on that gleaming destiny, and she would share her gifts with everyone around her, Melody sensed. The crew members watched the producer pass respectfully, as if they felt it, too, waiting there beside cameras and microphones. Hair man reluctantly stepped back, adjusted his bow tie and stroked his own wing of hair, as if reassuring a small animal.

'Lights. Three, two, one …'

Anthea lowered her arm towards Melody like she was casting a spell, and Melody slid her eyes to the camera. She felt calm. Playing the spiritual seer was not difficult. In truth, it just meant going to her happy place and taking a deep breath. These were not her horoscopes, but then this was just an audition. If she did get the gig, she would write authentic horoscopes; precise divinations of the constellations with the power to help thousands of television watchers. Maybe *this* was what the universe meant her to do. Maybe this was why it had brought her to Melbourne and dragged her through the muck of televisual and kindergarten-mother ignominy. She took a deep breath.

'Let me remind you *not* to look outside yourself by taking on the victim role or pointing the finger of blame. Take *full* responsibility for your own actions and thoughts.' She read from the teleprompter and stared into the eye of the camera, drawing the unmanifested deep from within that black pool and, as Anthea had asked, spreading her open hand towards the viewer. *Come.* She would imagine someone. Grace maybe, who had been so grumpy that morning, and claimed she was weak from not eating meat. Who said she was fed up with legumes and couldn't think of a single idea for a vegetarian meal that interested her. Who said children living without television would miss out on valuable cultural socialising experiences, and be isolated by their peers, and that she, personally, was sick of having to go down the road to Anna's house to watch *Farmer Needs A Wife*.

Now, Melody imagined Grace before her, and summoned all her inner forgiveness and love. 'Continue to delegate your tasks if you have the opportunity to do so in your workplace,' she told her friend. 'This will free up an *immense* amount of time and give you a chance to do what you do best. If you're at home, you need to *put* your foot *down* and *demand* that others play their part in contributing to the household chores.' Who had written this atrocity? Since when did the stars mediate over whose turn it was to take the rubbish out? But she held the gaze of the camera's eye, as if pressing a loving question to the sulky Grace. Off to the side, Anthea nodded enthusiastically, raising her fist in a silent cheer. She was nailing it. Hair man templed his fingertips together as if in prayer, and whispered to makeup lady. Makeup raised her eyebrows and nodded, her expression saying *Although I generally think you're a fool, hair man, you've got an indisputable point there.* They beamed at her. Maybe they all had jobs riding on this. Obviously the Grace thing was working, so Melody stuck with it. She leaned forward and focused on her invisible friend, talking to her as if she were handing down the tablet of Moses from the Mount.

'Leo. You have forgotten some of your best talents and *what it is* that made you great,' she admonished, lowering her voice a little to sound mysterious. Husky. Wild waves of approval from Anthea; hair man turned away helplessly and touched his fingertips to his forehead, as if she were just too divine for human eyes. Makeup lady smiled smugly as if watching her own best work. This was an absolute hoot. Melody experimented with another hand gesture, this one a sort of opening and spreading of both hands, as if to invite Grace inwards. She was owning this studio; there was not a soul in it escaping her spell. 'Think back to a time when your power was at its peak. If you're run-down, low in spirits or even diminished in self-confidence, recollecting the past will be of *great value* to you today.'

God, Skip would go crazy when he saw this. Was the universe really going to dump a telly job right in her lap?

But Melody already knew the answer to that, even as she kept reading. '... Taurus, you feel confronted by challenge, but rest assured, *you can do it*. You will be amazed at your own strength ...' She glanced over at Anthea's triumphant face. When the take was finished, and the bright lights were turned off, the crew burst into spontaneous and genuine applause, a slow clap, and Melody blushed and arranged her face into a disingenuous question: So, how did I go? But she didn't need a horoscope to tell her what was coming her way. A big, fat gift from the universe, bless its complicated and generous soul.

CHAPTER SIXTEEN

Eddy sat in a city restaurant, and watched the world go by down on Swanston Street. Outside his first-floor window pigeons wheeled around a canyon between city buildings, as if marking out territory. They flew at the height of his window, sometimes so close he could see the black gleam of an eye, and hear the swish of feathers.

Eddy ate a mouthful of kofta and rice, and felt so full he put down his fork. He was reminded of a post-birth friend who said she ate one lifesaver during a twenty-four-hour labour, and felt like she had stuffed in a three-course meal.

Full. Full of that mouthful, and full of thoughts of Laura. Two nights it had been; the first night an Italian restaurant, the second night Mexican. They had not touched, just talked. They were meeting again that night — French. He felt more peaceful than he had for weeks, as if his whole body was relaxing for the first time, letting go of all its traumas. He was still so young. There was so much life ahead.

His phone rang and he reached for it, pressing the green

handset button before checking who it was, hoping it was her.

'It's me.' A woman's voice. A sad, quiet, disappointed voice. Not Laura.

'Romy?' He held the phone back quickly and stared at the little screen in disbelief. *Romymobile*, it said. Oh God, he should have checked. The second call in two weeks. 'What's wrong?'

'I'm in trouble. Can I talk to you?'

In his newly relaxed state, she seemed like a stranger. Did he really have a diamond ring somewhere at home, with this woman's name figuratively on it? He was getting over her, he realised.

'Is this to tell me again how I did everything wrong, how it was my fault for being too caring?'

'No.'

'Okay.'

'I'm sorry. I shouldn't have said that.'

'No. Well.'

'Things are shit, Eddy. Absolutely shit.'

'Really?'

'I miss you.'

The birds flew past again, their circling suddenly seeming frenzied and deranged. 'How's Van?'

She started to cry and Eddy silently consulted his watch. His leisurely lunch break was almost over, and he either had to wrap this up within three minutes or be late for a meeting with clients.

'Please can I come over when you finish work? I need to talk.'

'Really? You're not out robbing a 7/11, or trafficking drugs, or zooming off into the sunset on your motorbike?'

'No,' she whispered. 'I'm not.'

'I have a date tonight. I'm going out for dinner.'
'Oh. With a ... woman?'
'Yes.'
'Who?'
'No one you know. So, you said you needed to talk? Because I have to get back to work now.'
'Oh. Sorry. Could I meet you straight after work, just for a drink? Before you go out for dinner. We could meet at four-thirty, at that little bar with the weird lights?'

Eddy slapped a fifty-dollar bill on the counter of the restaurant and nodded to them as he left, the phone still held to his ear. She knew he didn't finish at four-thirty, never before five-thirty.

'Five,' he said sullenly. 'And I can't stay long.' He felt resentful.

'Thanks so much, Eddy.'

He slapped the phone shut and walked off down the city streets. Above him now, the birds flew their mad laps, while around him people walked theirs, up and down, to work, from work. None of us ever really get off our merry-go-round, he reflected. We just have moments, glorious moments, where we think that we do.

Romy sidled into the bar wearing a sunhat and glasses, combined oddly with a woolen scarf and an overcoat. She walked too casually around the premises, staring at patches of nothing on the wall, and casting quick, fierce glances at other patrons. She finally wandered close to Eddy and then sat in his booth.

'Are you in disguise?' Eddy said.
'Shh!'

'No one's listening.'

'The cops are after me.'

'Oh?' said Eddy. Romy had always loved a bit of drama. However, he had to admit, she may have a point. Just yesterday she and Van had featured in a *Crimestoppers* item. *Have you seen these people?*

Romy slid off her glasses and impatiently unwound the scarf. She left the hat on and gazed at Eddy.

She appeared to have put back the weight she had lost earlier that year, during her incarnation as a criminal. Her face was thinner, her shoulders sharper, and yet the rest of her looked fatter, under a loose top. Large, even. Eddy's mother was a big woman and, to Eddy, real women had curves and bulges. Bits moved when they walked, flesh yielded to touch. They took up space.

'You look well.'

'I'm not well,' she hissed angrily. 'I am permanently stressed. The police raided the squat where Van and I were staying. We only just got out the back door in the nick of time, and then we spent three hours hiding in bushes under a bridge while the police searched for us. Everywhere I go, I feel like people are watching me. There's a *reward* out. Did you know that?'

'No,' he lied. He stroked one finger down the frosted beer glass before him.

'Can you imagine how frightening it is to be pursued, all day, every day?'

Her breathing was ragged, her eyes looked bloodshot and scared. Faint sympathy washed over him, despite himself.

'Probably pretty terrifying to be a kid working in a shop and have someone point a gun at you.' He tore open a foil packet of nuts.

'I know.' Romy wept silently for a couple of minutes.

Eddy passed her a serviette. She wiped her eyes. 'I can't believe what I've become this year. It was fun at first. It felt daring, adventurous. But I feel so sorry now for these frightened people. And Van ... when he's the one holding the gun, I'm scared he's going to lose it and hurt someone.'

'Well.' He was hearing all this as if it were coming from far away. 'You could stop. Turn yourself in.'

She stirred the peanuts with her fingertips and stared down at them for a moment. 'I'm pregnant.'

Eddy was just lifting his beer to his mouth and her words forced his eyes back to her face. Was she joking? His beer was suddenly jolted back to the floor of the glass, from whence it returned like a small tidal wave and flooded his nostrils. He coughed, he spluttered, he put down the glass and wiped his face with a serviette.

'What?'

'I'm pregnant.'

He was stabbed with a ridiculous wild hope and terror, before he realised.

'To who?' Not to him. Not to him.

'To Van.' She let her coat fall open and he saw her belly.

'You're having a child with Van?' His own stomach felt horribly empty, and yet he might need to throw up.

'Well, *I'm* having a child. I don't think Van's that interested in it.'

'Why not?'

'He's got other things on his mind. Like staying out of jail.' She started to cry. 'Oh, Eddy, I don't want to go to jail. I would ... I can't ...'

Eddy looked around the bar. A group of women a few years younger than Romy had just floated in, slim and cool, casting their eyes over the various tables to find spare seats. One wall of the bar was filled with tiny canvases; some local artist's exhibition. Tiny squares featuring simple moments. A quarter of a face, one smiling eye. The moon, through a window frame. A plate, with knife and fork neatly paired in the middle. A fat baby's hand, reaching for an adult finger.

'So how far pregnant are you?'

'Maybe eight months. Maybe less. It's a bit unclear. What with hiding out all the time, I sort of lost track of things.'

He stared for a full minute at a sign, which advertised the bar's upcoming karaoke night.

'Are you going to say anything?' she whispered.

'When's it due?' It was November, but he was too shocked for simple calculations. The incident with the truckie and Romy the bunny, three or four months ago — had she looked different then? Larger? Not that he had noticed.

'December. Next month.'

Eddy tapped his fingers on the table and checked his watch. He felt like someone had told him about the death of a beloved friend, and yet he no longer had any right to grieve. Thirty minutes and he would leave to meet Laura. Could he still face her? He felt like crawling under a rock. 'Well. Thanks for telling me.'

She reached out for his hand, her face suddenly tense. 'I made a huge mistake, Eddy.'

'You did?'

'I should have stayed with you. This should have been your baby.' She was pale, her eyes abnormally large. 'I don't know if you've ever made a mistake this big, Eddy, if you've ever felt regret so strong that it has you writhing in your bed at night, thinking about the way things could have been. But that's how I feel.'

Something about the words focused Eddy. It was as if,

for the first time since she had sat down before him, he could see Romy clearly. Thoughts of Laura fell away. 'What do you want?'

'I want to come back.'

'I don't think I can forgive you.'

She sighed heavily and leaned back, her hand on her belly. 'I want to come home.'

'Home?'

'We chose that house together, Eddy.'

It was in his name and all the loan repayments had come from his salary. But that was nitpicking, he knew. Both in his own moral world, and in a court of law. They had lived together for over two years, what was his was hers, too.

'You were so insistent on a fireplace, do you remember?'

She smiled. 'And we hardly had any fires after all, did we?'

'We *never* had one.' He had never trusted the chimney.

'We could now.'

'It's nearly summer.'

'I know.'

He glanced at his watch again. 'Do you need somewhere to live? Is that it?'

'I do. But I also want you. I want us to get back together.'

'Well.' He rubbed his forehead and got wearily to his feet. 'I'm seeing someone.'

She nodded. 'For how long?'

He wasn't going to say only two dates. It had been two of the most intense, intimate, revealing nights of his life, and they hadn't even touched. 'For a while.'

'How long is a while?'

He shook his head. 'Romy,' he said gently, 'it's no longer any of your business.'

She exhaled sharply, and her eyes filled with tears.

'I don't mean to hurt you,' he said. 'And I understand that you're in trouble. Listen, if you want to come stay for a while, you can sleep in the spare room. Just until you work out something permanent. But one week, that's all. I'll help you look for a place.'

'Oh.' She dropped her gaze to the table top. 'I see.'

'Do you still have your key?'

'I do.'

'Is that okay?'

'That's great. Thank you so much. Just for a week, Ed. Until I find my feet. Find a place to stay, get some Centrelink payments happening.'

Of course. No money left, after her little stint holding up shops. Couldn't she have saved a bit for a rainy day? He would not offer her money. He would not.

'Do you need money?'

She shook her head bravely. 'I've got a bit.'

'When do you think you'll move in?'

'Is tonight okay?'

He blinked. He had had visions of bringing Laura back that night, but maybe they could go to her place instead. 'Fine,' he said, just as he remembered that Laura lived with her parents. *Damn.*

'Thanks.'

He hesitated, but pulled a couple of fifties from his wallet, and laid them before her. 'Don't go hungry,' he said. He knew he shouldn't. But he had loved her, once.

CHAPTER SEVENTEEN

Melody stared for a long time at the laptop. Grace waited beside her, fingers poised, sitting with one knee drawn beneath her. She looked from Melody's face to the computer screen, and back. The kitchen table was a mess. The laptop was a sleek, shiny island in an ocean of children's drawings, Star Wars figurines, dry-crusted porridge bowls and piles of folded washing. The scent of rising bread mixed with the smell of rising mould. Glass panes rattled in rotting window panes; the light flickered every now and then, probably rats in the ceiling chewing happily away at the wires. Grace tapped her fingers on the tabletop. 'Well?'

Melody nodded carefully, her eyes narrowed. She looked so serious, so focused, she could have been drafting the national budget. Finally, she exhaled. 'Sagittarius seems to have a pretty good outlook at the moment. It's moving into the seventh house. Which governs relationships.'

'Excellent.' Grace frowned for a while into the corners of the ceiling, tapping the pen end on her teeth. She wrote: *Expect to meet new love, or shed an old one. Pay close attention to the people around you.*

Melody read over her shoulder doubtfully. 'Oh. That's a bit ... I don't know.'

'What? We should all pay close attention to the people around us. Anyway. All the time. It's good general advice. And you know; either you meet a new love or you shed an old one. That's sort of the story of relationships, isn't it?'

'What about all the relationships that stay together? Where nothing happens?'

Grace stared down at the page. Yes, what about them? Damn them. Maybe her view was a little jaundiced. 'Okay, how's this. You *farewell* an old one, instead of shed. That way you could be, you know, seeing them off at the station for work.'

'Hmm ...'

'Anyway, moving on. What's in store for Capricorn?'

'Shouldn't we do more on Sagittarius?'

Grace shook her head. 'Relationships. Good outlook. Meet, farewell. I'll flesh it out later. Think about Capricorn.'

Melody stared at the computer again, clicking through incomprehensible charts. Grace put aside the pen and checked emails on her phone; the kindergarten needed parents to make sets for the kindy Christmas concert. Volunteers could contact Tom Ellison! Her Tom! Well! Mr Bloody Wonderful Kindy Dad, was he now? Mr Fucking Community. Bet those divorced mothers were getting all gooey over the wonderfulness of Tom Ellison; she could just imagine the coy emails now. *Hi Tom! Love to arrange some hay on set, let's meet and discuss?*

'Ah. Goodness me,' Melody said finally. Grace roused herself from silent fury and picked up the pen.

'Jupiter is entering the house of Cancer,' Melody said, swinging around from the computer to eye Grace meaningfully.

'Gosh. And ...'

'That's *huge*. That's like, I don't know, it's like the biggest event for Capricorns in about ninety years.'

Grace raised her eyebrows politely. 'Really? How super. So that means ...'

'Cancer is the house of honours, achievement, fame. Jupiter brings good fortune to all he touches.'

'Jupiter is a he?'

'It's an amazingly lucky mixture of events. Historic.'

Grace nodded carefully, like someone humouring a child. So, what, one-twelfth of the population would have their biggest thingummy in ninety years? How did she write that?

Melody made a *however* sort of face. '*However*, before all this good fortune can come, we need the new moon to sort of prod it into action.'

Luckily there'd been one of those every month since creation, so they were in business. Grace bit her lip and wrote: *Cancer, Jupiter, good fortune, need new moon.*

'And the new moon is when?'

Melody toggled screens. 'On the eighth, when the moon moves house. Honestly, this is a once-in-a-lifetime opportunity for Capricorns. Really. Do we know any Capricorns?'

'Tom,' said Grace tonelessly. She wrote *8th, new moon, cancer*. 'So what does it mean for Tom? He'll find new love? Get a cheap divorce?'

Melody sighed and rubbed her eyes. Her fingers covered the top of her face for a few minutes, prodding and pushing her pale skin, until finally her eyes emerged again, open and deep blue, fringed with her long black lashes. Grace wondered what her hair would look like out of dreadlocks.

Melody murmured, 'I'm so tired.'

Grace felt guilty. Reading horoscopes was probably a spiritually draining business, and here she was, sapping Melody with her cynicism. But she was Mel's agent now, and her manager, and she needed to have a spine for them both. 'Well, we need to finish these horoscopes before lunch. Then we've got to take the kids to prep orientation. Then we'll set you up with Twitter and Facebook accounts.'

'No? Really?'

'If you're not interested, I'll run them for you. And at 3pm, we've got the phone interview. With the newspaper.'

'No, I did that already. Yesterday.'

'This is another one.'

'Oh, please. I can't bear them. Can you do it?'

'What? Pretend to be you?'

'Why not? It's over the phone, they'll never know. It's not like I'm really being me anyway.'

'Okay. If you trust me. Also, Anthea's asked for your bank details.'

Melody wriggled uncomfortably. 'You're my manager. Can she pay your account, and you pay me?'

Grace frowned at her. 'Have you *still* not set up a bank account?'

'I keep meaning to.'

She hesitated. 'Are you sure you want to give me this much— I don't know.' Power seemed like the wrong word. Nobody could have power over Melody. She slipped away from such things like she was coated in teflon.

'Please. I would love you to. And we'll share the money. Fifty-fifty.'

Grace opened her mouth to argue, and then shut it. She had a lot to get done today. She simply did not have the time.

Grace was forced to go to her mother and ask for a loan.

'Oh, Grace. Your life is terrible.' Dawn took her daughter's hand with her own bony one and stroked it. Grace in turn watched her mother, the way her hair had receded from her forehead in recent times, and how Dawn was still bothering to dye her frail wispy hair orange, as evidenced by the inch of white at the roots. Dawn was growing old, and one day she would die and leave Grace all alone. Grace pulled her hand out from under her mother's, picked up Dawn's hand instead and kissed the thin skin on the back, feeling the frail metacarpals beneath her lips. How shocking, that within everyone you loved, there were bones.

'Thanks, Mum. I know.' She took a deep breath and smiled bravely. This, this was the lowest point she could reach. She had hit rock bottom.

'Well, I ran into Tom yesterday, in the IGA.'

Grace felt her heart clench. 'And how was that?'

Dawn lowered her voice and looked around, as if they were not alone in the house. 'He was with a woman.'

'A woman.' Grace silently corrected herself: no *this* was now the lowest point she could reach.

'A girl.' Dawn viewed any female younger than herself as a girl. 'Tight pants,' she said meaningfully. 'And my iPhone says it's Tom's birthday this weekend.'

So it was. Grace nodded dully. A girl in tight pants. Dawn leaned close.

'Midlife crisis,' she pronounced. 'And the girl is *very unattractive*. Not a patch on you.'

Grace shuffled her chair close and slid her arms around her mother's bony body, sank her head onto her shoulder and inhaled the scent which had not changed since Grace's childhood. A smell of spring days, of Trix dishwashing liquid and faintly of onions. *Unattractive. Not a patch on you. Midlife crisis.* The sheer *kindness* of her mother; the solidarity of women, across the generations. Like Melody, begging for Grace's help with the TV job. Not just dumping the childcaring on Grace, but drawing her in, calling her her agent, making Grace truly a part of it in these, the lowest, lowest days of her life. Grace was not totally fooled, much as she would like to have been. As if Melody had ever needed anybody's help, really. She slipped her fingers under her mother's arm. It was enough to turn the hardest heart to marshmallow. It was enough to save you. She wept until her mother's apron grew damp and Dawn rubbed her back for a long time on the same spot, until Grace's tears dried and it felt like one more second of being rubbed on that same spot would make her scream.

But still, Grace did look after the children while Melody learned lines and spent long days in at the studio. It was Grace who packed kindy lunches, laid out clothes and arranged playdates. She bought a big day-at-a-page diary and mapped out Melody's time down to the last half-hour. Anthea Schulberg began to ring Grace, not Melody, to finalise details, and seemed quite relieved to have a practical intermediary for her dreamy new television star. Grace carried the diary and phone with her everywhere. She had been known to stop in the kindy foyer to answer a call, maybe pushing aside Big Ted on the tiny table to open the diary and frown over her scrawls for the days ahead. 'I can give you a half-hour for that interview on the Thursday, but it must be eleven, not ten, as I've told you before.' Melody did a half-hour of meditation every day at ten, and it was immovable. 'And as for the fashion shoot, only if it's vegan clothing.'

It was Grace who took the children to the primary school orientation day, because Melody had a week of voice training. Grace walked Lotte and Skip to the little school they would attend next year, every day, all on their own. Kindy would soon be over; their babies were growing up. In the school playground, a girl who would have been taller than Grace clasped hands with a shorter girl and spun around in a ray of sunshine. The girl had long hair, and small, new breasts rose beneath her shirt. She was almost a woman. Maybe the girl she played with was her little sister. They spun with their feet together, the girl's hair swinging down as she leaned back. The playground swarmed with enormous children; it seemed the bulk of them were little boys, although the official statistics didn't reflect this at all, Grace knew. She watched the tall girl; she looked way too old for the school, although she would be just twelve, maybe close to thirteen. Grade six, on the verge of the big world beyond, like a plane going down the runway. Her last weeks of primary school. Did her mother share Grace's half-nauseous mix of excitement and grief at the prospect? This girl must have started school as a round-tummied, big-eyed four-year-old like Lotte, who had stretched like chewing gum over the years into this long-boned, elegant girl, tucking locks of straight glossy hair behind her ears.

Grace left the children, feeling a little disconsolate and yet relieved to get some work time. She spread herself out in a nearby café, and was quickly immersed in paperwork;

contracts, Melody's diary, costume sketches, an iPad on which she was fleshing out horoscopes.

Anna, Nina and Verity, whose children were also doing prep orientation, knocked on the window and crowded into the café, dragging clattery chairs up to her table and excitedly describing their children's responses to school.

'And is it true Melody's got some job on the telly?' asked Verity.

Grace described it to them, and their faces froze into varying comic masks of shock.

'An on-air job? On *Round Up*?'

'Surely they'll cut her hair?'

'They must be paying her a *fortune*.'

'And you're her what ...?'

'I'm just helping her,' said Grace modestly. She picked up Verity's newspaper and scanned the front page headlines: *Cat and Pirate: Police closing in*. A close up of the masked bandits. She folded the paper in half and laid it aside.

'Who did she sleep with to get that?'

'She was headhunted. Spotted. She was on screen after the thing with Lotte and then they realised she had that *thing*. That screen thing.' Grace couldn't help but feel a little proud. *Melody lit up the screen like a power station*, Anthea Schulberg had confided in her. *Some people are beautiful in real life, but they get on screen and their wattage sort of ... dims. But Melody, oh Melody, she had the opposite. A sort of visual broadcast charisma unseen since Minogue. It was a freak of chemistry; money could not buy such a thing, nor could it be created*. Anthea's only fear was that *Round Up* wouldn't keep her, that she would be snatched away by talent scouts.

'Headhunted,' whispered Anna disbelievingly.

'Can we come into the studio, watch them filming?'

'I *always* thought she had some special quality about her,' said Verity. 'Such a *nice* person.'

The women finished their coffees and left Grace to work. She watched them set off down the street, handbags on shoulders, heads tilting back and forth as they talked. She wondered what they were saying. Opposite her café was the ice-cream shop where a year ago Lotte had made her mad dash into the future, running towards danger and friendship and a brand-new life, trailing everyone behind her. It had been the worst moment of Grace's life, the absolute worst. And yet. Sometimes the worst moments were portals into whole new worlds. She went back to writing. *Taurus. Sometimes the worst moments can be portals into whole new worlds …*

Grace took Lotte to buy her father a birthday present. She remembered how long Tom could take to open a present from either herself or Lotte. How he would get down and sniff it like a dog, his expression quizzical, Lotte helpless with giggles, nearly wetting herself. Then he would shake it for ages, peer at it, knock at it, rub it against his cheek questioningly, until both Lotte and Grace were begging him, Open it! And whatever it was, he would almost collapse on the floor with gratitude. It was always the *best* present he had ever had. Always his favourite birthday ever. They were always the best two girls Nature had ever made. His girls.

Who would Tom spend his birthday with this year? she wondered.

'I want to buy Daddy this.' In the two-dollar shop, Lotte brought Grace a plastic sleeve thing, filled with blue liquid and two black spiders which floated inside it. You apparently could wear it on your wrist, and roll it up and down your arm. It was the ugliest and most useless thing Grace had ever seen. This shop smelled so fiercely of the chemicals used to make all this plastic crap that it actually hurt the back of her throat to breathe. She looked at the thing doubtfully. Was it maybe a spectacularly awful masturbation device? Lotte jumped up and down, the spiders on her wrist jiggling about in their blue pool. 'Oh please, Mum! It's so beautiful! He'll love it!'

Grace sighed and opened her wallet.

She stopped to buy printing paper from the newsagent and a radio muttered away behind the counter as she paid. 'The two armed criminals known as Cat and Pirate ... police say they have had some very strong leads ... just announced a $30,000 reward for further information ... Held up a store manager who hours later had a heart attack ... In a 3YPA exclusive, we can reveal that that store manager has passed away ... police say these criminals are very dangerous and could now be charged with manslaughter ... Victorian police have come under fire for their inability to catch the two criminals, who have been wanted and on the loose now for eight months ...'

'Useless druggies,' said the newsagent, passing Grace her change.

'Oh, yes,' said Grace absently, glancing again at the newspapers. Romy. It was unbelievable. Front page. This story that began at her dining table was now unfolding in the national news. Thirty thousand dollars! That was a lot of money. A lot. Anybody might start to reconsider their loyalties for that amount of money. Not that Grace had any loyalties, to either of them.

Van had dropped by once, a week or two back, when she was at home with the children. Melody had apparently told him their new address. Grace had been half-heartedly weeding the vegetable garden when she heard the front doorbell ring. When she reached the door, there was no one there. She returned to the back yard and a man sat in the rusted outdoor setting, a hood pulled up over his head, hanging down to shield his eyes. She started, and then realised who it was.

'Oh. Yes?' she said primly.

'I'm a friend of Melody's,' said his voice, from the depth of the hood.

'I know who you are,' she said scornfully. 'You need a better disguise than that. Melody's not here.'

He glanced at her quickly, through sunglasses. 'When will she be back?' he said in a low voice.

'Later.' Grace said, stony-eyed.

'Can I see Skipper?'

Grace narrowed her eyes at him and called to Skip, who ran out to her. She whisked him up onto her hip and held him so tight that he wriggled.

'Hey, mate.' Van drew closer, tucked the boy's small hand into his own. He pushed back the hood and lifted the glasses to reveal bloodshot eyes.

'Hi, Van.' Skipper looked pleasantly surprised, if a little shy.

'Do you want to come for a ride with Vanny?' He reached out towards Skip, his fingers slipping under the little armpits, and Grace jumped backwards, shocked.

'No!' she shouted. The last person she had seen ride off with this man had ended up as a front-page news story.

'Steady on—'

'Leave! Right now.'

'I was just wanted to say hi—'

'My mobile is in my pocket and I can press one button

to reach emergency, and have police here in two minutes,' she hissed, slipping her hand into her pocket. Her mobile was inside, on the charger. She formed a fist around a packet of mint-flavoured chewing gum.

Van pulled his hood up, and shot her a menacing look. But he melted away and Grace made the children play inside for the rest of the week.

CHAPTER EIGHTEEN

Eddy put on his coat and stopped at the door of Alf Tankhouse's office. Alf had fully recovered from being abandoned by his wife, and a framed picture of his new girlfriend sat beside another of his children. These days he was building his share and property portfolio at the same time as holding down his role as Risk, Routing and Co's swaggering company attorney, a job he did with ease.

'She looks nice,' said Eddy, touching the girlfriend's photo. 'Nice eyes.'

Eddy raised his eyebrows wickedly. 'She is sooo nice. I can't tell you. The *nice* things she does.'

'Okay,' said Eddy hastily. He had never been comfortable with blokey disclosure about intimate details of women. For himself, he had been flat out for the past week with finding excuses for Laura *not* to come home with him, despite going out with her every second night, and going almost insane with lust. Romy was sleeping in his spare room, something he had not quite mentioned to Laura. He was losing sleep at night, lying there thinking of Laura while Romy got up every hour to go to the toilet. Once, Romy had paused outside Eddy's bedroom door, in the silent hours of the night, while Eddy lay in the room that had been theirs. He held his breath and willed her footsteps to move on. What would he do if she came in, and laid her body down beside him? Her *pregnant* body. There was a part of him that wanted to touch that round belly, to feel Romy hard in the place where she had always been soft. And maybe to feel her heart soft, where it had for so long been hard.

But he knew now that Romy's vulnerability was his own. He had fallen in love with Romy in need, and Romy in need was back again. He must not weaken.

'Have you got a minute?' he asked Alf.

'Steady Eddy, never fear. My minute is yours. What can I do you for? Are those bastards paying what you're worth yet?'

Eddy stepped into the office, glancing over his shoulder as he did. 'Well. I just wanted to ask you a question. It's not work-related, but—'

'Women? Shares? Law? Shoot away.'

'I've got this mate called Tom; an inventor. He's invented this thing, it's a solar panel made out of old plastic bottles. You can build it into a roof.'

'Phew. Sounds like a gold mine. Or a piece of crap.'

'I'm meeting him in a few minutes and we're going to meet with a potential buyer. A big buyer. He wanted me to come, because ...' Eddy paused. He wasn't quite sure why Tom had wanted him to come, and he shrugged to finish the sentence. 'Because, you know. He's a mate. Company. Anyway, I'm meant to be in that Jefferson meeting at two, and I was wondering whether you could make up some excuse and cover for me? Tell them I got called away.'

'Sure, sure. But does your mate have a lawyer? Who's the potential?'

'Universal Materials Incorporated.'

'Oh, fuck. *Tell* me he's got a lawyer. *Tell* me he's not going to meet with UMI without a lawyer. Button, they'll eat him for breakfast.'

'Well, I think it's early stages.'

'Show them you mean business. Bring a top-flight contracts man.' Tank swung into his coat and adjusted his cufflinks. 'In fact, bring *me*. Marion can tell the Jefferson people we were both called out at short notice.'

'Err ...' Eddy trailed out after Tank, who was already at his secretary's desk, issuing orders. 'It's just, um, Tom wasn't really expecting ... Tom may not want ...' They were already in the lift and Alf punched the ground-floor button with the side of his fist.

'Sweet. That Jefferson meeting was going to be a snooze anyway. This sounds like fun.'

'Um ... I'm just a bit ... Tom might be feeling a bit ... confidential about it.'

'I *am* confidential — and to you, I'm free. You're telling me this man is about to sign a valuable business contract, yes?'

'Er, uh, well, hopefully ...' Probably not, reflected Eddy, and Alf would be wasting his precious time, and standing up the valued Jefferson clients, and probably pissing Tom off, too.

'And does he have a lawyer?'

'Er, uh, no. Not that I know of.'

'Then he needs one.'

They arrived at the offices of UMI only a few minutes before the meeting was due to start, and Eddy hastily explained who Alf was to Tom, and Tom looked bewildered, but shrugged and said okay, a lawyer might be good, and handed over some documents which Alf coolly flicked through in the remaining thirty seconds. Then the door opened and they were welcomed into a boardroom. Eddy's heart was racing, on Tom's behalf. They sat, Alf, Tom and Eddy, looking, he realised, like a cohesive, well-dressed team of young men; men from the generation about to take power, the ones starting to run companies and invent things and take the driving seat of the world. No one would guess that Tom was sleeping in a filthy warehouse, or that Eddy had been living alongside pizza boxes and beer cans and the regrets of a failed relationship, or that Alf, all white shirt-front and strong jaw, had only come on board five minutes ago.

Opposite them sat three more men, another reason why it was good Alf had come. They weren't outnumbered. One of them proceeded to deliver a brain-numbing speech to Tom about the merits of the panels, what they hoped to do with them, how far around the world they could be sold, how they could be a boon to parts of the third world. Tom looked dazed, and the man opposite him leaned forward.

'To get to the point, we are willing to offer you three million dollars for your invention.'

The atmosphere in the room changed. There was silence and Tom paled. He looked like he might burst into tears. He opened his mouth to speak.

Alf cut through him.

'That would be a deposit on national rights only, surely?'

'Worldwide, of course. Total rights. It's a generous price.'

Alf chuckled, as if highly amused. 'And royalties?'

'This generous offer would buy those out.'

Tom opened his mouth again, and Alf put his hand on his shoulder and spoke over him.

'I would advise my client not to accept.'

Tom stared at him in horror, and Alf stood. 'Could we have a few minutes alone, gentlemen?'

'Of course.' A secretary showed them into an adjoining room and closed the door.

Tom snapped at Alf. 'My *client*? Mate, no offence, but I don't think we need you here.'

'*Au contraire*, you most certainly do.'

'No, I don't think I do, actually. I'm about to make three million dollars. Piss off.'

'I will, if you're sure you want to sell your invention for a twentieth, or possibly a fiftieth of what it's worth.'

'How the fuck would you know what it's worth? Do you even know what it is?'

'Yeah. Eddy told me; I read your little prospectus. But, to be honest, I don't even need to know what it is. If this is UMI's first offer, they'll fully expect you to come back and ask for a better one. And if your invention is any bloody good at all, you won't sell it outright, you'll hang out for royalties. No inventor with any brain would give up their royalties. I would suggest you come back with a proposal for twenty million, Australia and New Zealand rights only, *plus* a ten percent take in every unit that's sold for the rest of its commercial life.'

'They're not going to give me that!'

'How do you know until you ask? I think they will at least go away and think about it. They'll have to take it to their board, they can't just dismiss it.'

'I don't want to wait around for weeks.'

'Days, mate, if not hours.'

'I don't want to wait for *one* hour.'

'Jesus, what are you, a businessman or a kid wanting an ice cream?'

'Mate, just hold off on the fucking insults.'

'Seriously. How long have you been working on this thing — a year? And you don't want to wait a few days to get potentially millions more out of them?

'Bird in the hand ...'

'Forget that shit. You have kids, right?'

'What's that got to do with anything?'

'A lot. So what, two, three kids?'

'One.'

'You could hand her an income for life, long after you're dead. Cheques arriving quarterly, to remind her of Daddy, right up to when she's an old lady. She'll pass those onto her children, and it will be your legacy. Alternatively, you could lose half of what you get in tax, pay off your mortgage on some suburban house, and go back to your job as a wage slave. Big deal, so what. Your choice.'

Tom looked at Eddy. Eddy sighed. He wanted to say, *I know, I know, he's an arrogant moron, but he's also really, really smart, and he's right, you should have brought a lawyer to something like this, and he may actually be in the ballpark here* ... He did his best to convey this with raised eyebrows and rueful glances, which Tom, by the disheartened set of his sagging shoulders, seemed to reluctantly get.

'But if we ask for more, don't we risk losing the whole deal?'

Tank shrugged. 'Hard to say. But if you've been trying to invent machines, I'm guessing you're not a man to shy away from a risk.'

'Okay, okay. Let me think.' Tom shook his head and rubbed his forehead. 'You really think there's a chance in hell they might go for that? They won't just laugh us out of the place?'

'I think there's a good chance that the actions of the next

few minutes will determine whether you merely repay your debts, or become a millionaire.'

'Or whether you lose the whole deal,' murmured Eddy. He was, after all, a risk analyst. But no one heard him.

Tom stared at Alf and took a deep breath. 'Okay. Okay. Do it.'

Eddy sat in the back seat of Tank's car and held the phone to his ear. Laura had to shout above a gaggle of four-year-olds.

'Where are you?' she said.

'I'm with a couple of friends. We're just driving out to a pub in the country.'

'You've finished work already?'

Eddy watched the suburbs flash past, thinning out to the country. 'We finished a bit early. I'm actually with Tom, er, Lotte's dad. He's had an offer on his invention and he's ... well, it's a waiting game now.' Too complicated to explain that the firm members had asked for a night to consider his request, and that Alf had, on leaving, insisted on taking Tom to a pub where he could get pissed and wait out the night under Alf's watchful eye, without caving in. Eddy could hear Alf right now demanding Tom hand over his mobile phone.

'Sounds exciting,' said Laura. 'Well, here in the Possum group we're experiencing tactile sensations; exploring the different feelings of wet, dry, furry, gooey, sticky, warm, and cold.' There was no mistaking the playful note in her voice. 'It's fun.'

'Goodness. It does sound ... fun.' He was suddenly weak with desire, and joy that she felt safe enough with him to sound so suggestive. They had had a few dinners out, one movie, and he had spent one Sunday helping her paint a set for the end-of-year concert. The rest of the time he could hardly stop thinking about her.

'Facilitates brain connections, they say.'

'Oh! I was just thinking my brain felt a bit disconnected. Could we maybe ...?'

'Mmm?'

'Could I see you tonight?'

'Aren't you en route to the country?'

'I could— Damn. Actually I think Tom needs me. I can't leave.' He was worried Tom and Alf might rip each other to shreds if left alone. 'Why don't you come out to Healesville and meet us for dinner?'

'Or I could meet you back at your place?'

Oh my God. Was she hinting that ... *Dammit*, Romy was at his place. He tried to match her suggestive tone. 'Well maybe if we have a drink it will be better to stay in a *hotel*.' God, *when* was Romy going to move out? She was only meant to have been there briefly; he hadn't even told anyone she was there.

'It's not a boys' night?'

'I really hope not.'

'You sure? It sounds like it is.'

'Does it?' Eddy heard the gloom in his own voice. He didn't really like boys' nights, with all their fraught competitiveness and veiled anger and the unsettling sense that anything was possible. 'I don't want it to be. In fact, I think we need a woman here. It's all a bit tense.' Oh God, he shouldn't have said that. She would run a mile. 'I mean, not tense. Too boyish, you know.' Oh, God, he sounded like a fucking Girl Guide.

But she just laughed. 'Okay.'

'Really?' He grinned madly out at the paddocks. 'That

would be great.' She liked him. She must. Even if he was a Girl Guide.

'I'll see you there.'

'My brain will be ready. For those new connections. All that tactile stuff.'

'Hmm. Dr Laura is on her way.'

Grace knocked on Eddy's front door. A crate of beer bottles sat out the front alongside a stack of empty pizza boxes. Eddy's car was here, but that meant nothing, she knew. He could be working late, or he might have gone out after work. It was almost nine, and Tom had said earlier that he would call her back that evening. She had rung him that morning to tell him that there was an excursion fee due for kindy, it was his turn to pay, that Lotte needed new clothes, that Grace needed help. He had sounded distracted, said he would call her back, and then he had not answered calls all day. She had left message after message, and she had gone beyond angry to worried. Was he alright? Had he been electrocuted while working on his invention? Hit by a car? Had he committed suicide with grief from being apart from her? Well, probably not that. Worse, was he in bed with a woman? The tight pants girl from the IGA? A kindy mum? Oh God. Eddy might know where he was. She pounded on the door.

She was about to turn away when she heard a noise and the handle rattled. The door opened a few inches to reveal a woman. For a moment, Grace couldn't place her.

'Romy!' It was Eddy's old girlfriend, who had vanished from Grace's own home that long-ago night last summer. The one who had sailed off into the darkness on a motorbike and only appeared since in newspaper photographs, blurry convenience-store security pictures. Grace was shocked. 'Are you and Eddy, er?'

'No, no.' Romy glanced nervously up the street and pulled Grace inside. She locked the door again, and leaned back against the wall, resting her hand on her stomach. Her very large, pregnant stomach.

'Oh, my God!' said Grace. 'You're ... Is that ...? Does Eddy ...?'

'It's Van's,' said Romy, sighing heavily. Despite her pregnancy her face looked thinner, her eyes larger and more serious, and Grace recognised the heavy breathing of late gestation.

'Oh!' Grace was momentarily back in that far-off dinner party. And now this.

Romy nodded ruefully. 'Can I make you a cup of something? Please don't rush off. I've been alone here all day, I'm going out of my mind.'

'How long have you been living back with Eddy for?'

'For a few days now. I had nowhere else to go and he said I could stay here for a week until I get somewhere else, but ...'

'So you're not ... together, then?'

Romy shook her head. 'He doesn't want me back.'

It was all so calm, so undramatically stated. So unlike the drama queen who had roared off from the front of Grace's home. Romy walked awkwardly to the kitchen and sank into a chair. She moved like someone trying to conserve energy, someone hanging on by their fingernails. Grace well remembered this state of pregnancy, the belly solid like a stone shrink-wrapped in plastic. The vibrating in the thighs and shoulders, as if the guy ropes of the whole structure were anchored there. The visibility of it, providing a spectacle everywhere you went.

'Are you alright?'

Romy slumped on the table. 'Terrified. Every time I hear a police chopper. I can't sleep, what with the baby kicking, and the fear that the cops could burst in the door any minute. They're after me. Have you heard? It's on the news. They've got a reward out. It's like a bad dream.'

Grace stared at her. 'But surely they'd have some sympathy ... I mean look at you. They couldn't send you to prison like that.'

'Are you kidding? There are women's prisons, where people keep their babies with them. Oh no, they won't let a little thing like pregnancy stop them.'

There was a thud outside the kitchen window and Romy jumped, wild-eyed. 'Shit.'

Grace went to the window and pushed the curtain aside with one finger. 'Just your neighbour, putting out the rubbish.'

'Oh, God, I'm a wreck.' Romy wept silently. 'Why, why did I ever meet that man? It was the worst thing that ever happened to me. That dinner at your house ... it was the crossroads of my life.'

Grace looked at her. She sympathised, and yet she had been there when Romy had dumped her boyfriend at her dinner party, behaving like the most spoilt of children, the most self-indulgent of girls. She had seen Eddy broken-hearted for the best part of a year. She couldn't believe he had taken her back into his home.

'Ah, well. Do you know where Eddy is?'

Romy shook her head, sniffling. 'No. But he's got his mobile on him.'

'I'm looking for Tom. He's been missing all day and I

thought maybe he was with Eddy.' Grace sat down. 'We broke up, Tom and I. You probably heard.'

'Eddy mentioned it. Do you want his mobile number?'

Grace shook her head. 'I've got it.'

'You all became pretty good friends this year, didn't you?' said Romy. 'After that dinner where I took off.'

'It was more after my daughter almost got killed by a bus, and Eddy and Melody were there.' It wasn't about you, you silly cow. Although if the bus hadn't hit Lotte, she wouldn't have had them all for dinner, and Romy wouldn't have run off with Van, and now she wouldn't be sitting here in front of her, her shirt riding up over a belly so taut and huge that lines were snaking their way upwards, like elastic fabric stretched too hard. Grace wouldn't have gotten such a fright that she demanded Tom keep his job for two years so she could have a baby. Tom wouldn't have decided she was a controlling cow, and Melody wouldn't have been on the scene to tell Tom about the universe providing, and Tom might not have left Grace. Eddy might have presented his ring and he and Romy might be married right this minute, with this pregnancy not Van's, but Eddy's ...

'I'm scared, Grace.' Romy stared at her. 'Eddy's left me here alone and I could go into labour. I can't call a hospital, in case they turn me into the police.'

'Take my number,' said Grace, writing it down distractedly. She was desperate to speak to Tom, and dialed Eddy.

'Eddy? It's Grace.' She paused. Was Eddy in a nightclub or something? She could hear shouting and laughter and the unmistakable volume of drinkers. 'I'm just sitting here with Romy.'

'What's happening? Is she alright?'

'Fine. Pregnant. As you know.'

'Hang on, let me find a quiet place.'

'I'm after Tom, have you seen him?'

'Sure!' Eddy was almost shouting with relief. 'I'll put him on.' And there was Tom's voice, slightly slurred. 'Yair, hello?'

'It's me. You were going to call me back. Where are you?'

'Errr ... Pub in Healesville. With a few fellas.'

Romy leaned over. 'Can I speak to Eddy?'

Tom brightened. 'Is that Romy? At Eddy's house?'

'She's staying with him. She's pregnant.'

'Pregnant!'

'Hey, I need money. I need to talk to you about Lotte and her kindy fees.'

'Kindy! Well, let me put you onto the woman herself.' There was a shout and laughter and Grace stared at the phone in confusion. Then a voice said, 'Hello, Grace? It's Miss Laura.'

There was a burst of rowdy laughter and Grace glared furiously at Eddy's kitchen wall. 'What are you doing with Tom?' she asked Laura. Oh God. Her child's kindergarten teacher was in a relationship with her ex-husband. Did all the other mothers know already? Had they all been tiptoeing around her? *Does Grace know yet? I don't want to be the one to tell her ... but someone has to ...*

'We're just having a few drinks.'

Right.

A strange man's voice came on the line and said, 'Mrs Tom, you're going to be a millionaire. And your children have one sexy kindergarten teacher.' There was a hoot of laughter that sounded like it came from Laura, and then Eddy's voice in the background sounding a little injured. 'Mate. Show a bit of respect.'

'I have plenty of respect for beautiful women.'

God, they were all *horribly* drunk. Messily, awfully. What

the hell was Miss Laura doing out there with them, laughing like she was a pole dancer for hire rather than a role model to small children? How could Miss Laura have a sexuality at all, and, if she did have one, why did she have to exercise it on Tom? Truly, nothing was sacred. And what was that? She could hear another familiar voice as well.

'Is Melody there?' she demanded indignantly. If there was going to be a party at some out-of-the-way country pub, they could at least have invited her.

'Melody? No. Oh, shit. Look! Look! It's Melody on the telly!' said Eddy.

Grace ran to turn on Eddy's own set. There was Melody, angelic in white with gold stars woven through her blonde dreadlocks; like some heavenly bride. Her face was a treat to watch, utterly serene and yet fired through with emotion. She could see what Anthea Schulberg had meant about the camera loving Mel. You wanted her to never leave the screen. In her ear, the pub fell silent, except for Melody's calm voice.

'Aquarius ... You need not feel that you are obliged to stay forever with what was once agreed — but nor can you just walk away,' Melody said, her crystal ball turning before her. Dreamy music played in the background. A mobile of stars and moons hung from the studio ceiling above. *'Over the next few days you will take part in a significant conversation and begin a new way forward that will prove both reassuring and comfortable'.* She spread her hands before her to denote the pleasantness of the new route ahead, flat and smooth and easy.

Grace held onto the remote, Romy stood beside her, and they watched Melody on the small screen, like some goddess bringing messages from a world far beyond.

CHAPTER NINETEEN

She wore tight jeans, over a bottom resplendently, generously curvaceous. A floral shirt unbuttoned to show the inner curves of peachy breast. Shiny brown hair and no makeup, or none that Eddy could detect. Rosy-cheeked, pale-skinned, dark-lashed. Eddy couldn't take his eyes off Laura. Except to scowl at Alf, the big-talking show-off.

'So there I am, camping alone in the German countryside, when in the middle of the night I hear footsteps.'

Laura widened her eyes and sucked on her straw. Her lips pursed. Her ice rattled. She wrinkled her nose in a friendly way at Eddy, but she watched Tank as he relived some alpha-male adventure in Europe.

'My heart's pounding, and then there's a rustle at my tent door. Someone takes hold of my tent zipper and starts pulling it up, very slowly.'

Three strangers, other drinkers at the bar, leaned in close. Tom wasn't one of them. He was over by the juke box, leaning on it as he argued with a man in a biker jacket over the sounds of Dead or Alive's 'You Spin Me Right Round'.

'So we don't all like the same music, mate. 'sa free whirl, mate, a free whirl,' he shouted.

Biker jacket thrust his fat, unshaven chin towards Tom's face. He thumped the juke box. 'It's a poofter song,' he growled.

Tom danced loosely, clicked his fingers in the air and sang. 'Right round, baby, right round, like a record baby, right round round round round ...'

'*Fuck*. That's a fucking shit fucking song.' The biker turned around and snarled at the world. *Hornets*, read the back of his jacket. Crimson letters stitched on black leather, sewed in a symmetrical arch. His back was so wide that the H and the S disappeared around his sides. *ornet*.

Eddy looked back at Tank. His girl, Laura, was getting seduced by another man, a manlier man than he. His mate was about to get punched. Great night. All he needed was Romy to go into labour. Grace had scared him with her call; he must check that Romy had some plan for birth that didn't involve him.

Alf said: 'So it's pitch black. Silent. Then there's a sound. It's a zipper, going up. I manage to reach out, noiselessly, and find my pocket knife.'

'Oh, of course you do,' sneered Eddy, glancing quickly at Laura.

'Luckily I know every surface of my knife off by heart ...'

'Yeah, right.' Eddy tried to look loftily contemptuous, but Laura was too enthralled by the story to notice.

'Sorry, mate?' Alf looked sideways at Eddy, as if at an irritating child.

'Er nothing, nothing.' Eddy subsided resentfully.

'... and I can open it in the dark. Then, the other guy

rustles around a bit outside and I use the cover of his noise to sit up and feel for my headlamp, stick it on my head.'

Laura was panting with suspense. She finished her drink and picked up the full glass Eddy had placed before her, barely moving her eyes from Alf's face. She transferred the straw and resumed sucking. The straw flattened out and the level of pink drink plummeted, like water down a sinkhole. Alf continued.

'I turn on the torch and there it is — a hand.'

'Oooh!' Laura guided the straw-end proboscis over the bottom of the glass, and it sniffed around the ice blocks for any last morsel of alcohol.

'A big, hairy man's hand, reaching through the tent door. Within a second I grab it, throw my knees on the fingers and start stabbing at it! He's shouting something in German, and I hear footsteps! He had a mate, you see, and the mate ran off.'

'Oh, my God,' said Laura. 'I can't believe you held onto him.'

'And then what?' Eddy interjected, sounding as bored as he could. Let's just get the bloody story over with and fast-forward to the ending, which would paint Alf as the hero.

'Then I beat the shit out of him.' Alf casually sculled his beer and grinned. Laura recoiled, revolted, and Eddy seized his chance.

'You punched him in the head or you stabbed him in the belly?' he inquired.

Alf shrugged. 'Oh mate, details. Let's just say that, while I can't speak German, I reckon all that jibberish could pretty easily be translated into *Let me go, please — you win this round, big fella.*'

'Are you hungry?' Eddy spoke in a low voice to Laura, so

she had to turn towards him. 'We could scoot off to the bistro and get a bite to eat.'

'Bistro's closed,' reported Tank loudly.

'I wasn't *talking* to you.'

'Oh, I'm starving,' wailed Laura.

'Have another cocktail, that'll fill you up.' Alf tossed her a packet of potato chips. 'Shit, what is our budding Thomas Edison doing now?'

Tom had climbed on a table and was reaching his hands to the roof. 'People! People!' There were guffaws from the bikers who sat nearby in a thick knot of bellies, leather and hair.

Tom pressed on portentously. 'I am about. To Become. A Rich. Man.'

Eddy groaned, and dragged his feet towards Tom. 'Mate.' He stood beside him, as far from the bikers as he could, and reached up to tug at his friend's sleeve. 'Get down. Please. I'm begging you.'

Tom shouted on. '*Because* I have discovered a universal truth, that the universe will provide everything you need. I want to make that truth ... I want to pass that on ... I want to provide something to you, you good people, you people here to share my joy. I want to buy *every single person in this bar* a free drink.'

Luckily the bar was so crowded and noisy that only those immediately nearby heard, most of them bikers. They trotted to line up along the bar as obediently as school children and ordered triple shots of spirits, followed by spirit chasers. Eddy helped Tom down from the table.

'That's going to be really expensive.'

'I don't care. Because they're going to take the offer, aren't they? Eddy? What do you think?'

'I honestly don't know.' A set of antlers adorned the wall beside them, emerging right at the level of Tom's head.

'Would you have taken the risk? Would you have gone for the jackpot or would you have taken their offer?'

Eddy shrugged. 'Well, personally three million sounds like a helluva lot of money to me.'

Tom's face fell into a mask of horror. 'Oh. My. God. You're right. What have I done?'

'I don't— Hey, watch out!'

Tom clutched his head, which had hit the antlers. 'You're right. You're right. What have I done? Have I really walked away from an offer of three million dollars?' He was wild-eyed, and Eddy felt Laura near his elbow, her silent offer of help. Alf meanwhile had, thankfully, moved on and was chatting up another woman.

'You'd better get your wallet out, you're buying these guys drinks.' He looked down at Tom's jeans and was grateful to see a wallet-sized bulge in the pocket.

'Oh, Jesus. Oh, God. Three million dollars! I said no to three million dollars.'

'You're apparently paying for these drinks, mate?' the bar man asked him.

'No! Oh, God, I'll pay for what's done, but no more! Stop ordering! Happy hour's over!'

'Happy fucking minute more like it,' said one bikie.

Eddy said: 'There's still time, Tom. You've got the guy's number.'

Tom was crying, as he pawed at his groin, trying to dig his wallet out of his pocket. 'What have I done? I see it now, Eddy, I've fucked up totally. After all these years, after losing my marriage, I was there, I was there on the doorstep of greatness, of wealth, and what happens? I fuck it up. I get greedy and fuck it up.'

'It's not that bad.'

'It's not?'

'Well, I don't know that you were ever on the doorstep of greatness.'

Tom wept on. 'It's Grace. She would never have let me do that. She would have made me take that first offer, and she would have been right. She's my compass, she's my business sense. I am nothing without her, nothing.'

'She's—'

'I wanted to teach her a lesson mate. I wanted to punish her, so I left. I owe her everything. I owed it to her not to fuck it up at the last minute, but I did. I did.'

'Well, I don't—' Eddy exchanged glances with Laura.

'You're right! You're absolutely right! It was that arsehole ...' Tom pointed bitterly across the room at Tank. 'It's his fault. I'm going to *have* him.' He lunged across the table, tripped on a chair and fell.

Eddy pulled him into an upright position. 'Calm down.'

Tom was searching his pockets. 'I'm going to ring them now. I'm going to accept their offer. Maybe it's not too late.'

'Tom, it's nearly midnight, man. Might be a bit late to call. And you're not exactly at your best.'

'I must! I have to do it for Grace.' He turned his pockets inside out and looked around wildly. 'That fucker! He took my phone, didn't he! I remember now. Who the fuck is he, coming out of nowhere and fucking up my whole life? Why did you bring him, Eddy? Why?'

Eddy looked at Laura, who winced sympathetically. 'He just sort of came, Tom. I couldn't stop him.'

Tom shook his head. 'Never leave a good woman. Never leave a good woman, mate.' He beckoned Eddy forward and made an exaggerated attempt to speak behind his hand, although the words came out loud and clear. 'I heard

Romy's come back to you. Heard she's living back at your place.'

Eddy froze, his eyes swiveling towards Laura. She paled, her mouth slack and open. She stared back at him. He turned to her and spoke hastily.

'It's my ex-girlfriend, she had nowhere to go. She means nothing to me.'

Tom leaned forward again. 'And I heard she's pregnant. Due any minute. God, is that a moment.' He slumped back in the chair and stared unseeingly up at the ceiling of the pub. 'Watching your baby born. Watching her slither into the world, better than the best fortune you'll ever have. That, that is better than three million dollars, better than ...'

Eddy didn't hear any more, because he was chasing Laura as she marched, white-faced, out of the hotel. 'Laura, stop! Let me explain.'

Outside, the air was sweet and fresh after the fug of the bar. Lights streamed through the door, making a golden rectangle on the bitumen under his feet. He stepped out into the dark, towards her back, thankful she had stopped walking. Stars twinkled above the car park. God, he was drunk. Please don't let him throw up.

She turned to face him, her arms crossed over her chest, her eyes filled with tears.

'I thought you were different. Why do I always meet the arseholes?'

He was shocked by her grief, touched by it. He took her shoulders gently and hunched his tall frame to stare into her eyes.

'Romy is my old girlfriend. She dumped me almost a year ago and she turned up the other day, pregnant to another guy and about to give birth, with nowhere to stay.

She asked if she could come back, just until she found somewhere else to live, and I said yes.'

Laura turned on him a silent look. *Sure*, that look said. *Like I'd believe that.* Then she looked down at her feet.

'It's true. What else could I have said?'

There was a long silence, while they stood inches apart. A car reversed out and drove away. A couple swung past them, entered the bar and silence resumed.

'I could have said no,' Eddy answered himself thoughtfully. 'It's not my baby.'

Laura met his eyes.

Eddy shrugged, suddenly exhausted and dispirited and tired of his failures with women. Tired of the inevitable ruin. 'You can ask Grace if you want to. Call her now and ask her, she knows the story.'

Laura spoke, her voice thin and tremulous. 'Why would you take her back, if she dumped you and came back pregnant to another guy? No one would do that.'

He stared at her, grim and resigned. Okay, now it would all turn to shit. Just like Romy, Laura had seen him for the spineless wimp he was. Too soft. His father was right. And yet, that was who he was. He couldn't have done things any differently.

'I guess that's the sort of dickhead I am.' And he turned and walked back to the door of the pub. He was sick of apologising for himself. Sick of feeling guilty for caring about people. Stupid, selfish people, who didn't deserve it.

She ran after him and grabbed him by the arm, pulled him back and made him turn around.

'I believe you,' she whispered. 'It *is* just the sort of dickhead you are.'

Eddy sighed. 'She is nothing to me anymore.'

'Good.'

And they kissed, out there under the stars, the door opening and closing behind them, a motorbike revving away, oblivious to it all.

Skipper spoke from the back of the car. 'Nemen, when the lights are green, you go.'

'Okay.' Melody agreed. She settled into the passenger seat of Grace's car and directed her eyes away from the dashboard clock. Had they really had to leave at six? Was she ever going to get into the spirit of the dreaming camp with Grace on board? She breathed deep, and felt oxygen enter her lower lungs. At least they could have a couple of days away to celebrate all the work of the past few weeks.

'An', nemen, when they're red, you have to stop.'

'Sure, Skip. So! Here we are!'

Grace frowned and clung to the steering wheel. 'Do you know the way? I need to stop and get the oil checked.'

Melody breathed deeply and exhaled slowly. Grace had been able to borrow a car, and while Melody had planned to catch the train and hitchhike to the dreaming camp, a close look at the map had revealed that there would be little traffic going to such an out-of-the-way place. The universe might provide, but, then again, she could find herself on the side of the road with a four-year-old and a backpack, in the middle of a rainy night. The universe might provide little more than a stern lesson, which Melody wasn't really in the mood for receiving. And maybe Grace's presence was the universe's way of providing. She tucked a feather back into the nest of her dreadlocks. 'Shall we play I-spy, kids?'

'Yeah!' shouted Lotte. 'I spy wi mi-liddli ...'

'Can you tune in the radio, so we get the weather forecast?'

Melody ignored Grace and felt her spirits lift. With feathers threaded through her hair, she wore flared purple leggings with a short striped dress over the top. She had Indian chains on her ankles, a new gold ring in her nose, and she liked the sensation of being Melody, herself, again. She was shaking off all that TV energy. Melody tried not to think of it as negative energy, because it had brought her positive things. It had brought them money, and they had met some good people. But it was a weird space to be in.

She tuned in to a good song.

'No, no, we need the weather,' said Grace.

'I'll give you the forecast, oh spacey Gracey. A weekend of vegetarian food around a forest fire, with the retelling of Aboriginal dreaming stories by a wise elder of the tribe. Kindred spirits, the gentle crunch of leaf litter underfoot, our children running wild and feral, eating from the communal pot and playing in the communal teepee—'

Grace groaned. 'Followed by chanting and group sex, after which we smear ourselves with the semen of the guru and await the end of the world—'

'What's semen, Mummy?'

'It's a man of the sea, darling. Like a sailor.'

'Is he going to be there?'

'Who?'

'The semen?'

'No. I mean, yes ... I hope the studio can cope without us.'

'I don't need to be back in the studio until Sunday.'

'Are you sure we're all going to fit in your tent? It didn't look very big.'

'What tent?' Melody sat back and watched the paddocks

turn green. She wondered if Van might turn up to the camp. Probably not with that reward out on his head.

'The one in the back. That big bag, thing.'

'That's not a tent. It's a swag. You don't need a tent with a swag.'

Grace stared at her furiously. 'You said you'd organise a tent!'

'And I will! Don't stress!' Melody reached out and patted the shoulder of this woman who had become her unlikely friend. For whatever reason, they had been brought together, and Grace was being taken to a corner of the world that she would never have visited before. Melody was overcome with a feeling of warmth towards her, and shame for scaring her. 'There's teepees there, Grace. You and Lotte will be able to find a place inside them, no problem.'

'I'm not sharing with strangers.'

Melody sighed and watched a strip of shops flash past. This wasn't the way. 'Where are you going?'

'I just want to drop by Eddy's, and ... borrow some camping gear.'

'It's seven o'clock! And I just *told* you ...'

'Okay, okay, I want to see if he's back yet, from wherever they all were last night. My God, they sounded drunk. It won't take a minute.'

'Grace! What do you really want from Eddy's?'

Grace sighed. 'I want to find out whether Miss Laura was out on a date with Tom last night.'

'Oh, who cares? Let's just go to the camp. Please?'

'Okay.' Grace subsided sulkily.

CHAPTER TWENTY

Eddy had had four very different orgasms throughout the night. One, he would have described as a sort of purple colour, as if the long evening of his arousal by Miss Laura had inflamed the world. The next orgasm had been a light grassy green, a sweet, spiritual floating through space, under golden tree arbors and through fern. Looking back, he thought he might have smiled at the moment of climax. The third had come after a short sleep, when he had woken with a mad itch in his genitals, driven crazy by the woman beside him, her full breasts, her dark nipples, the territory which he jealously wanted to claim all over again. He had fucked then like a teenager, selfishly and wildly wanting to scratch that itch. Then she had woken him at dawn, her naked body crouched over his, kissing his mouth, down his chest, down his stomach ... He was a lost man, drowning in pleasure, and his fourth orgasm was a gently blissful one, pale pink and deliciously sleepy as she sat astride him.

He held her as if she might fly away, the force of her orgasm sending her into another land, her eyes closing, her neck stretching. He saw her face twist and thought, I did that. She fell down across him and he stroked her shoulder, shrinking comfortably inside her. Come back, he called to her silently. Come back.

At last she breathed deeply and lifted herself. Dragged her wrist out of the tangle of limbs and bedclothes and blinked at her watch.

'Shit.' She lay back beside him, in the hotel room bed. Her breathing was long and deep, the skin of her arm touching his the whole way along. He smiled at the ceiling, feeling the tendrils of her life entwining with his already. She was going to be late for work, he would help if he could. From such small foundations, big things grew. He lay on his side so he could see her face.

'Hello.'

'Mmm. Hello.' She smiled sleepily, wrinkling her nose. Her cheeks were pink.

'Can we do room service breakfast? Or should I call you a taxi to get to work?' He felt washed clean of his frantic lust, enough to self-consciously wonder whether he had revealed too much of himself, been too much of an animal. He wanted, now, to be a gentleman. With Romy, he had nurtured and cared for her, and if he had performed well enough in this regard, and a suitable period of time had passed since the last encounter, she might consent to have sex. There was always a sort of rolled-eye tolerance of his male urges, and he always felt slightly guilty afterwards. Sex four times in one night, as just committed, would have incurred a frighteningly large nurturing liability. Thus, he attempted to quickly start repayments.

She leaned over and kissed him. 'Don't *you* have to get to work?'

'No one will care if I'm late.' This wasn't strictly true, but he could easily text Alf and ask him to cover for him.

Although who knew where Alf might be, and whether he had made it back to the city in time for work. 'I want to take you to kindy, Miss Laura.' He kissed her on the shoulder, butterfly kisses.

He was getting hard again. It was a national miracle. He was probably going to do himself some sort of damage. And she had a job to get to. He sat up, and pulled her to a sitting position. 'Okay, I'm going to stop this now. There are a whole bunch of four-year-olds waiting for you.'

Laura rolled her eyes and swung her feet to the floor. She pulled on her panties slowly, sensible white Bonds-style numbers, and then settled her breasts into a serviceable, flesh-coloured bra, all the while eyeing his erection. 'I don't think you really want me to go to work, Eddy.'

He looked at her sternly and pulled on his pants. 'I most certainly do.'

Melody stirred the lentils and sighed. The canvas shelter covering the camp kitchen sagged with the weight of the morning's rain, and water dripped perilously close to the sacks of basmati rice. Somehow the kitchen, stocked with food and apparently no one to cook it, had become the domain of herself and Grace. Not that Grace was present at that moment; she was immersed in a session on kundalini energy in the tent next door, which Melody could hear over the gentle drizzle of rain falling from soaked eucalyptus trees.

'Reach down and feel the base of your spine, where your kundalini energy sits coiled, ready to spring up and cleanse you to the top of your skull with white light. Only your inner blockages are stopping you from achieving your full power, your inner emotional and spiritual plugs, like clogs of phlegm stopping you from achieving a full life of abundance ...'

They had arrived that morning, after a trip in which Lotte had vomited in the car and they had had to drive for the rest of the trip with the windows open to escape the smell. When they finally bumped down the last stretch of dirt track, they encountered the sign *Camp*. The words *Aboriginal Dreamtime*, which had once preceded the word *Camp*, had been crossed out and slapped with a flier across the top of it. Melody got out and read the fine print.

The indigenous people of this area, being the tribes of Moorta Moorta and Taten Wurrung, would like to advise participants of this function that there has been NO involvement by local indigenous groups, and NO permission given to tell our dreaming stories. We demand that the organisers refrain from continuing the despicable and insidious practice of colonising our culture. If participants want to spend their money in support of the Koori community, we suggest they do so through reputable means.

'Is this the Abiginaldeamtum camp?' demanded Skip, standing behind her.

'Well, it's the camp.' Grace had said wryly. 'I'm so glad I brought my gumboots.'

Now, Melody added asafoetida powder and wondered whether the city was corrupting her. There were voices in her head, expressing cynicism and doubt about everything. Okay, so this camp wasn't quite what they had paid for. Okay, so it didn't have quite the feel she had imagined. The leader, Pemangku Lodan, had not been seen and had spent the whole time in his teepee, with two girls in their early twenties, flushed with smug importance (and hopefully nothing else) coming and going to him with food and drinks and joints. A woman had had a terrible acid trip that morning and had lain in a foetal position on the ground weeping, convinced that the clouds were on their way down to crush them all with their force and beauty. An ambulance had arrived to collect her, bumping down the track and ejecting paramedics who looked about them with disapproval. A bevy of local lads had turned up with a slab of beer in the transparent hope of picking up hippy chicks, and had been sternly sent packing by a couple of thin young men in dreadlocks. (They're *our* hippy chicks, was the unspoken rebuff.) The removal of Aboriginal Dreamtime from the syllabus had left a massive hole in proceedings, hastily filled with a mish-mash of kabbalah teachings, kundalini exercises, and a tantric workshop. The children, initially promised an enlightening programme of dreamtime stories, boomerang throwing and indigenous painting, were probably having the best time of anyone. They had been gathered, many of them plastered now with mud, beside a vast granite rock where they were painting pictures on the surface with paints that the hippy running it assured Melody would wash off in the next storm, which looked set to be in about five minutes. Melody stirred her pot and watched them absently.

It was at this point that Grace's phone, sitting on a sack of basmati rice where she had left it, rang. Melody picked it up. 'Hello?'

Nothing. Was that heavy breathing, or just the wind preceding the next storm? 'Hello?'

'Hell— Ohhh ... Grace?'

It was a woman's voice, either crying or under great strain. Melody froze? 'Romy?'

'Can I — speak — to Grace.'

'Wait. I'll get her.'

She entered the big tent, and was faced by a strange sight. All the members of this workshop, about forty in total, had been seated in a circle on the floor with their legs ahead of them and parted, their bottoms neatly pressed up against the crotch of the person behind. They were fully clothed, thankfully, but the sexual element in the air was present, and a couple of men and women were groaning, whether in discomfort or pleasure was hard to deduce.

Melody sought through the half-light for her friend and found her on the other side of the tent, looking pained. She paused, standing close to the instructor, and noticed the sign *tantric* beside her. The instructor, a man in a loin cloth and a white T-shirt was ordering everyone to close their mouths and breathe through their noses only.

'Faster! Faster!'

What on earth would Grace be making of this? wondered Melody, straining to see her friend's expression. It didn't seem like her thing at all. The man spoke again.

'Now, everyone lie back. Lie back and relax on the front of the person behind you. Open your legs and make room for the person in front. Arch your back if you need.'

The tent filled with movement, some grunts and a few murmured apologies. Melody edged around the side to see Grace.

She found her sandwiched between a man who would have been aged no more than 20 on the bottom, and a big man in his fifties on the top. Grace was flailing helplessly, tears in her eyes as she pushed against the shoulder of the big man, who seemed to be trying but unable to gain the momentum to pull himself up.

Melody gave him a big push sideways into the centre of the circle, and he rolled off Grace and onto his hands and knees, apologising profusely. Grace quickly rolled out of the circle and crouched over her groin. Melody squatted beside her. 'Are you alright?'

'God, he was *crushing* me. I'm going to be bruised all over. What *is* this thing?'

Melody sighed. 'Sorry. Hey, you've got a call from Romy, on the mobile.'

Grace stared. Melody said: 'I think she might be in labour.'

Minutes later, still furtively rubbing her groin and wincing, Grace rejoined Melody at the camp stove.

'Rom's having the baby.'

'Now?'

'She wants us to come. She has no one.'

'And what did you say?'

Grace winced. 'I said I didn't know if we could. I mean, you've been looking forward to this all year. We've only just arrived.'

Melody stared around herself at the mud, the soggy tents, the water now leaking into the basmati rice and the children's rock painting, already running down the sandstone face.

Grace said: 'She should have had someone organised. I hardly know her. It's only that I saw her last night.'

'Eddy?'

'She said she tried him. He's not home, and he didn't answer.'

'Should we call her an ambulance? They'd be there long

before us anyway. It would take us an hour to pack up. And an hour more to get back to her.'

'She's worried about the police. There's a reward out on her. She'd be arrested if they found her.'

'I guess it wouldn't take us a whole hour to pack up.'

'No?'

'Actually we could do it in five minutes.' Melody stared at Grace, and the two of them grew still, thinking.

'Maybe ...'

'Let's go. Let's get out of here.' Melody turned the gas stove off and put a lid on the lentils.

'Just like that?' Grace looked breathlessly hopeful.

Melody took one last look around herself and knew that it would indeed be just like that. In a life where she had always honored her impulses, she knew she had to embrace the one now gripping her; to get out of this scene and never come back, ever, to anything like it. Romy's baby was merely the best of excuses.

'Just like that.'

Tom gradually became aware of a ringing sound. It went on and on, and then it stopped. Then it started again. He wondered if it was coming from his head. He opened one eye, and found himself in close visual proximity to a tussock of grass, that appeared to be growing through a crack in the dirt. Or was it not dirt, but bitumen? Whatever it was, he was lying on it and it was hard. He blinked slowly, and it hurt. Everything hurt. He spent some time watching a couple of ants going up and down the grass blades, moving erratically and fast. Maybe the ringing was coming from the ants. Then it stopped.

He tried to move, and pain surged through his body and his head. If he was lying on bitumen, was he on a road? That was not good. Could a car come? Should he roll off? He forced himself to lift his head. Two adult shoes with feet and legs in them appeared to be not far from him, the soles at right angles to the bitumen. He craned his neck back more, and groaned with pain as he did. He could see a whole man now, in a suit, lying on the road. He looked familiar, although the sight of him provoked in Tom an antipathy, the cause of which he had yet to put his finger on. How had they got here? The ringing started again. Maybe it was not from the ants. It seemed to be coming from the man.

It was that lawyer guy, who worked with Eddy. The wanker. Tom collapsed back onto the road in pain. He rolled onto his back and started to feel his arms, his shoulders, his chest. Was he dead? Did he have any broken bones?

Alf Tankhouse opened his eyes, and reached inside his dusty suit jacket. He struggled to one elbow, and winced with pain, although he climbed to his feet more quickly than Tom could have contemplated for his own body, and held a phone to his ear.

'Alf Tankhouse.' His voice was clear, and authoritative. He could have been in an office with city views and thick carpet, rather than on a road verge with blood and dirt on his face. He looked down and met Tom's eyes.

'I see. No, my client is in a meeting at the moment …' Tom sagged back on his arm, and watched a baby magpie land on the road nearby, eyeing him as if he might be a giant and tasty worm. Alf continued. 'It's a pity you can't come to the table on what we've asked …' Tom remembered all now. Jesus Christ. He wished he didn't. *You can't come to the table* … And that would be the sound of three million dollars swirling down the plughole. 'But he may be prepared to at least hear your new offer. Although I must say he is in discussions with another group at the moment, so you might be too late. Oh actually here he is, he's just coming out of that meeting. If he's got a spare minute he might even be able to talk to you himself. Stephanie, could you hold Mr Ellison's calls for the next ten minutes ...' Alf turned to address the baby magpie, who skittered over the bitumen and eyed him back. 'Mr Ellison, can you possibly spare a minute to talk to Simon Factor, UMI?'

Tom's mouth fell open. He struggled up to a sitting position, and looked down at himself. His suit pants were torn slightly at the crotch seam; and again in the lower right leg. His good shoes were scratched, the knuckles of his right hand had blood on them. The last thing he remembered was trying to hug one of the bikies, and then Alf and someone else was fighting, and then there were a lot of boots swinging at him ... He struggled to his feet, staggered to the right and caught hold of a tree, before sinking gratefully into a bush.

Tank watched stonefaced, still holding the phone. 'Actually he may have to rush off to a meeting ...'

Tom staggered up and seized the phone from the lawyer. He glowered at him and cleared his throat. 'Hello. Mr Factor. Tom Ellison here. I'm glad you rang, I've been wanting to talk to you about your offer of yesterday. It's—'

The voice on the phone cut through him. 'I'm glad you can spare me the time, Mr Ellison. I just wanted to say that while we can't *quite* meet your price of twenty million with ten per cent royalties ...'

'Yes, that was what I ...' Tom croaked, his voice breaking up again. The trees were spinning and Mr Factor talked on.

'We've talked with our board and we can improve our original offer. We could offer *eight* million dollars, with ten per cent royalties, for a South Pacific market ...'

'Eight million dollars?' Tom blinked and shook his head. Did he have concussion? 'With ten per cent royalties ...'

Tank grinned. He gave Tom a thumbs-up sign and held out his hand, raising his eyebrows in a question.

Tom nodded. Dizziness and nausea were just about to overcome him, but with his eyes locked on Tank's, he made his voice as brisk as he could. 'Well, Mr Factor, that sounds ... acceptable. How about I pass you back to my lawyer and he can sort out the small print with you? I've got a meeting to attend.'

He handed Alf the phone and stumbled through the bush, trying to get a few metres away before he threw up. Afterwards, he leaned on a tree, stared out over a view of the far-off city skyline and the rolling hills, and he felt what it was to reach his own personal mountain top. Battered, hungover, weary and heartsick, he tried to make it matter. Eight million dollars! Eight million dollars! What would he do with it all? But really, he was faking. It didn't feel as good as he had imagined. There were only two people he wanted to be with right now, sharing this news. And only when he told them, and crowded them both into his arms, would it feel real.

CHAPTER TWENTY-ONE

Grace looked out the window of Eddy Plenty's lounge room and wiped her forehead. Eddy's bedroom, which she had just left, looked like a slaughterhouse. The sheets, carpet and mattress would all need to be thrown away. Romy was screaming for Eddy.

'You couldn't just drop by for five minutes? It would really, really help her to see you,' Grace had pleaded with Eddy earlier.

'Grace, she's in labour. There's only one thing that's going to help her.'

'Drugs?'

'Well yes, but I meant having the baby. Would help.'

'She keeps calling for you.'

'It's a verbal tic. She spent five years calling for me in every crisis of her life. "Eddy" is just another word for "Mummy". She doesn't know who she's calling for.'

'Oh yes she does. Please.'

'No. I'm with Laura, we're having a day together.'

'Are you scared? Do you think if you see her on this day, you might become ensnared?'

'Maybe. No.'

'I thought you were a stronger man than that.'

'Well, you were wrong.'

In the lounge room, Skip circled the room with a digital camera, and clicked relentlessly at puzzling things. He took pictures of pictures, he lined up Lotte, who was sucking an icy pole in front of the television. He took pictures of her feet, knees and face.

'Mmmmrrrrwwaaaaggghhh!' screamed Romy, from the bedroom. Skip took a photo of the nearest door, as if testing to see whether he could capture a noise that did indeed almost seem tangible. Lotte turned an anxious face.

'Mummy?'

Grace sat behind her, on the couch. 'Don't worry. The lady's having a baby.'

'When?'

'Soon.'

'Why is she so noisy?'

'Because it hurts.'

'It didn't hurt you.'

'When you were born?' Grace said. 'Oh yes it did.'

'Why?'

'It always does.'

'Then why do people do it?'

Grace sighed. 'I don't know. It's what we do.'

Skip brought a bowl and put it in Lotte's lap, to catch the drips from her icy pole. There was another scream from the rooms beyond, and Grace buried her face in her daughter's silken hair, and turned up the television. Skip snapped his way around the lounge room. Lotte's butterfly shoes; snap. He lined up three remote controls and leaned over them; snap.

'Can I see your photos?'

He handed Grace the camera and showed her how to flick back through the hundreds of shots he had taken. Some of herself and Melody. Every adult's face taken from below; with double chins from looking down at him, their smiles genuine and affectionate. About twenty of a bowl of chips.

'Aaaarrrgghhh!' The cry was a higher-pitched one, and Grace hoped things were moving along. It might be time she went back and offered to relieve Melody.

'Mummy, there's a man at the door.'

Grace sat on the corrugated iron of Eddy's garage roof and watched as Tom, her ex-husband, stood at the back door and frowned. He was wearing a suit. She was hidden by an overgrown jasmine vine and she could smell the tiny white-petalled flowers. She had fled on tiptoe out the back of Eddy's house, and up a trellis to this place. She had glimpsed Eddy and Tom and Laura as Lotte ran to let them in, and she had run away, like the most foolish of girls. Tom was with Lotte's kindergarten teacher; how *could* he? An easy, uncomplicated, child-loving woman. A tear rolled down her cheek and she leaned back a little, to ensure she was covered by the overhanging branch of the cherry tree from next door. The cherries were ripe and bursting off the branches; some had fallen on the iron roof and baked on. Melody would be collecting these if she lived here, gathering the fruit and dropping them all in a saucepan on the stove, until the flesh melted away and the pips could be scooped out with a slotted spoon. She would make jam. Grace found a dark one and took a tentative nibble, the juice dribbling onto her bare legs. The branch suddenly shook alarmingly, and she looked through the leaves to see Tom, climbing up to her.

She nervously moved along a little, to give him room to swing onto the roof. The branches arched over them in a protective shelter of green-filtered light, providing spyholes onto the back yard.

'I think Skip kicked a ball up here,' she said. 'I was just looking for it.'

'Can I help?'

She shrugged. 'Whatever.'

He lowered himself onto the roof, and placed his bottom, clad in what she knew to be his only suit pants, onto a patch of burst plums. Never had a man cared less about clothes, or had less value for possessions. Would the same things drive Laura crazy? Maybe she was more relaxed, more young and carefree than Grace. Oh, Grace had been young and carefree once, but then the mortgage and the baby came, and the hunger, the hunger for more of everything that for so long had seemed insatiable. Had it eased? She couldn't exactly say, although maybe she had managed to put an arm's length between her and it. The hunger was like an irritating neighbour now, rather than a tenant.

Tom appeared to register the sensation of wet fruit through his pants, looked and wrinkled up his nose, and moved aside a little. 'I knew you were out here somewhere.' His only suit, now she could see it clearly, was dusty and smelled faintly of beer. The hem of his right trouser leg had come down, a thread trailing from the flapping material. There was a hole around the crotch. Close up, he looked like a street hobo. He settled and looked at her. 'How's things?'

'Oh, you know. Just waiting.'

'For what?'

'For Romy to have her baby.'

'Ah.' He looked back toward the house. 'I think she's at the business end.'

'Can you hear her?' He had always had better hearing than she; they had joked that she would be the deaf old lady and he would be her ear trumpet.

He cocked his head and nodded. 'You can't?'

She shook her head and he smiled.

'So, how's Laura?' she asked.

He blinked. 'She's good, I think. She's here, inside.'

Grace nodded, bravely. 'Right.' Why was he suddenly so friendly? Then she realised. He was going to tell her about Laura. About their new love. He knew it would hurt her. This was why he was being kind. So unlike the last times.

He took a leaf in his hand and tore it into small pieces, his forearms resting on his knees as he did. 'I've got some pretty unbelievable news.'

'Oh?' she said stiffly. Her head spun. She was too high off the ground, to hear such news. Especially if it involved Laura. 'I might just climb down to the ground, actually.'

'I've sold the invention. The roof.'

She stared at him. The plastic-bottle solar powered roof. His dream. 'To who?'

'United Materials Inc.' He leaned close. 'Eight. Million. Dollars.'

Eight million dollars?

'Eight million dollars.'

She felt her stomach falling out of her body, down through the roof beneath her and into the earth. 'You're ... You can't ...'

'I signed the paperwork this afternoon. Eight. Million. Dollars.'

She tried to take it in. Her mouth had fallen open; she closed it. He stared at her face, as if drinking in every change of expression.

'Oh, Tom.' She shook her head finally. 'That's ... Well, congratulations.'

'Yeah.'

'You earned it.' Grace felt a lump in her throat. She was so proud of him.

He nodded, his eyes full of tears, his whole being focused on her. 'Grace ...'

The screen door banged shut and Laura stood, hands in her jeans pockets, her face screwed up against the sun. Looking for Tom, no doubt. Grace had a dull ache in her stomach, in the place where her love for Tom lived. Guilt. Disappointment in herself. Not a new feeling, not at all. But all she could really do was watch Laura as she wandered closer, until she was standing right below them. Any moment now Tom would call out to her. But Tom kept staring at her, Grace.

The door slammed again and Eddy strode out, urgent and pale, rubbing his face. Laura turned to him and, to Grace's amazement, Eddy loped across his backyard to Laura and wrapped his arms around her.

She turned to Tom. 'Oh.'

'What?'

'Are Eddy and Laura ...?'

'Oh. Yeah. Apparently.' He shrugged, not interested.

'Eddy's seeing Laura? Not you?'

'Me? No!'

'Oh.'

'I haven't seen anyone since we split up. All I've done is work on the solar roof.'

'But my mother saw you with someone! In the IGA.'

He frowned. 'That's right. She was a woman I used to work with. We had just run into each other when we were shopping and then your mother walked past while we were talking.'

'It wasn't Laura?'

He looked incredulous. 'What's all this about Miss Laura?'

'Nothing. *Eight million dollars?* Is that what you said?'

'It is.'

'I'm sorry. I can't ...'

'I know. I can't either. And Grace? I couldn't have done it without you.'

She shook her head. 'But you *did* do it without me. I'm *so* sorry. I doubted you. You did it, and I doubted you. I'm ashamed of myself. Not just because you made it. I've been ashamed of myself for ages. I should have believed in you. Even if you failed a hundred times over, I should have believed in you.'

'You did believe in me. I know you did.'

'No, I didn't. I mean I did for a while, but then ... I lost faith.'

'You helped me,' he said, taking her hand. 'Truly. You and Lotte. You are the reason I kept trying. You believed in me for so long, I wouldn't have got this far without you believing in me for so long, back before all this. Gracie, when I heard the news about the deal, after all this time, it meant nothing to me without you. It meant nothing until I could tell you, and share it with you. I don't care about it, even, actually!' He shook his head in disbelief. 'All I want is to be back with you. And Lotte. Like we were. I would give up all the money.'

His face was ruddy with dirt; she could see dark specks in his pores. His eyes were wide and unblinking. She realised she had been waiting, through this whole conversation, for him to get up and leave her, head off to something or someone more interesting, more important. And yet here he was, totally focused on her, breathing quickly, staring into her eyes as if searching for something lost down a well.

He was back.

'Really?'

'I *miss* you, Grace.'

'Oh, me, too. I miss you, too, so much.' She pressed her fingers into her eyes, a sob rising from her chest like a bubble, embarrassing her with its noise.

Laura and Eddy's anxious voices rose beneath them, and there was a crash inside the house. Eddy squinted up at them. 'Romy's had a baby boy,' he said. 'Healthy. And Van's here.'

'Van,' said Tom, massaging Grace's fingers, and she raised wet eyes to his.

Van. The baby's father.

Inside the house, Melody watched Van hold his brand-new baby son. He gently unwound the white flannel wrap and there was the tiny little boy, a peg on his umbilical cord, streaks of blood on his bloated stomach, and vernix in the creases of his rubbery doll legs. The baby's eyelids parted, and the swimming black eyes inside seemed to float across the surface of his father's face, as if digitally scanning him. He rested safe in Van's tattooed and muscular arms. Van, who had initially looked as though he would run in the front door of the house and out just as quickly, gently lowered himself into a chair, as if he might, after all, stay some time.

'Van, you shouldn't stay,' Melody murmured. Her skin

prickled. The air was full of warning; the curtains rustled with danger, the wardrobe urged flight. Never had a domestic bedroom felt so loaded, as if it were the very innards of a gun, waiting to fire. Van had burst in the door, looking behind him as if the angels of Hell were chasing him, terror on his face. Melody had gently closed and locked the door behind him, her heart pounding faster and faster, even as Van and Romy grew utterly hypnotised by the small creature they had created. Romy picked up a little wrist and turned over the hand; Van leaned in to study the baby's eyes, as if he could hear the baby speaking some language beyond the world, some message being passed from one life to the next.

Melody heard a car roll to a gentle stop out the front of the house. She knew straight away; didn't have to go look out the front to see. A shadow passed the window and she stared at it; heard the leaves rustling below the window.

Police were surrounding the house.

No, no, she was delirious. She was delusional, overtired from hours of watching a labouring woman; she should shut up and get out and leave Van and Romy alone with their new baby. What on earth was wrong with her?

She left and shut the bedroom door behind her. She lifted a corner of the lounge-room blind. Just evening peak-hour traffic, cars passing in each direction. An ordinary suburban car was parked out the front; no lights. The roof was bare. In fact there were two cars of the same make. She was just lowering the blind when she glimpsed a strange black stick protruding from a grove of trees in the corner of the front yard. Then a black knee. A gloved hand was raised and a signal made across the yard.

She had been right. The shadows were surrounding them.

She ran on tiptoe back to the room, not wanting the floorboards to give away her haste. Opening the bedroom door, she took the baby firmly from Van and handed him back to Romy. She pulled Van to his feet and pointed to the window.

'Police. They're surrounding the house. Go out the back. *Run.*'

Van met Romy's eyes, and for a second Melody thought Romy might try to run with him, might drag her sorry body and her newly born fragment of flesh out into the world, to join him as the hunted, as the prey. But then Romy folded the bunny rug over the little boy and, tears rolling down her face, she put her fingers on Van's chest, on his leather jacket and pushed him.

'Go.'

Outside, Eddy bit into a cherry, the rust from the roof of the garage scraping the backs of his legs. He and Laura had climbed the tree and onto the roof, to this perch which overlooked the yard, the road over the fence, and the back door of his home.

He had never seen his house from this vantage point before. He really needed to clean the gutters. And then he raised his eyes further.

Why was there a man all in black standing on his next-door neighbour's roof, with a gun trained on his garden? In fact, not one man, but two?

The back door suddenly flew open to release Van, a streak of black leather legs and black T-shirt, a streak of red and blue tattoo on his upper arm, where the leather jacket was falling off his shoulder, and a belt which glinted in the western sun. A face still young, too young and tender for the fierceness upon it, the bitter focus, the fear.

Eddy looked back at the two men on his neighbour's roof and realised all. He could hear but not yet see an approaching helicopter. Pirate and Cat had finally been cornered. He and Tom and Laura and Grace inhaled and clambered to their knees and their feet, rising like the crowd at a football game.

It happened so quickly. Van fled across the back yard and one policeman fired, missed and fell, sliding down the roof and dropping on his back into the bush. The other cop crouched to one knee and fired wildly, but Van had ducked behind the barbecue and was now leaping up the cherry tree to their eyrie, making it shake as he landed on it with his biker boots, and crossed it in two strides, for one moment agonisingly open to fire. Grace and Laura shrieked and dropped to the roof, covering their heads. Van stepped from the roof to the fence, teetered along it for a moment, like a cat, and jumped off it, down to the footpath and the road, out of sight and away.

Eddy held his breath, watching the cop on the roof swivel with his gun. Only the copper's trained eye on the gun's sights told him Van had recovered from the jump, was winding his way through traffic that they could hear but not see, and that he stood a chance yet of making it to the other side. The police helicopter was right overhead now, its belly low, beating the air with its blades.

And then, a massive crash. Not a gunshot, but cars colliding. The cop on the roof froze for a second and then loosened up, and slung his rifle over his shoulder. He began carefully and methodically making his way down from the roof. These things told Eddy the end of the story. A woman screamed. More cars screeched to a halt, and there was a second smash, then a third. Eddy was thrown back to the moment at the beginning of that year, when little Lotte had also made a dash for freedom, throwing herself into the river of traffic like a bomb, changing his life forever. Running. Running for dear life. Running for the joy of it, for escape, running towards her own future.

Romy appeared at the back door of his house, a bundle in her arms, and screamed.

'Van! No!'

Skipper appeared behind her, a camera held to his eye, and in the silence after Romy's scream, Eddy heard the camera click.

CHAPTER TWENTY-TWO

Q*antas today laid off four hundred employees, in the latest mass jobs casualty to hit Australian workers. Unions said the cuts would bring to sixteen hundred the number out of work in the aviation industry this year, and accused the airline of using the global financial crisis as a Trojan horse to bring in low-service air travel. Meanwhile, Qantas shares jumped two point five per cent at news of the cut ...*

Melody shut her eyes and submitted her face to the last-minute ministrations of the makeup artist. The air on the back of her neck felt strangely cool, and carried too much of the world in it. The brush dabbed intimately into the corners of her eyes, beneath her jaw, behind her ears. Lights flashed, glinting across black metal and glass, sliding on silent wheels. Men in sagging jeans and torn runners pushed million-dollar machinery about. She felt thin, stripped naked without her dreadlocks, lost within a low-cut red dress, and, most of all, hammered and crushed beneath the weight of Van's death. She had died a little with him the day before, she knew, had seen a part of her own soul fly up above the snarls of twisted metal on that road, a bumper bar clanging as it fell on the bitumen, that last car skidding into place as if it were hurrying to complete a puzzle. It turned side-on and smashed into the other three already piled up in a mess of spinning wheels and smoking engines. Even as Van flew up in the air like a doll, gone before he fell back onto the car which had hit him, she had felt part of her soul leave her, fly off with his own as it parted with his body and ran for whatever heavenly hills it could see.

Can we cut your hair? the television people had asked, when they rang soon after. The weather presenter had gone into early labour and they needed a fill-in. Sure, she had said dully.

We might have to change your, er, image a little. Dress you differently. That's fine, she had said.

'But the horoscopes? You'll need your dreadlocks for that,' Grace had said, panicked.

Anthea Schulberg had cleared her throat. 'Well, I was going to tell you next week, but horoscopes have actually been axed,' she had confessed. 'The board didn't like it. So this weather gig could save Melody's job.'

Melody couldn't care less. Suck me into the future, life, because this pain of separation, violence and loss has left me for dead. Let me hand this body over to the ghouls of television, because if Van has been crucified, so have I.

'How are you feeling?' Anthea leaned before her, and smiled warmly. 'Not nervous?'

'Not at all,' said Melody. There was not room for nervousness in her soul, aching as it was. She could see the headlines of the stories as they passed on the monitor, and she rose to her feet, gently stopping the makeup artist, as the words began.

A three-car smash on Manning Hill Road last night has marked the end of the police hunt for known thief and drug trafficker Van Anderson, half of the Cat and Pirate armed robbery team. The wanted criminal was fleeing police pursuit when he leapt off a roof and into traffic yesterday, throwing himself into the path of oncoming cars in his attempt to flee. Witnesses said vehicles skidded to avoid him, and multiple smashes ensued. Police had surrounded a nearby suburban home where Anderson was believed to have taken shelter, when he unexpectedly burst from the back of the home and made his deadly dash. His accomplice, known as Cat, has not been arrested, although a woman is helping police with their inquiries.

A mirror was held before Melody. A stranger looked back at her. Anthea popped past to see her. 'Two minutes! Wow, look at you!'

Melody stared. She could not recognise herself. The nose ring had been taken out, the piercing easily covered with the makeup caked on her face. Her eyes had been unnaturally enlarged by skilful shading, her lips coated in red lipstick. The dress highlighted her square shoulders, and clung to her lean frame. Her hair was a silvery blonde pixie cap on her head that made her look ten years younger. Her bitten nails had been carefully painted in a neutral polish. She held a clipboard someone had handed her, and for ten seconds she stared into the mirror, a breath away from dropping the clipboard, stepping out of the high heels and running for the door.

And then she heard laughter and it was Van, over near the door. She turned, and it wasn't Van, just a big comfortable sound guy with the same laugh, but when Melody turned back to the mirror, she found she was smiling. There would be a time for running, but it wasn't now. She turned to see Skipper, waiting over to the side with Grace and Tom and Lotte, and her little boy caught her eye and waved madly, pressing his face against the glass between them. Tom gave her the thumbs-up and Grace waved both hands, and pressed them against her mouth, her eyes wide. A crew member led Melody towards the set where weather charts flashed high and low fronts, with cloudy swirls over a green and brown Australia. Melody took one last look back at her friends, and turned and walked onto the set, her footsteps firm, her heart full.

... and Victoria can expect warm northeasterlies as a trough in the west moves across the state. There will be isolated afternoon showers, and a coastal waters wind warning has been issued for Victorian waters between Lakes Entrance and sixty nautical miles East of Gabo Island ...

It was a strange way to grieve for someone. But everywhere she looked, every teleprompt, every map, every camera's square black eye, she could see Van's face, the way it had looked bathed in the light beaming from his newborn baby; Skipper's half-brother. It was a face of joy, and she felt her face crease in the reflection of its love and hope, until the weather became like the horoscopes, a communion with all those she loved. She read the words and laid them at the feet of Van, of Skipper, of Grace and Tom and Eddy and Lotte and Miss Laura. She had not felt a glimpse of the divine in that rainy, fraudulent dreaming camp. Yet here in this jungle of technology and people and face paint, the words of sunshine and rain poured forth from her like a sacrament.

CHAPTER TWENTY-THREE

Two months later, Eddy cradled baby Minh and walked back and forth across his lounge room. With great care, he tilted his arm to check the time. Only ten minutes since Romy had left to meet her parole officer. A thirty-minute meeting, a ten-minute walk from Eddy's to the station and another ten back, fifty minutes, he did the math for the eighth time and it worked out the same.

'Relax,' he told baby Minh, who despite his chaotic arrival into the world, looked at this point much more relaxed than Eddy felt. He was sated by the last-minute feed Romy had given him, but fighting sleep, sliding his eyes over the ceiling lights, Eddy's face, the window and back again.

'We're going to be just fine,' Eddy informed Minh. 'Mate, there's just forty minutes to go.' Talk to the baby, Romy had recommended, as she swung out the door more like a woman escaping custody than one meeting a weekly commitment with the law. She had moved into an apartment. Laura meanwhile had moved in with Eddy, and his dining table had been colonised with engagement party guest lists, weighty brochures from reception venues and fabric samples. It was Laura who had said to Romy, let us mind the baby, any time you need a break. Now Laura was working late to prepare to shepherd last year's kinder kids into school tomorrow, Skipper and Lotte amongst them, and it was Eddy who found himself holding this little scrap of human. Van and Romy's baby.

What a thought. He remembered that dinner party, the first time Van had appeared on the scene, almost exactly one year ago, Romy virtually walking straight out the door with him. 'Your dad,' he began to tell Minh. 'He ...' And then he thought better of it, unsure of the karmic energies swirling around an eight-week-old baby whose father had died in the minutes after his birth. Van hadn't been so bad anyway, apart from the theft and the suspected drug trafficking. It wasn't his fault he'd encountered a middle-class girl more desperate for adventure than anyone had dreamed. In fact, Eddy decided he should after all feel grateful to Van — without his interference, Eddy may never have met Laura. Quite satisfied to have reached this charitable resolution with baby Minh in his arms, Eddy started to feel a whole lot better. As if sensing his relief, Minh slid angelically into sleep and Eddy risked slowly lowering himself onto the couch and turning on the television news, babe still in arms. There was footage of a little girl wearing a stiff new gingham dress and shiny shoes; it was the first day of school tomorrow for thousands of small children across the state.

And now for the weather.

He watched Melody, elfin-faced and elegantly dressed. Pearl earrings, neat facial features, and that calm, steady stare, even as she read the forecast. She was getting better at it, more relaxed night by night. Was this the same woman who had climbed a railway bridge in the dark, leaving her child in his arms, the arms of a man she barely knew? He would miss her crazy ballgowns, her dreadlocks, her nose-rings. This woman who had once stood armed with a spray can in the moonlight, fearless on the rails between the brick side of a factory and the shadows and lights of a city and its mountains. *Risk Being Alive*, she had written. He smiled at the memory and snuggled back, the baby warm and nicely soap-smelling in his arms. Then he felt suddenly concerned that time had flown and Romy would return, just as he and Minh were starting to hit it off. No no, his watch reassured him, he had another twenty minutes. That was enough time, for starters, between blokes. Much could still be shared. *Risk Being Alive.*

... the winds will drop to four hundred isobars, and the high pressure front will bypass Adelaide but meet us by mid-morning tomorrow, this new, polished Melody told him gravely, her face poised, but with a hint of a smile.

And the weather ahead looks fine and sunny, all the way.

ABOUT THE AUTHOR

Fran Cusworth is a writer based in Melbourne, Australia.

She is the author of three previous novels: *The Love Child*, *Hopetoun Wives* and *Sisters of Spicefield*.

www.francusworth.com

ACKNOWLEDGMENTS

Thanks to Olga Lorenzo, Myfanwy Jones, Paddy O'Reilly and Kelly Gardiner for writing advice and friendship, and to La Trobe University's English faculty, who hosted me to write a later draft. Thanks to Red for letting me borrow Mr Sumper, and Ewen for taking me to Alfred Nuttall Kindy, and Simon for all the things. Ten Mile was inspired by Buchan. I had the privilege of living in a co-operative up near Nimbin at one time in my life, and Melody's commune experiences are a little touched by that time in Tuntable Falls. Thanks to Tara Wynne at Curtis Brown, for her support and friendship through four novels, and Anna Valdinger, Vanessa Williams and Kate Stone at Harper Collins for their work on the digital edition of this book, which is available through their Impulse imprint.

This is a work of fiction, and any resemblance of these fictional characters to living people is coincidence.

If you enjoyed reading this book, please consider leaving a review online at Goodreads.

www.ingramcontent.com/pod-product-compliance
Lightning Source LLC
LaVergne TN
LVHW091532060526
838200LV00036B/584